"What did my mother say to you?"

Roxy forced herself to look at Steve. "Your mother's worried. She thinks you're falling in love with me."

"I am."

Those two words turned her world topsy-turvy. "You can't be. We said neither of us wanted a relationship."

"I didn't think I was ready. I thought all my heart could hold was grief, but I was wrong. There's space for you there, Roxy."

Roxy's shoulders stiffened. "Don't love me, Steve," she said. "Your mother's afraid I'll break your heart, and I will if you love me."

"If you're about to tell me that you don't care about me, then I won't believe you," he said.

"I do care about you," she admitted. "I care about you more than I've ever cared about a man, but that doesn't change the fact that I never intend to invite a man into my life."

"What are you afraid of, Roxy? Why are you so afraid to love...to be loved?"

Men of Wolf Creek: Small-town lawmen charged with finding the lost...and uncovering true love.

Dear Reader,

Last year my husband and I got the opportunity to take a road trip through Pennsylvania, where we fell in love with the beauty of the countryside, the Amish settlements and chocolate.

The Men of Wolf Creek series was born from the places we saw and the people we met. I've taken poetic license in many cases, but hopefully you'll find these books filled with hot heroes, strong heroines and enough suspense to keep you on the edge of your chair.

Thanks and happy reading!

Carla Cassidy

COLD CASE,
HOT ACCOMPLICE

Carla Cassidy

HARLEQUIN® ROMANTIC SUSPENSE

Recycling programs
for this product may
not exist in your area.

ISBN-13: 978-0-373-27849-7

COLD CASE, HOT ACCOMPLICE

Copyright © 2013 by Carla Bracale

Printed in U.S.A.

Books by Carla Cassidy

Harlequin Romantic Suspense

Silhouette Romantic Suspense

Other titles by this author
available in ebook format.

CARLA CASSIDY

is an award-winning author who has written more than one hundred books for Harlequin. In 1995 she won Best Silhouette Romance from *RT Book Reviews* for *Anything for Danny*. In 1998 she also won a Career Achievement Award for Best Innovative Series from *RT Book Reviews*.

Carla believes the only thing better than curling up with a good book to read is sitting down at the computer with a good story to write. She's looking forward to writing many more books and bringing hours of pleasure to readers.

To all the people in Pennsylvania who welcomed us into their homes with love and warmth.
I love you all and hope you find these stories as entertaining as we found all of you!

Love, Carla

Chapter 1

For the first time in three and a half years, Aunt Liz was late. Roxy Marcoli checked her watch for the third time in the past five minutes and tried not to panic.

The older woman had never been late delivering the baked goods that were offered each day to the customers of the Dollhouse. She always arrived at six-thirty, a half hour before Roxy turned the closed sign to Open, signaling the beginning of another day at the restaurant.

It was now quarter till seven and still no sign of Aunt Liz. Roxy had already called her aunt's house twice, and there had been no answer. She'd also tried Liz's cell phone, but it had gone directly to voice mail.

"Maybe she's held up in traffic," Josephine Landers, Roxy's manager, said as she checked the quiches that baked in the oven.

"Yeah, because traffic jams are such an issue in Wolf Creek, Pennsylvania," Roxy replied drily. She couldn't remember the last time she'd heard of a traffic snarl in the relatively small tourist town twenty miles up the mountain from the bigger city of Hershey.

"You know she'd never answer her cell phone if she was driving. She'll probably be walking in here any minute now," Josie said, obviously unconcerned about Liz Marcoli's punctuality or lack thereof.

What worried Roxy was that her aunt Liz was the one person in the entire world she'd always depended on, the one person who had always been there for her. She checked her watch once again. Almost seven. This was so out of character for Aunt Liz.

A thousand scenarios played out in Roxy's head, one worse than the other. Maybe she'd slipped and fallen in the shower. Or she'd been in a car accident and was at the hospital. Half the time she forgot to carry her purse with her, so if she was in an accident and rendered unconscious, it was possible that nobody would know her identity.

Stop it, Roxy commanded herself. *Stop thinking so negatively.* She'd been told often enough by both of her sisters and her aunt that she was prone to always seeing the bad side of any situation.

Maybe for once in her life, Aunt Liz had simply overslept. But then why hadn't she heard the phone ring? "Maybe I'll just give Marlene a call and have her run over and check in at Aunt Liz's," she said, more to herself than to Josie.

"Whatever you're going to do, you'd better do it fast because our first customers should be coming in any minute." Josie pulled the tray of homemade quiches from the oven.

Roxy grabbed her cell phone from her apron pocket and punched in her middle sister's number. Marlene picked up on the third ring, her voice groggy with sleep.

"You'd better be profusely bleeding or on fire," she said to Roxy.

"Neither, and I'm sorry to bother you so early, but I can't find Aunt Liz," Roxy replied. She leaned one hip against the large butcher-block island in the center of the kitchen.

"What do you mean you can't find Aunt Liz?"

Roxy could hear the rustle of bedsheets and could easily imagine her blond-haired, beautiful sister sitting up in her bed in her tiny walk-up apartment bedroom. "She didn't come this morning with the baked goods, and I've tried to call the house and her cell phone, but I get no answer." Roxy tried to keep the worry from her voice, but it was obvious Marlene heard it.

"You want me to go over there and check things out?"

"Would you mind? I'm just about to open my doors, and I can't imagine what's held her up this morning. This has never happened before."

"It will take me a few minutes to pull myself together and get over there, but I'll call you back as soon as I know something."

Roxy released a small sigh of relief. "Thanks, Marlene. And if she shows up here in the meantime, I'll give you a call back."

Roxy hung up at the same time she heard a rapid

knock come from the front door of the three-story Victorian home she'd turned into a restaurant.

For the past year, the first three customers at the door every Monday, Wednesday and Friday were three of Hershey's finest who, before beginning their shifts as detectives, started their day with a hearty Dollhouse breakfast.

As Roxy left the kitchen to open the front door, pride of ownership filled her heart. The restaurant consisted of three seating rooms, the large kitchen and a small storage area that had once served as a mudroom.

She was open six days a week, from seven in the morning until five in the evening. She'd initially envisioned the intimate restaurant to be popular with small women's groups and lunching ladies. She'd never expected the men who showed up for breakfast, and as a result, her morning offerings had become bigger in size, heartier than the lunch menu.

When she reached the front door, she was unsurprised to see the three familiar men standing on the porch. Jim Carmani, Frank Delaney and Steven Kincaid were all detectives with the Wolf Creek police force. As she opened the door to let them in, her stomach twisted into a small knot of tension.

She busied herself turning the sign from Closed to Open in the glass pane of the front door, and the three men seated themselves where they always did, at the round table nearest the front window.

Knowing they would want coffee all around, she hurried to the kitchen to grab a serving pot of the fresh-brewed drink and then returned to their table and placed the silver pot in the center.

Jim and Frank both murmured a good morning. Steve eyed her with bright blue eyes and a sexy smile that should be considered illegal. "Foxy Roxy, you're looking stunning this morning as usual."

This was the man who twisted the knot in her stomach. Half the time after serving them, she wasn't sure if she wanted to pull out his shaggy surfer blond hair or her own black curly strands.

"Don't call me Foxy Roxy," she snapped.

"Why not?" he asked. A light of amusement shone in his ocean-blue eyes as his gaze perused her from head to toe.

"Because I told you not to," she said and then smiled at Jimmy and Frank. Both of them were dressed in black slacks, white shirts and lightweight suit jackets, while Steve was clad in a pair of slacks and a blue dress shirt that emphasized the color of his eyes and the shoulder holster that held his gun.

"What can I get for you this morning?" she asked Jimmy. "I'm afraid I don't have any cinnamon rolls or muffins. They haven't been delivered yet." She tamped down a new burst of worry about her aunt. Where could she be?

"I'll take your breakfast special, scrambled eggs with bacon and white toast," Jimmy said.

"And those Belgian waffles are calling to me, the ones smothered with bananas and caramel topping," Frank added.

Roxy nodded and turned to Steve. He grinned at her, and the knot in her stomach twisted a little bit tighter. "I'd like a plate of your long gorgeous legs and a hint of your pretty smile."

"Vegetable quiche," she said as she wrote on her pad, knowing few men ordered the delicate dish.

"No, wait!" Steve released a low rumble of laughter. "Give me the same as Frank."

"That's what I thought you said," she said drily and then twirled on her heels and left the table. "That man," she exclaimed as she entered the kitchen where Josie and Gregory Stillwell, another employee, were manning the oven.

"Let me guess," Josie said as she took the order sheet from Roxy. "Detective Steve Kincaid?" She didn't wait for Roxy's answer, but instead pointed Gregory to the waffle maker while she got eggs from the fridge. "I don't know why you let him get under your skin. Every woman in town thinks he's hot and sexy and would love to get a little of his flirtation and a taste of his lush lips, but we all know he's not really the serious type."

"He looks like some surfer dude who wandered in from a beach instead of a detective on the police force."

Josie grinned at her. "And you look like a hot, take-me-to-bed-right-now kind of woman instead of the man-hater you really are."

"I'm not a man-hater," Roxy grumbled. "I just refuse to buy into anything any of them are trying to sell."

Josie looked down at the wedding ring that had adorned her finger for the past three months. "Sometimes they're just selling you love," she replied, her voice gooey with sentiment.

The honeymoon stage, that's all it was, Roxy thought. Josie had married her high school sweetheart three months ago. Sooner or later the honeymoon would pass and real life would intrude—and that's when everything went to hell.

Roxy knew…. She'd lived it with her mother for the first seven years of her life. Men had led her mother to utter destruction, and Roxy wasn't about to make those same kinds of mistakes. She was good by herself, thank you very much.

It took only minutes for the three meals to be prepared and served, and by that time other diners had entered to get breakfast and enjoy the ambiance of the cozy eatery.

The three dining areas were named by the wallpaper and color theme in each room. The main area was the blue room, papered in a rich blue satin paper with antique glassware and trinkets on display on various shelves. The second biggest room was mauve, also decorated with a variety of antiques, old hats and framed news articles that chronicled the history of Wolf Creek.

The final dining area was the green room, which hinted of an outdoor eating experience with lush plants and the requisite antiques used to flavor the room.

For years this had been Roxy's dream. She'd worked two jobs since the age of eighteen in order to have a healthy down payment on a place.

The Dollhouse only used the best and freshest ingredients, utilizing local farmers and the nearby Amish community to assure quality in every dish they prepared.

She'd been open less than four years, and already she was functioning firmly in the black. This place wasn't just her dream; it, along with spending time with her two younger sisters and her aunt, was her very life.

For another half an hour she took orders and served customers. Allie Jenkins, one of her part-time waitresses, worked the crowd, as well.

Roxy was standing in the kitchen doorway waiting for an order to be ready for delivery when her cell phone rang. It was Marlene.

"Roxy, she's not here. The door was unlocked. I've gone through the entire house and she isn't here, but her car is in the driveway and her purse and all the baked goods are on the counter ready to transport."

A thrum of thick anxiety shot off in the pit of Roxy's stomach. "But she has to be there someplace if her car is there."

"Roxy, I've checked every room in the house. I even went down to the basement, and there's no sign of her." Marlene's voice rang with a touch of the anxiety that grew bigger and bigger inside Roxy. "What do you want me to do?"

"Have you called Sheri?" she asked, referring to their youngest sister.

"I did, and she hasn't heard from Aunt Liz since around two o'clock yesterday afternoon."

The simmer of anxiety moved into full chest-crunching alarm. "Go home and try not to worry," Roxy told her sister. "I'm sure there's a logical explanation. I'll take care of things." That's what Roxy did—she took care of things when her aunt wasn't available.

And why wasn't she available? Had Roxy's mother, Ramona, showed up after all these years and asked Liz to go someplace with her? Or had Ramona called and Liz gone running with no thought of anything else?

That could only mean bad news. Where Ramona went, chaos followed.

Liz had a soft and forgiving heart for everyone, and despite everything Ramona had done over the years, Liz would easily want to believe the best of her much younger sister. Liz would definitely drop everything if Ramona had called.

It had now been an hour and a half since she'd expected Liz to show up, and the alarm inside Roxy could no longer be ignored. There was only one thing she knew to do.

With stiff shoulders and the feeling that the world was suddenly all wrong, she went back into the blue room, where the three detectives were just finishing up their breakfasts.

"I need your help," she said without preamble. "We can't find my aunt. She's missing, and I need you all to go to her house and see if you can find out what's happened to her."

Jimmy, a handsome Italian, frowned. "How long has she been missing?"

"Almost two hours," Roxy replied. "My sister has been over to her house and can't find her anywhere. Aunt Liz's car is there, but she isn't. Something is wrong."

"Roxy, we can't check out someone who has only been missing for a couple of hours," Frank said kindly. "She's an adult. She's allowed to be missing if she wants to be."

"I'll go." Steve drained his coffee cup and then stood and looked at Roxy expectantly.

Both of his partners looked at him in surprise, and a sinking feeling swept through Roxy.

Of the three men at the table, the last one she wanted to have anything to do with was Detective Steve Kincaid. But at the moment her concern for her aunt overweighed her disgust at having to deal with the handsome devil.

Steve had no idea what he was doing. Why had he offered to check this out for a woman who had made it clear in a hundred different ways that she didn't think much of him?

The minute she climbed into his unmarked car, the scent of her filled the confines. She smelled of some kind of fresh floral perfume and a combination of exotic spice scents, and he was glad that the passenger seat hadn't been covered with the usual fast-food wrappers that normally adorned it.

He knew there were three Marcoli sisters, but he didn't know any of them well. They had all been younger than him, and the only interaction he'd had with any of them had been Roxy, who both fascinated and repelled him at the same time.

She was slamming hot with her short, curly dark hair, full lush lips and figure meant for lovemaking. But her tongue was sharp enough to slice a tough cut of meat, and she'd made it clear that she didn't particularly like him.

"So I gather your aunt comes in each morning and delivers baked goods for you to put on the menu?" he asked as she pointed in the direction of her aunt's house.

"She comes in every morning at six-thirty like

clockwork. In the three and a half years that the Dollhouse has been open, she's never, ever been late," Roxy said.

"So she's responsible for that coffee cake I like."

Roxy nodded. "And the pies and cakes that I serve throughout each day. She's always loved to bake, so when I decided to open the restaurant we came to an agreement about her baking for me." She began absently chewing on a fingernail.

"How old is this aunt of yours?"

"A very spry sixty-five." She continued working the fingernail.

"If you draw blood, we'll have to waste time at the hospital before we get to your aunt's house," he observed with a pointed stare.

She flushed and dropped her hand into her lap. "Aunt Liz always tells me that it's unbecoming for a thirty-four-year-old to chew her nails, but I've been doing it since I was a kid."

"I'll bet you were a cute kid," he replied, the charm easily falling from his lips from long habit.

He felt her glare on him. "You have a reputation for being a great flirt. I don't find it great—I find it quite tedious."

"Ouch," he responded with a mock wince.

For a few minutes they rode in silence, the only communication nonverbal as she directed him where to turn on the winding mountain roads that led to her aunt's home.

"So what exactly is your relationship with your aunt besides your business arrangement?" he asked, eager to break the uncomfortable silence between them.

"Aunt Liz raised me and my sisters from the time

we were little. For all intents and purposes, she's my mother figure, and she's always been the most dependable person in my life. That's why this is so unlike her. She's never late. She's never unreliable. That's why I'm afraid something bad has happened." She raised her hand up toward her mouth as if to begin to gnaw her fingernail again, but then quickly dropped it back into her lap.

"You said your sister already checked things out at the house?"

Roxy nodded, her rich dark hair gleaming in the late April sun that drifted through the passenger window. "Marlene. I called her when Aunt Liz was almost half an hour late. She called me just a little while ago to tell me she'd checked out the entire house and Aunt Liz wasn't there."

She sat forward against the seat belt. "That's it. That's her place." She pointed to a neat brick ranch house with beige trim and a well-manicured yard. "That's her car in the driveway."

He felt Roxy's tension rolling off her as he pulled the car in behind the older Buick and parked. Before he'd shut off the engine, she was out the door and running toward the front porch.

"Roxy," he called after her, halting her before she could enter the house. Her sister had already been inside, stirring things up. Although there was no reason to believe that anyone nefarious might be in the house, he didn't want Roxy just bursting through the front door without knowing what might be on the other side.

Even though he believed that nothing bad was going on, he pulled his gun from his holster and motioned for her to get behind him.

"Don't shoot my aunt," she said from behind him, and he fought the impulse to turn and stare at her in disbelief. Did she really think him so inept that he might shoot a helpless older woman?

"I don't intend to shoot anyone," he said. "I think you're probably overreacting to all of this."

"I'm not the one who has a gun in my hand," she retorted.

Steve gritted his teeth and tried the doorknob, which turned easily beneath his hand. "Did your sister say if the door was locked or unlocked when she arrived?"

"Unlocked," Roxy replied.

Steve gave the door a good look but saw no indication of forced entry. In the back of his mind he knew he was probably investigating a crime that hadn't happened, looking for a person who wasn't really missing.

So what was he doing there? Why had he agreed to this? He thought it might have to do with his physical attraction to Roxy Marcoli and an attempt to ease some of the obvious distaste she held for him.

Not that he really cared what she thought about him. The last thing he would ever want was another crazy woman in his life. Been there, done that, and he still paid the price in a shattered heart that found no respite from pain.

It took him only moments to make sure the house was clear, and after that he and Roxy stood in the kitchen, facing each other. "Her purse is here." He pointed to the brown oversize bag on the counter next to a set of keys.

"She is constantly forgetting her purse, and she keeps her cell phone inside it," Roxy replied. Her dark eyes held strain and the barest whisper of fear. "Look, the cakes and pies and muffins are all packaged and ready for delivery." She pointed to the countertop, where the items were in plastic carrying cases. "She obviously had the intention of bringing those things in first thing this morning just like always. Something terrible has happened to her, and you have to do something about it."

"Officially I can't do anything about it." He saw the flash of irritation that darkened her eyes even more. "Roxy, right now all we have is a grown woman who has been missing for less than three hours. There might have been an emergency with one of her friends. Somebody could have picked her up here, and she forgot her purse or to lock the door after her."

"So you aren't going to do anything," she said flatly.

"I've already done what I can at this point."

She stared at him for a long moment and then headed toward the front door. "You're obviously a better flirt than you are a detective," she said, and he winced once again as he heard the front door slam shut.

He followed her back outside, locking the door and pulling it closed behind him. She stood at the side of his car, her arms crossed over her voluptuous breasts and her expression mirroring that of a beast from hell.

She got into the passenger seat as he settled in behind the wheel; the silence in the air was as thick as honey turned to sugar. Unfortunately there was no honey in Roxy Marcoli.

She had a reputation for being a tough woman, both in business and in her personal life. He knew that several police officers had asked her out at various times and had always been cut off at the knees.

While Steve found himself drawn to her on a physical level, he wasn't looking for a woman in his life, and in any case he was certain that Foxy Roxy would shut him down even more easily than she had others.

"Roxy, I'm sorry I can't do anything more for you at this point. I suggest you call your aunt's friends, check in with neighbors and see if they've heard from her this morning. I'm sure she'll show up and there will be a logical explanation for her absence."

Roxy shook her head. "You don't understand. You don't know my aunt Liz. She would never just disappear like this and not get in touch with me or my sisters to let us know what was going on. She's not that irresponsible. She's just not that kind of person."

Steve drove her back toward her place of business. For the rest of the ride she chewed on her nails without acknowledging that he was in the car with her.

As he pulled up in front of the Dollhouse, she got out of the car. "Thanks for nothing," she said and slammed the door.

Steve watched her as she disappeared into the restaurant. He'd done what he could for her at this moment in time, and he hoped that by the afternoon Liz Marcoli would reappear with apologies for making Roxy worry, and all would be right in the Marcoli world.

The last thing Steve wanted to work on was a missing-persons case. He tried to avoid those whenever possible. He might be a shameless flirt, but he was a damn good detective, and along with his partners, Frank and Jim, his solve rate was enviable.

But missing-persons cases usually ended badly, or didn't end at all, leaving questions that would forever remain unanswered, leaving behind broken hearts that couldn't even begin to go through the healing process until they knew what had happened to their loved ones.

Steve knew all about the lack of closure when a person went missing. He understood the questions that nagged, the gnawing need for answers. He tried not to tap into the well of pain inside himself, preferring to keep up a superficial ladies' man mask to keep people at bay.

How could he work a missing-persons case when he had one in his own life, one that he'd been working for the past two years and couldn't solve?

Roxy just might be right—he was probably a better flirt than detective when it came to finding somebody who'd gone missing.

Chapter 2

At precisely five o'clock that evening Roxy changed the open sign to Closed and locked the front door. It had been a busy afternoon that had kept her jumping from one dining room to another to assure that all her customers had what they needed.

Throughout the afternoon, whenever there was a lull in business, Roxy had been on the phone, calling her aunt's friends, the nearest hospitals and her sisters, but nobody had seen or heard from Liz all day.

After locking the restaurant, she raced up the two sets of stairs that led to her private quarters. The second floor was strictly storage and the top floor was her personal sanctuary, but as she opened the door to the large apartment she knew there would be no peace at the moment.

She called her sisters, Marlene and Sheri, and then

grabbed her purse and car keys. Hopefully by the time they all arrived at the Wolf Creek police station, Detective Steve Kincaid would be off duty. Somebody had to take her seriously about Liz's disappearance, and if he wouldn't, then she'd find somebody who would. There was no way she intended the night to pass without somebody official out looking for Aunt Liz. She didn't care about some stupid twenty-four-hour rule.

She had to stay calm. Nobody would take her seriously if she lost it.

To the outside world Liz Marcoli was a pleasant, kind woman who excelled at baking and quilting, but to Roxy she was the person who had made order out of chaos, security out of danger. She had saved Roxy's life and the lives of her sisters, and now Roxy wouldn't rest until somebody was doing something to find her.

Where could she be? What could have possibly happened to her? Since the age of seven, a day had never gone by that Roxy hadn't seen or spoken to her aunt.

She tightened her hands on the steering wheel as she thought of the handsome detective who had been like a chigger under her skin for months.

She didn't know how any crime got solved with men like him on the job; not that there was that much violent crime in the area. Still, if he investigated as often as he flirted with all the women in town, they would have no unsolved crimes on the books.

The Dollhouse was at the opposite end of town from the police station, but it only took her minutes to get there, for the business district of Main Street was only three blocks long.

She parked in front of the brick building and sat to wait for her sisters to arrive. They would be a force of three, and hopefully somebody would take their concerns seriously.

Lowering her window, she breathed in the late spring air, trying to staunch the panic that threatened to crawl up the back of her throat and release itself in a scream.

She tapped the steering wheel impatiently. Marlene would arrive first. She rented an apartment above a shop that sold antiques, trinkets and souvenirs. She'd moved there almost a year ago after her divorce.

Roxy frowned as she thought of Marlene. She'd left Wolf Creek as a happy bride to move to Pittsburgh with her new husband and had returned home two years later a different woman, not only divorced, but withdrawn and unwilling to talk about the failure of her marriage.

It would take longer for the youngest of the sisters to arrive. Sheri lived farther up the mountain in a small cabin surrounded by thick woods.

Roxy was in the process of tapping the leather right off her steering wheel when Marlene pulled up next to her. She got out of her car and slid into the passenger seat in Roxy's.

She met Roxy's gaze, the frantic worry inside Roxy's stomach reflected in her sister's blue eyes. "What do you think happened to her?" Marlene asked.

"I don't have a clue, but I'm not leaving here until we have a full investigation under way to find out where she is," Roxy said.

The two sat silently as they waited for Sheri.

"How's business?" Roxy finally asked when she could take the silence no longer.

Marlene and Sheri owned a roadside storefront closer to Hershey that specialized in Amish-made furniture, cheeses and fresh-grown fruits and vegetables.

"Getting better every day now that the weather is warming up," she replied. "Abe and Jennifer are working this evening. Sheri called them in to take over after we found out Aunt Liz was missing."

Missing.

The word hung in the air, horrifying...heartbreaking. At that moment Sheri's black pickup pulled into a parking space nearby. The youngest of the three got out and approached them, her shoulder-length chestnut hair shimmering in the sunshine.

When the three women stood side by side, few people realized they were sisters. While they all shared the same mother, they each had different fathers.

Roxy was short and compact, with dark hair and dark eyes. Marlene was a tall blonde with ice-blue eyes, and Sheri liked to refer to herself as an ordinary mutt, with brown hair and whiskey-colored eyes.

Roxy and Marlene got out of Roxy's car and greeted Sheri, who looked younger than usual with worry darkening her large eyes.

Roxy knew she would be the one to take the lead here. She'd always been the strong one, the big sister who would take care of her younger siblings at any cost.

"Okay, let's do this," Roxy said. She wouldn't be turned away. She refused to be dismissed like she had been that morning by Steve. She wanted boots on the ground and search parties beating the bushes.

More than anything, she wanted Aunt Liz to be found safe and sound.

With a deep breath and her sisters following just behind her, Roxy stepped into the police station, where plastic chairs lined a wall and a uniformed officer she didn't know sat at a desk. A door to his right led to the room that she knew all the other members of law enforcement called home away from home.

"We're here to file a missing-persons report," Roxy said, relieved that her voice sounded strong and confident, even though she wanted to melt into a puddle of worried goo.

"Then you need to speak to one of our detectives." There was a sound of a buzzer, and he gestured toward the door. "They're at the desks on the right side of the room."

Roxy nodded and pushed through the door. Her gaze automatically went to the three desks on the right, and her heart sank to her toes as she saw that the only one occupied was by her shaggy-haired nemesis.

An attractive long-legged blonde in the traditional blue police officer uniform leaned over his desk, and they were laughing as if they didn't have a care in the world.

Roxy was vaguely aware of other people in the room as she cleared her throat with the force of a snorting bull. The smile on Steve's face fell as he turned partway in his chair to see the three of them standing there.

He said something to the blonde, who sauntered away with a sexy swing of her hips. Roxy marched toward him, trying to balance temper and fear.

She wasn't sure why it irritated her that he'd obviously been enjoying the company of the blonde bombshell, but it did. "We hate to mess with your social life, but we want to file a missing-persons report," she said as he got up from his desk.

He frowned. "You still haven't heard anything from your aunt?"

"Not a word, and I don't care that it hasn't been twenty-four hours. She's in trouble, and you need to put out an Amber Alert."

"That's for kids. A Silver Alert is for adults and is usually put into effect when an elderly or disoriented person goes missing."

"She's disoriented," Roxy exclaimed. "She has a touch of early onset dementia." Sheri gasped at the blatant lie, while Marlene merely released a small groan.

Roxy would do whatever it took to get somebody to look for her aunt, even if it meant telling a little white lie, even if it meant Aunt Liz would kill her if she ever heard what Roxy had said about her.

Roxy raised her chin as Steve's eyes narrowed in obvious disbelief. "Early onset dementia. Well then, if that's the case I guess we'd better file a report," he finally said. He pulled up two more chairs to join the one that sat before his desk and gestured for the three to have a seat.

"I don't just want to file a report," Roxy said as she sat down in the chair directly opposite him. She leaned toward him. "I want a search party started. I want a full investigation going. I want…I need…" To her horror, tears burned at her eyes.

"How about we start with some paperwork," Steve replied with a hint of kindness in his voice.

"Fine, and then we'll start a search party," Roxy exclaimed as she quickly reined in her emotions. The last thing she wanted to do was show weakness in front of her sisters. Still, Sheri placed a gentling hand on Roxy's arm, and Roxy drew a deep breath and leaned back in the chair.

For the next hour and a half Roxy held on to her patience as Steve asked question after question about the missing woman. Even though she was screaming inside for some kind of action to be taken, she knew that each and every question he asked and the answers they could all provide might hold a clue as to where Aunt Liz might be.

Twilight had fallen when Steve finally asked for a picture. As Roxy pulled a photo of her aunt out of her wallet, the encroaching darkness of night crept deep into her soul.

"So what happens now?" Marlene asked.

"You all go home," he said.

Roxy stared at him in stunned surprise. "Go home? How can we just go home? We haven't found her yet."

"I suggest you go home and continue to contact friends and acquaintances, and let me know if you hear any information that might help me in the investigation." He stood, and it was obviously a dismissal.

"Are you sure you're going to be able to fit an investigation into your busy social life?" Roxy asked as she noticed the blonde pointedly looking at her watch and then at him from across the room.

Marlene shot her an elbow in the side. Roxy's cheeks warmed as she realized she was insulting the very man she needed to help her, to help them.

* * *

It had been the most frustrating hour and a half Steve had spent in recent years. While he'd found Marlene and Sheri to be simmering with anxiety, yet calm and cooperative, Roxy had been like a bomb on the verge of explosion.

She'd bitten her nails, snarled out answers and insulted his work ethic, but looking into the depths of her beautiful dark eyes, with lashes that were sinfully long, he could tell a panic screamed inside her and he knew that feeling intimately.

When the three of them left, it was as if Roxy sucked all the energy out of the room with her. He leaned back in his chair and only looked up from the notes he'd taken when Officer Chelsea Loren sidled up to the side of his desk once again.

"I thought maybe you'd like to head out of here and get a drink with me," she said, her sexy smile attempting to lure him in. She'd been trying to entice him into a relationship for months without success.

He grinned at her. "Ah, Chelsea, how many times do we have to go through this? You know you're utterly irresistible, but I don't do workplace romances."

Her enhanced lips puffed into a pout. "Obviously I'm not that utterly irresistible if you always turn me down."

"Go find somebody else to play with, Chelsea. I've got work to do," he said, his mind instantly filling with a vision of dark eyes and that barely suppressed panic that had lit them from within.

Chelsea flounced back across the room, and within minutes she had left with a couple of other uniforms getting off duty. Steve looked toward the window, where darkness had completely fallen.

The first night of dealing with a missing loved one was the absolute worst. There would be little or no sleep for the Marcoli sisters tonight. It would be the most agonizing night they'd probably ever suffer.

They would jump at every phone call and hear every creak and groan of their homes, anticipating some answer, a sudden appearance of their aunt Liz. By morning they'd all be exhausted, and still the fear would be like a living, breathing entity eating at their insides.

He shoved aside those thoughts and got up from his desk. There wasn't much he could do this late at night as far as a real investigation, and he still wasn't sure that any foul play was involved or that Chief of Police Brad Krause would even issue orders for an investigation.

But it was time for Steve to get out of there, and it wouldn't hurt him to take a drive for the next hour or two and look for a woman who had somehow gotten lost from her home. Most nights he either met with his work buddies for a few beers or drove around, putting off returning to his own house until the very last minute.

He left the building and got into his car, and he thought of Roxy telling him that Liz Marcoli had early onset dementia. It had obviously been a lie, but he'd forgive her, as he knew the forces that were driving her at the moment.

The woman who for the past three and a half years had been responsible for the luscious cakes, pies, pastries and muffins at the Dollhouse didn't suffer early onset dementia or anything else, except maybe a touch of arthritis. The sisters had mentioned no other health issues, but rather had insisted that Liz was in perfect health.

He was just about to start his car engine when Officer Joe Jamison pulled his patrol car in next to Steve's car. As Joe got out, Steve rolled down his window and grinned at the bear of a man.

"What's up, big man?"

Joe shrugged broad shoulders. "The usual, writing warnings and tickets for folks who can't read speed limit signs. Later I'll be looking out for the usual Friday night drunks. What about you? Who's the lucky lady tonight?"

Steve laughed. "You know my reputation is mostly based on rumor and fiction, but actually there is a lady on my mind this evening, and I'm going to do a little hunting for her."

Joe raised a dark eyebrow. "Hunting? Since when did you ever have to hunt for a woman? It seems to me that every time we're out together, there are a couple of hot women throwing themselves at you."

"You don't do so bad yourself," Steve replied with a grin. Joe often joined Steve, Frank and Jimmy for Saturday night drinks at the Wolf's Head, a popular local tavern.

"For me it's got to be the uniform. We all know women like guys in uniforms, even if they do look like grizzly bears."

Steve laughed. "You don't look like a grizzly bear. You look like a big guy who can take care of any trouble a damsel in distress might have. And speaking of damsels in distress…"

Steve quickly explained about Liz Marcoli. "I'm planning on driving around a bit now before heading home to see if she's anywhere on the streets. I'd appreciate you and anyone else who's working the night shift doing the same on the nightly patrols. There's a photo of her on my desk."

"Will do," Joe agreed. He backed away from Steve's car. With a wave Steve pulled out of the parking lot and headed slowly down Main Street.

He'd learned from the sisters that Liz Marcoli had been a young widow; she'd lost the love of her life in a car accident when she'd been only thirty. According to the sisters, Liz had never dated again, had never expressed any interest in marrying or having any kind of a romantic relationship.

But would Liz share the details of a man in her life with her nieces? Wasn't it possible that Liz might have a secret lover? That she'd been whisked away for a spontaneous romantic couple of days and hadn't told her nieces anything about it?

Still, that didn't explain the baked items neatly packed for delivery and her purse on the kitchen counter. Although walking away from responsibilities was not a crime, it was also not normal, and anything abnormal like this had the potential to be a crime.

However, a friend the women didn't know about might have needed emergency help, and the possibility of a spontaneous absence because of a man in her life was equally plausible.

He knew how busy Roxy stayed at her restaurant, and from what he'd learned talking with Marlene and Sheri, they were business owners, as well. Running the roadside building near town would require a lot of time and energy on their part.

So how well did they really know their aunt? What he needed to do tomorrow was talk to the friends and neighbors the ladies had provided him with in a list and see what Liz Marcoli did when she wasn't with her nieces.

Steve knew better than most that you could think you knew somebody, that you could love and trust somebody, and in the end realize that person had secrets and that you really didn't know them at all.

A thick band of pain inched around his chest, and for a moment it felt like an old familiar friend. There were now days at a time when he stayed so busy that he didn't feel the ever-present heartache—minutes in time when he almost forgot, but not quite.

He shoved away thoughts of his own issues and instead focused on the street he slowly cruised, looking for a sixty-five-year-old woman who might be walking in the dark after suffering a head injury or some other medical issue that might have her disoriented.

The streets were nearly deserted. The small town of Wolf Creek closed up early, with most stores shutting down by eight in the evenings. Although many of the businesses were geared toward the tourism the town enjoyed, there were also the normal stores found anywhere.

He drove slowly, occasionally using his high beams to peer into an alley or a recessed storefront.

At this point he didn't feel the frantic panic over the missing woman that he'd seen in Roxy's eyes. It was too early to panic.

As he passed the Dollhouse, his gaze went up to

the third floor, where lights appeared to glow from every window, like beacons calling out in the night to the missing woman.

He couldn't help but think of the woman who lived on that third floor. Roxy was a wildcat, driven by her emotions, and while he found himself impossibly attracted to her, at the same time she scared the hell out of him.

Right now what he felt toward her was an empathy born in a common trauma. Hopefully Liz Marcoli would be found soon, alive and well, and this vanishing would have simply been some sort of miscommunication.

His own missing-persons case was an ongoing heartache that he wouldn't wish on his worst enemy. The pain of the absence of a loved one had built a shell around his heart, forcing him to pull on the facade of a carefree, flirtatious, shallow man in order to survive his emotional pain.

He hoped Roxy and her sisters never had to deal with days, weeks, months of such ongoing agony. He knew better than anyone that the lack of closure in such an event transformed a person—and, in his case, had the power to completely break a man emotionally.

Chapter 3

Roxy jerked awake just after five in the morning. She was on the sofa, still dressed in her clothes from the day before and appalled that she'd fallen asleep at all.

She'd spent most of the night before on the phone with her sisters and then checking and rechecking with Liz's friends until it had gotten too late to make any more calls. Then she'd paced the floor, waiting to hear something, anything, about Liz's whereabouts.

Her body's need to rest had apparently finally overwhelmed her panicked fear, and even though she'd only been asleep a couple of hours, she felt guilty for sleeping any length of time while her aunt was still missing.

As she roused herself from her awkward position on the sofa, muscles ached and protested the time spent on the sofa and not in her comfortable bed.

Coffee, her brain screamed. Coffee and then a long, hot shower. Although she'd like to call Detective Steve Kincaid and see what he'd done the night before to find her aunt, she knew it was an unreasonable thought at an unreasonable hour of the morning. She doubted that much work had been done overnight, and, in any case, if he'd found out something pertinent, surely he would have called her.

She turned on the kitchen light and stumbled across the room to the coffeemaker. This was her usual time to get up in the mornings, and she normally enjoyed the half hour or forty-five minutes she gave herself before heading downstairs to start the prep work for the day.

Even though it was Saturday, the busiest day in the Dollhouse, Roxy had told Josie to make arrangements for extra help, as Roxy wouldn't be working. She *couldn't* work with her head in utter turmoil, with the fear that had already begun to possess her entire body as she thought of the one woman in the world who had always managed to center her.

It was too early to call her sisters, too early to do anything but sit at her table and sip her coffee and think, but she quickly realized she had no viable ideas about where Aunt Liz might be or what might have happened to her. She'd already considered most of the possibilities, and they'd proved fruitless.

She leaned back in the black-cushioned chrome chair and gazed around the kitchen. It was funny, really, that she'd decorated her restaurant with antiques and kitschy items, but her personal domain was sleek and modern, from the stainless steel kitchen appliances to the glass-topped tables and black-and-white decor of her living room.

Even her bedroom was simple, a king-size bed covered in a black-and-white patterned spread, a dresser holding a couple of bottles of perfume, a jewelry holder and two nightstands with small black-and-silver lamps.

She'd always found the rather austere, impersonal aura of her private quarters comforting and peaceful, but this morning was definitely an exception.

She rarely cooked up here, given the industrial kitchen in the restaurant, where she usually nibbled and picked her way through the day from whatever was on the menu.

The last thing on her mind was food, either for herself or her customers. What she really wanted to know was what time Detective Kincaid began his day at work, or if he was off on Saturdays.

Since the three detectives usually had their first meal at the restaurant around seven and were always on their way out the door within forty-five minutes, she assumed their daily schedule began at eight.

Steve Kincaid didn't strike her as a man who would be on time. He probably lollygagged to his desk sometime between eight-fifteen and eight-thirty. Roxy had never been late for anything in her life, and she wouldn't have a hard time believing that Steve Kincaid had never been on time for anything in his life. His laid-back aura was in direct opposition to her driving energy.

She frowned and got up to pour herself a second cup of coffee, her mind still filled with the shaggy-haired, blue-eyed detective, who for some reason irritated her by his mere existence whenever she saw him.

It was, for the most part, an irrational reaction, and that's what made it all the more irritating. Despite his outrageous flirting with her, he would never mean anything to her in life. No man ever would. Besides, she knew his stupid flirting was just for show.

But she was aware of the fact that she needed him right now, that she was depending on him to fix her world and make it right. She just wasn't used to needing anyone.

She also realized that in all their talk about Aunt Liz and her friends and acquaintances the day before, they hadn't mentioned Ramona and the potential that Liz might have run off to meet her young sister somewhere. In fact, Roxy thought perhaps they'd given Steve the impression that their mother was dead, and as much as she hated it, she needed to be clear about the woman who was their mother.

After finishing her second cup of coffee, she left the kitchen and headed for the bathroom, where she took a long, hot shower and then dressed in a pair of jeans and a navy T-shirt that advertised the Dollhouse in bold pink letters.

By that time she knew Josie had arrived in the kitchen downstairs, for the scent of boiling chicken and simmering roast drifted up the stairway as Roxy headed downstairs.

When she entered the kitchen, Josie stood in front of the stove, her feet moving and arms flailing to the music coming in from her earbuds.

She nearly jumped out of her shoes when Roxy tapped her on the shoulder. Roxy might have laughed on any other day, but today there was no laughter to be found anyplace inside her.

Josie yanked out her earbuds, her cute features instantly transforming into concern. "Roxy, how are you doing?"

It took a moment for Roxy to reply. How was she doing? "I think I'm kind of numb right now," she finally said.

"So there wasn't any word overnight?"

Roxy shook her head. "No, nothing. Are you going to be okay here without me today?"

"I've got it covered." Josie stepped back to the stove and turned down the flames beneath the boiling chicken that would later be deboned and prepared as chicken salad for the lunch fare. "I've called in Allie and Nancy to waitress. Greg will help me out here in the kitchen, and Gus said he'd try to show up a little early this afternoon to help with anything we need and with closing up."

She moved closer to Roxy, her brown eyes soft with sympathy. "We have this, Roxy. For as long as you need us, we'll all pull together and keep this place running just as if you were here snapping the whip."

Roxy smiled faintly, knowing that she was, indeed, a tough taskmaster. She was first and foremost a businesswoman, driven and determined to succeed.

"You know I have full confidence in you to keep the standards high and service impeccable," Roxy said. "Besides, I'm hoping we'll figure things out this morning, or at least by the end of the day, and Aunt Liz will be home and I'll be back in the kitchen in the morning."

"Are you meeting up with your sisters?"

"No, I insisted they open the store today as usual. There's no point in all three of us running amok trying to find answers. Besides, Marlene hasn't been herself since her divorce, and Sheri would be too shy and polite to demand things get done unless somebody threatened one of her woodland creatures."

Josie shot her a wry grin. "And we know you don't have that problem. Actually, Marlene called me a little while ago and said she'd been up all night and had baked some pies and pastries to bring in this morning."

Roxy looked at her in surprise, although she supposed she shouldn't be startled. Marlene had always been at Aunt Liz's side when she baked goodies and had at one time dreamed of opening her own bakery, a dream that had seemed to die along with her marriage.

"She said she'll bring in the baked goodies every morning until your aunt can do it again," Josie said.

Roxy's heart expanded with love for her sister, who had probably been up all night worrying and had used that time to make sure Roxy had what she needed for her business.

Josie looked at the large clock on the kitchen wall. "Actually, she should be here anytime."

It was just after six-thirty, and so Roxy sat at the prep table to wait for her sister and tried not to focus on how wrong everything felt.

She should be cooking, waiting for Aunt Liz to arrive, while Marlene should be in bed, snoozing until heading into the roadside shop at noon. Roxy should be cutting up vegetables or adding a secret herb to a soup or planning new specialties.

Sheri was probably already outside, filling squirrel and bird feeders and taking care of all the other woodland creatures that brought her far more comfort than people ever had.

Sheri had been a stutterer for the first twelve years of her life, and Roxy couldn't count the number of times she'd beaten up some ignorant bully for making fun of her kid sister. The stutter had gradually gone away and now only appeared when she was particularly stressed or excited.

A knock on the back door signaled Marlene's arrival. Roxy hurried to let her sister in, as her arms were filled with pie carriers and boxed pastries.

"Let me take those from you," Roxy said, noting that Marlene looked utterly exhausted. Dark circles shadowed the porcelain skin beneath her eyes, although the long blond hair that fell to her shoulders was clean and silky. Her lips quivered slightly as she attempted a smile.

"You didn't need to do this, Marlene," Roxy said as she and her sister placed the baked goods on a nearby table.

"I know, but I couldn't sleep and I couldn't just do nothing, so I drove to Aunt Liz's and used her kitchen to bake. I can do this for you, Roxy, at least until Aunt Liz comes back. It will make me feel useful, and I don't mind at all."

"But you can't get up early in the morning and bake for me and then be at the store all day," Roxy said.

"Sheri and I have already figured it all out so that I can bake in the morning and work the evening shift at the store. All you have to know is that you can depend on me for the baked goods every morning until things are back to normal." Marlene's eyes deepened to a midnight blue and shimmered with a hint of unshed tears. "Things will get back to normal, won't they, Roxy?"

Roxy grabbed her sister into a tight embrace. "I'll find her, Marlene. One way or another, I'll see that she gets home. Don't I always fix everything? I swear I'm going to fix this, and everything will be back to normal," Roxy exclaimed fervently.

She released her hold on her sister. "Now go home and try to get some sleep. I'll check in at the store later this evening, and if I find out something before then, I'll call either you or Sheri."

She and Marlene shared a final hug, and then Marlene left through the back door. Roxy forced a smile at Josie. "I'm going to take off, too."

It was close to seven, and she wanted to be sitting in the police station waiting room when Steve decided to show up for work. There was no way she intended for him to take this slow and easy. She wanted action, and sooner rather than later.

Steve had awakened long before dawn with thoughts of Liz Marcoli racing through his brain. Thank God it wasn't winter. The weather in Wolf Creek could be brutal in those months, and she wouldn't have lasted a night out on the streets or wandering in the woods.

Maybe she had haunted his dreams because she was the same age as Steve's mother, and he was very close to his mom. Most Sundays he ate lunch at the condo she'd moved into a couple of months before. There had been so much grief in the past two years that he knew his mother worried about him as he did her.

The unexpected death of his father eight months ago from a heart attack had hopefully been the last in a string of tragedies for what was left of the Kincaid family.

At six he rolled out of bed, downed two cups of coffee and then showered and dressed for the day. First thing this morning he intended to talk to Chief Krause and get the okay to pursue the Marcoli case.

He had nothing pressing on his desk, and once he had the chief's okay, the day would be spent interviewing anyone and everyone who knew Liz Marcoli. What he hoped was that somebody he spoke to today might know something that the three sisters Liz had raised didn't know about her.

Normally he wasn't due into his office until eight, but it was just after seven when he pulled up and parked, eager to get the day started.

As he walked in the front door, a rivulet of dismayed shock rode up his back at the sight of Roxy seated in one of the plastic chairs in the outer area.

She jumped to her feet, looking as surprised to see him as he was to see her. "You're early," she said.

"And you're earlier," he replied with an inward sigh. He'd hoped to get some plan in place, some action taken before he saw her or spoke to her again.

She followed him through the door that led to the inner sanctum and planted herself in the chair in front of his desk. "So the night has passed, and we still don't have any answers. What's your plan?"

"The first thing on my agenda is to get a cup of coffee. Would you like one?"

He was unsurprised by the slight flare of irritation that sparked in her eyes, and he wondered if she had any idea how sexy she looked with her T-shirt stretched across her full breasts, a faint pink flush filling her cheeks and her dark hair a curly halo around her head.

She sat back in the chair, and the hint of irritation disappeared. "Sure. A cup of coffee sounds fine. It will help to fortify us as we organize the search party."

He nodded and got up from his chair to go into the small break room where the coffeepot was located. He hated to give her the news, but he knew there would be no search party. The woods around the small town were too thick and massive and the resources of the department far too small to warrant an official search party in a case where they couldn't even be sure at this point that any foul play had actually occurred.

He hadn't asked her how she drank her coffee, so he grabbed the two foam cups, a packet of fake sugar and another of powdered creamer and then returned to the desk. The day had only just begun, and already he knew it was going to be a long one.

"I didn't know how you drank it, so I brought some cream and sugar," he said as he placed a cup in front of her.

"Thanks," she said grudgingly. "Black is fine."

"Just give me a minute to check in with my chief, and I'll be right back."

She half rose from the chair, as if expecting that he intended to pull a disappearing act on her. "I'll be right back," he repeated and then headed for the chief's office.

It took him only a few minutes of conversation with his boss to get the okay to conduct an investigation into Liz Marcoli's disappearance.

He returned to his chair and Roxy looked at him expectantly, as if waiting for him to wave a magic wand and fix her world.

It was only on closer examination of her lovely features that he saw the shadows beneath her eyes and the overall exhaustion that had her shoulders slumped slightly forward. Despite the obvious weariness, a white-hot energy emanated from her, an energy that warned him to tread carefully.

At least she appeared relatively calm at the moment, but Roxy's temper was legendary and he didn't want to be the one who stirred it up. It would do neither of them any good for her to get angry.

"Did you sleep last night?" he asked.

Her dark, well-shaped eyebrows lifted as if she was surprised by his question. "I fell asleep for about two hours sometime during the early morning." She spoke the words as if disgusted with herself, as though maybe if she hadn't slept, Liz Marcoli would be where she belonged this morning.

"You need to sleep and you need to eat during this ordeal. No matter how hard it is, you need to try to keep to your normal routine as much as possible. You won't be any help to me or anyone else if you don't take care of yourself."

She eyed him as if expecting a trick and then leaned forward, bringing with her the scent he always noticed around her—a whisper of spring flowers topped with a dash of exotic spices. "Speaking of being helpful, I think maybe we gave you the impression yesterday that our mother is dead."

"She's not?"

Roxy shook her head. "She's very much alive, and

probably the only person on the face of the earth who might call and have Aunt Liz running off someplace to her rescue."

This time it was Steve who looked at her in surprise. "I just assumed by what you told me about your aunt raising you all that your mother was dead." He pulled out a notepad. "What's her name?"

"Ramona Marcoli, although who knows at this time what her last name might be."

"Marcoli? I thought your aunt had been married."

"She was, but when her husband died she took back her maiden name." Softness swept into her eyes. It was there only a moment and then gone. "Her husband's name was Joe Arnoni, and he was the love of her life. When he died she couldn't stand to hear his name. It hurt too badly, so she went back to being Liz Marcoli."

"Do you know where your mother lives?"

"The last time I saw or spoke to my mother was when I was nine and she dropped off Sheri, who was a newborn, for Aunt Liz to take care of. Stop by, drop off the unwanted garbage and then get on with your life—that was apparently Ramona's motto." She didn't try to hide her bitterness.

"Do you have any idea where she was living the last time you saw her?" Steve asked.

"At that time I think she was living someplace in Harrisburg, but it's anyone's guess where she might be now."

"And you think that if your mother needed her, your aunt Liz would drop everything and go to wherever your mother might be?" Steve asked, a touch of relief flooding through him as this new scenario came to light.

"Yes, but if that had happened, Aunt Liz would have somehow managed to call one of us by now to let us know she was okay." Once again Roxy's eyes simmered with fresh panic. "She would have taken her purse and driven her car. I think we definitely need to get together a search party as quickly as possible."

So far she'd been relatively calm and reasonable, but Steve knew his next words would probably change all that. "Roxy, there isn't going to be a search party."

She stared at him as if he'd suddenly spoken an ancient language she didn't understand. "What are you talking about? Of course we need to get together a search party. We need to find Aunt Liz."

"It doesn't work that way, Roxy." He drew in a breath as he saw the narrowing of her eyes, and she sat back in the chair as if gathering her strength to throttle him.

He continued at his own peril. "At this point we can't even confirm that a crime has taken place. The first thing we need to do is locate your mother and see if perhaps your aunt is with her."

"And how do you suggest we do that?" she asked.

"I'll get Frank on it. He's the magic man when it comes to finding people through the internet. Do you know if she has any kind of a criminal record?"

"I have no idea, but it wouldn't surprise me."

"If she has a record, then we'll find her fairly easily. In the meantime, today I plan to speak in person with all of your aunt's friends to see if maybe they know some information about her personal life that might explain this absence. Finally, I'd like to take another look around inside your aunt's house. You said she had a cell phone that was probably in her purse. What about a computer?"

"She doesn't own one."

"I need to get her cell phone and see if maybe there's something on it that will help us."

Roxy's eyes blazed with the anger and helplessness he'd expected. "I don't know how you'll find my mother, but I'll take you back to Aunt Liz's house and you can see what we might have missed yesterday that might help figure this all out."

He nodded and started to speak, but she didn't give him a chance. "And if you're planning on interviewing Aunt Liz's friends, then I'm going with you."

"I already have two partners," Steve said.

She leaned forward, getting right in his face. "And now you have a third," she said in a voice that brooked no argument.

Chapter 4

Despite Roxy's desire for immediate action, it was almost nine by the time they finally left the police station. Frank had arrived and agreed to work on hunting up an address for Ramona, and he also planned to upload Liz's information into the missing-persons database.

The thought of Aunt Liz officially being part of a national missing-persons pool made everything more frightening and real than it already had been.

She opened the door to the passenger side of Steve's car to return to her aunt's house, and tossed the fast-food wrappers that were on the seat to the floor. "I should have figured you for a messy man," she said, at the same time trying to swallow against a new-found terror.

"Actually, you caught me on a good day. Usually

there's at least five times more trash in the car than there is now. That's the evidence of my dinner last night." He slid behind the steering wheel and cranked the engine while she tried to find a place for her feet amid the wrappers.

"You know that kind of food will eventually kill you," she said.

He cast her a quick smile. "Ah, Foxy Roxy, I didn't know you cared."

"I don't. And stop calling me that."

"It's just a little pet name," he said.

She glared at him. "Do you have pet names for all your girlfriends? Let me guess…there's Lucky Lucy and Boobsie Betty."

"And don't forget Willing Wendy," he supplied, and as he smiled at her again she realized exactly what he'd done. He'd taken her terror and transformed it into an aggravation toward him, an emotion that felt safer and far more familiar than the stifling fear.

She rolled down her window and for a moment they rode in silence. "Thank you," she finally said.

"You're welcome," he replied, apparently not needing an explanation for her gratitude. "I know it's tough, Roxy," he added softly.

She didn't reply. There was no way he could know all the feelings that she was experiencing at the moment. Aunt Liz had been missing for an entire day and night.

Even Marlene and Sheri wouldn't be feeling the full ache of emptiness, the utter horror that continuously tried to crawl up her throat. Sure, they'd be worried and afraid, but they weren't as emotionally tied to Aunt Liz as Roxy was. They didn't have the memories of what life had been like before Aunt Liz.

Horrific memories.

A childhood that no kid should have to suffer.

Roxy had spent her entire life making sure that Sheri and Marlene had only happiness in their lives. She had made caretaking for her sisters her number one priority, and she'd always known that while she was her sisters' emotional support, Aunt Liz was hers.

There was no way surfer dude knew the ache of absence, the fear of the unknown that had Roxy's emotions simmering with anxiety and terror. Probably the worst thing he'd ever suffered was a painful hangnail.

Still, as she gazed out the window she couldn't help but smell him, the scent of minty soap and shaving cream and a whisper of sandalwood cologne.

She shot him a surreptitious glance and then looked back out the window. There was no question that she found him more than a little bit attractive, as did most of the single and married women in town, although she'd never heard any gossip about him with any married woman.

That perpetually mussed, sun-streaked hair of his begged for fingers to dance through the shaggy length, and his eyes were the blue of Caribbean waters. He had a sensual mouth with a fuller lower lip that held the promise of kisses that could buckle a woman's knees.

With a new flash of irritation, she nibbled on her thumbnail until they pulled into Aunt Liz's driveway. Roxy dug a set of keys from her purse, and then together they got out of the car and approached the house.

Roxy unlocked the front door and shoved it open; the absence of sweet baking scents shot a stabbing pain through her center.

When they had been here the day before, they had only done a cursory search, looking for her aunt. She knew that today Steve would be looking for other things or the lack of items that might provide a clue as to what had happened yesterday morning that had kept Aunt Liz from her usual schedule.

He stopped her before she walked from the entry into the living room. "I want you to stand here and look around. See if anything looks out of place or is missing," he said.

She nodded and studied the living room as if seeing it for the first time. The sofa was a floral print, slightly worn and matching the overstuffed chair nearby. Behind the chair, a floor lamp sat to provide Liz additional light as she quilted or embroidered in neat little stitches. Her quilting material was all in a blue-flowered tote next to the chair, an embroidery hoop visible with a pattern half-completed by colorful threads.

The bookshelves that lined one wall held a variety of items, including photos of her and her sisters, mementoes from the time Liz had worked in Hershey at the Hershey factory and plenty of books.

"Nothing missing and nothing out of place," she announced. Nothing except her aunt, who wasn't in her chair with her quilting in her lap and her glasses propped down on the lower end of her nose.

"Okay, let's move into the kitchen." He placed a hand at the small of her back as they walked through the living room. Roxy wanted to protest the touch, but she found it oddly comforting.

When they reached the kitchen it was just as they'd left it the day before, the baked goods still on the countertop along with Liz's purse and car keys.

After looking around and seeing nothing else amiss, Roxy opened the pie containers. Lemon meringue and chocolate silk. "These need to be thrown out," she said, and he watched as she tossed the pies into the trash container. She opened the cake pan to see a black forest cake. "I can't serve this at the restaurant, but it's still good. Do you want to take it home with you?"

He looked at her suspiciously, as if perhaps she might be offering him a poisoned apple. "Why can't you serve it in the restaurant?"

"Because it's a day old. I promise you it's perfectly good. I just won't allow day-old desserts to be served at the Dollhouse."

"Okay, then I'll take it to Sunday lunch tomorrow at my mom's."

"Oh, your mother lives around here?"

"Yes, and I have lunch with her every Sunday. My father passed away eight months ago from a heart attack. Where did you think I came from? Under a rock?"

"Actually, I thought maybe you crawled out of a seashell. You've got the surfer dude attitude down pat," she replied honestly.

"Surfer dude?" His amazing blue eyes stared at her blankly.

"You know, the shaggy sun-streaked hair, the laid-back attitude, the chicks that follow you around everywhere…" She allowed her voice to trail off, wondering how they had gotten so far off track.

"You obviously know nothing about me or my life, whatever your impression or my reputation might indicate." There was a touch of irritation in his tone as he gestured her out of the room and down the hallway.

His cell phone rang, and he dug it out of his pocket and checked the caller identification. "I've got to take this. It's a private call." He ducked into the bathroom and closed the door behind him.

Probably one of those girlfriends of his, Roxy thought. She walked into the first bedroom that used to belong to Sheri and Marlene when they'd all been growing up together. It still held twin beds with pink spreads, two matching upright dressers and a single nightstand between the beds.

Rather than an array of clothing for two growing girls, the closet now held quilts already made and boxes of material and thread, along with a large standing hoop.

The bathroom door opened, and Steve rejoined her. "Sorry about that," he said.

"There's nothing missing." Roxy thought they were wasting time and was irrationally irritated by his private phone call.

The second bedroom had been Roxy's, but it had since been transformed into a storage area with shelves that held baking items, storage containers and utensils the small kitchen couldn't hold.

By the time they reached Liz's bedroom, Roxy had a mere finger grasp of patience left. Seeing the neatly made double bed where Roxy had often spent stormy nights snuggled with her aunt and younger sisters nearly cast her to her knees in worried grief.

She turned to Steve, who stood just outside the door in the hallway. "It's all the same. Nothing is missing, so whatever happened to her didn't involve a robbery. There are no signs of a struggle anywhere in the house. We're wasting time here. It's obvious she isn't here, and there's nothing to point to where she might be right now."

"Roxy, this is all going to be a process of elimination. We had to check the house in order to eliminate any clues that might be here." He spoke in slow, measured words, as if explaining something to a two-year-old.

Before she could respond, a knock sounded from the back door in the kitchen. Roxy started down the hallway to answer, but Steve grabbed her by the arm and pushed her behind him at the same time that he pulled his gun.

It was at that moment that Roxy realized two things—that Steve was taking this far more seriously than she'd thought he was, and that there was absolutely no guarantee of a happy ending.

The man at the back door wore a wide-brimmed straw hat, and a beard that instantly identified him as one of the Amish from the nearby settlement. The older man's eyes widened as he saw Steve with his gun through the door window.

"That's Mr. Zooker," Roxy said from behind Steve. "Put your gun away before you give the poor man a heart attack."

Steve holstered his gun and opened the door. The tall, muscular man was clad in the traditional white shirt and black trousers, and beyond him in the driveway Steve saw the horse and buggy that he'd arrived in.

His blue eyes softened as Roxy stepped in front of Steve. "Good morning to you, Mr. Zooker," she said.

He nodded. "A good day to you. I have a delivery for your aunt. Could I speak to her?"

"I'm Detective Steve Kincaid." Steve took control by once again stepping between Roxy and the man at the door.

"Abraham Zooker. Is there a problem with Mrs. Marcoli?" A line of concern deepened in his broad forehead.

"We aren't sure. When was the last time you saw or spoke to her?"

Zooker frowned and pulled on the end of his long salt-and-pepper beard. "It would have been three weeks ago. I was at the Roadside Stop delivering some of my furniture to Miss Marlene and Miss Sheri when Mrs. Marcoli approached me and ordered a piece from me."

"Was she expecting you today?" Steve asked.

"Not specifically. I told her I would deliver it once it was ready, and I'd planned a trip into town so I decided to attempt to deliver it today. If she isn't here, I can always come back another time."

"You're here now so you might as well drop off whatever you brought. Have you been paid?" Roxy asked.

Abraham nodded. "I was paid in full when your aunt ordered the piece." He backed away from the door. "I'll be right back."

Steve turned to Roxy. "What's the story?"

"He's one of the Amish who have been given permission to work with the English. He makes beautiful wooden furniture that Marlene and Sheri sell at their place, and he also has made several quilting racks for Aunt Liz."

Steve knew that the Amish community closest to Wolf Creek was a progressive order. Although they used no electricity and continued the old tradition of traveling by horse and buggy, he'd heard that some of them were allowed running water in their homes and many did a brisk commercial trade with business-people in town. They had large farms and ran a dairy operation, and their horses and buggies and wide-brimmed straw hats were common sights in town.

Although Steve had been out to the settlement many times in the past, he had never met Abraham Zooker before.

"I get a lot of my cheese and dairy products from Abraham's brother, Isaaic," Roxy explained.

By that time Abraham had returned, carrying a beautifully crafted quilt display rack. Steve opened the door to allow the man to set the piece inside the kitchen. "She paid me for two, so there is another one that I should have ready in a couple of weeks," he said.

"Why don't you hold off on that one for now," Roxy said, her eyes a simmering cauldron of emotion as she ran a hand lightly over the smooth wood of the piece. "I'll get in touch with you when it's time to start making the other one."

"Your aunt is ill?"

"She's missing. She hasn't been seen since yester-day morning," Steve replied.

"I will pray for her," Abraham said.

"I'd appreciate it if you'd ask around your community whether anyone has seen her in the past twenty-four hours," Steve said.

"Of course. We've always cooperated with authorities whenever necessary," Zooker said. He looked at Roxy, his blue eyes once again softening. "I'm sorry for your worries, and I hope your aunt turns up well."

"Thank you, Mr. Zooker," Roxy told him. Steve noted the hint of tears in her eyes.

It stunned him. In the past twenty-four hours he'd seen her combative and rude, anxious and fearful, but he hadn't seen tears.

As Abraham Zooker left, Roxy closed the door and leaned against it weakly, the glistening tears more pronounced as she stared at the quilt rack.

"Aunt Liz bought a rack and made a wedding ring quilt for Marlene when she got married. I'm guessing this one was in anticipation of whenever Sheri or I get married, even though I've told her a thousand times I have no intention of that." The tears that had shimmered in her eyes released and trekked down her cheeks. "Where could she be, Steve? What could have happened to her?"

Steve knew he was about to take his life in his own hands, but he'd never seen a woman who looked more like she needed to be held than Roxy looked at that moment.

Knowing the danger, but unable to stop himself, he reached out and pulled her into an embrace. She stiffened against him and he tensed, expecting a knee to his jewels or a jab to his jaw, but instead she relaxed into him as a deep sob escaped her.

He tightened his arms around her, trying not to

notice the press of her full breasts against his lower chest, how neatly her head fit just beneath his chin.

She felt good; she felt right in his arms, but she allowed it for only a handful of heartbeats and then she stepped back from him and swiped the tears off her cheeks.

"Wow, that won't happen again," she said, her voice filled with an appalled regret. "I never cry, and I definitely never cuddle." She raised her chin defensively.

"Fine, then we'll just chalk that up to you having something in your eye and we accidentally bumped into each other," he replied drily.

It was obvious that the last thing Roxy Marcoli wanted was to appear vulnerable in any way. The angry defiance he sensed in her would hold her in good stead in the days to come. Hopefully it would fill up part of the space inside her that otherwise would be screaming in fear, dying of anxiety.

Steve knew very well the maelstrom of emotions flooding through Roxy, and he also knew her body and mind could only endure the high state of anxiety for so long.

She was with him now because she was in the first stages of disbelief and fear. Eventually, if Liz Marcoli wasn't found, Roxy would have to figure out how to resume her life and work around the hole in her heart until some sort of closure was finally granted.

Steve was still waiting for closure in his own missing-persons case, and in the absence of that closure he'd adopted the laid-back "surfer dude" attitude to hide his own fear and pain. The day that his ex-girlfriend had kidnapped his son had been the moment Steve's world had shattered. That had been two years ago, and during that time Steve had never stopped looking for the little boy he loved more than anything else on earth.

"So what happens next?" Roxy asked, pulling him from his thoughts.

He gave himself a mental shake. He had to stay focused on *this* missing-persons case.

He walked over to the counter where Liz's purse was and looked inside. He pulled out her cell phone, punched a couple of numbers and frowned. "The history of incoming calls has been deleted."

"So we don't know who might have called Aunt Liz early Friday morning," Roxy said flatly.

"We'll drop the phone off at the station. Frank not only does magic with finding people—he's also a rock star at getting this kind of information. The calls might be deleted from the phone, but the cell phone company will have the records."

"And after we drop it off at the station?"

"Next we go talk to Patricia Burns. You told me yesterday that she was your aunt's closest friend. Maybe she'll know something about your aunt that you don't know."

Roxy shot him a tight grin. "Doubtful, but we have to do what we have to do."

What was happening? Steve asked himself minutes later when they were back in his car after dropping off the phone at the station and heading to Patricia Burns's house. What was he doing with Roxy like a mouse in his pocket, gnawing a tiny hole in his sanity?

He should have done the professional thing and sent her on her way that morning in the station. He wasn't sure exactly how *he* had become *we*. He had two perfectly good partners to work with, and he didn't need another one. He especially didn't need one who'd felt so right pulled tight against his body, one who sent his adrenaline rushing whenever her eyes snapped with fire.

As soon as he interviewed Patricia Burns, he was taking Roxy right back to her car at the station and carrying on alone. He'd promise her frequent check-ins, but he needed to get her out of his pocket.

Patricia Burns lived two blocks away from Liz Marcoli in a neat ranch house that was identical to Liz's except for the color.

Their knock was greeted by a petite woman with short salt-and-pepper hair and a worried expression in her brown eyes. She instantly grabbed Roxy's hand. "No word?"

"No, nothing."

Patricia nodded to Steve and then gestured them into a living room decorated in shades of blue. Steve introduced himself to her as he sat in a chair next to the sofa, where the two women sank down side by side.

"Can I get you something to drink?" Patricia asked.

"Thanks, but we're fine," Steve replied. "I understand you and Liz are good friends, Mrs. Burns," he continued.

"Best friends, and, please, call me Treetie." She smiled and patted Roxy's hand. "When the girls were little they had trouble saying Patricia, and so I became Treetie and the nickname stuck."

"Okay, Treetie, when was the last time you spoke to Liz?"

"Thursday night. We talked on the phone around eight."

"Anything unusual going on with her? Anything she was worried about?" Steve took out his little pad and pen, ready to take any notes that might be pertinent to the case.

"No, nothing unusual. The only thing Liz ever worried about was the girls. She worried that Marlene was never going to get over her divorce and that Sheri would wind up being all alone with only the chipmunks for company. And, of course, she worried that Roxy would keep any man from ever marrying her because of her sharp tongue and the scars left from her early life with her mother."

She patted Roxy's hand as Roxy's cheeks dusted with high color. "Sorry, honey, but that's the truth." She pulled her hand back from Roxy's. "Other than that, Liz was enjoying her life. She had her baking that she did for the Dollhouse, she was planning her flower and vegetable garden and she had Edward."

"Edward?" Steve asked.

"Edward?" Roxy parroted in confusion. "Who in the hell is Edward?"

Chapter 5

"Edward Cardell." Treetie frowned and shot a quick glance at Roxy and then looked back at Steve. She drew a deep, reluctant sigh. "She didn't want the girls to know about him."

"What about him?" Roxy asked, her head beginning to spin.

"They were dating. They've been dating for quite some time."

The air whooshed out of Roxy. Aunt Liz dating? She was positively stunned by the news. The very idea was as alien as a vegan in a meatpacking plant.

"Edward Cardell. Who exactly is he, and what do you know about him?" Steve asked, taking the words right out of Roxy's mouth.

"Oh, dear." Treetie looked worriedly at Roxy and then at Steve. "I told Liz she should have mentioned him to the girls a while ago, but she insisted that she wanted to keep things quiet for the time being. I think she was enjoying having a little secret all her own. Edward lives here in town. He's a very nice gentleman, retired from the post office a couple of years ago. He's been a widow for about three years, and he and Liz met one night at bingo about a year ago and hit it off."

"Aunt Liz has been dating for a year?" Roxy wondered what other secrets her aunt might have had.

"Were Liz and Edward having any problems?"

Treetie frowned. "Not any real problems. The only issue was that Edward thought it was past time for Liz to come clean about him with the girls. He was ready to be a part of the entire family and was beginning to pressure her a bit to make their relationship more public."

"And did that upset her?" Steve asked.

"No." Treetie smiled. "Liz is a strong-willed woman, and there was really no question that she'd tell the girls only when she was good and ready. Edward knew that, and he'd push a little and she'd push back, but they never really fought about it. They're wonderfully suited to each other."

"Why would she want to keep him a secret?" Roxy asked, still reeling with the shock.

"She never wanted you girls to believe that anything or anyone came before you."

Roxy's heart squeezed tight. "But we're all grown-up now. We'd be delighted if we knew that Aunt Liz had found somebody who made her happy. She deserved to have a life of her own after all the years she gave to us."

Treetie smiled at her. "You know Liz—to her you all were always going to be her baby girls."

The numbness that had washed over Roxy at various times since her aunt's vanishing now overwhelmed her as Steve continued to question Treetie.

Was it possible that Aunt Liz was someplace with this Edward Cardell? That perhaps he had swept her away somewhere for a romantic weekend without her knowing his plans? Maybe she'd been so flustered by the unexpected event that she'd left her purse and forgotten about delivering the usual items to the restaurant.

There was a certain relief in that thought, and yet she couldn't imagine Liz not insisting that before they go anywhere she take care of her duty in delivering the baked goods to Roxy for the day.

But look what men managed to do to your mother, a little voice whispered in the back of her head. Men and drugs had ruined Ramona's life. Men often caused women to make bad choices. Wasn't it possible Aunt Liz was so crazy in love that she'd been talked into being whisked away without any thought of Roxy or responsibilities?

By the time she and Steve got back in the car, the numbness that had overtaken Roxy had transformed to an excitement mixed with hopeful possibility. "We need to find this Edward Cardell," she said as Steve started the car. "Maybe he and Aunt Liz are together somewhere."

"Maybe," Steve replied. "But the first thing we're doing is heading back to the station. I want to check in with Frank and see if he's managed to get a location on your mother or any information from Liz's cell phone, and it's time for this partnership to end."

"What are you talking about?" Roxy asked. "We have a lead, Edward Cardell, and we should follow up on it immediately."

"*We* aren't doing anything, Roxy. I'm going to take you back to your car, and you need to get back to work at the Dollhouse or go talk to your sisters, or do whatever you want to do, but you aren't coming with me."

"Are you worried that being seen with me might make one of your other girlfriends mad?" she asked.

"Knock it off with the girlfriend thing, Roxy. It's getting old. I'm doing my job, and it isn't professional or right for you to be with me while I'm conducting an investigation."

"It's exactly right for me to be with you while you're interviewing my aunt's friends and acquaintances. If I hadn't been here, I wouldn't have known that Aunt Liz was seeing somebody." A frantic feeling rose up inside Roxy. She had to be a part of this. She *needed* to be a part of it.

"A fact she obviously didn't want you to know," he returned.

Roxy chewed her thumbnail thoughtfully and then dropped her hand to her lap. "There's only one reason why Aunt Liz would have kept her relationship with this Edward a secret, and that would have been because she thought we wouldn't approve of him. Which means Edward probably wasn't right for her. For all we know, he's a serial killer or a sexual deviant."

Steve shot her a quick glance, one of his dark blond eyebrows lifting. "Now you're a matchmaker who knows what's best for your aunt and an assassinator of character without even meeting this Edward?" he asked sarcastically.

"It's the only thing that makes sense," she countered.

"Maybe she just didn't want to introduce him to you because she was afraid you'd be rude, judgmental and a control freak. She was probably afraid you'd scare him off."

She drew in a sharp breath as he pulled his car to a halt in front of the police station. "And you're a jerk, just like I always thought you were." She got out of the car and slammed the door.

"Where are you going?" he asked as she headed for the station house door.

"I'm going to find out if your partner Frank has found out where my mother is." She blew through the front door with Steve at her heels.

The cop at the counter buzzed them through, and she was grateful to see Frank Delaney at his desk. He started to rise when he saw her, but she quickly motioned him back down.

Steve stood next to her, and she realized she'd managed to tick him off. Not that she cared; he'd ticked her off, as well. First by telling her he was dropping her off here, and second by telling her that she was rude and judgmental.

"Have you located my mother?" she asked Frank, who immediately cast his blue eyes to Steve as if asking his permission to give her any information.

After getting a nod from Steve, Frank looked back at her and shook his head. "I haven't been able to find out anything. Apparently she doesn't have a vehicle registered in her name, there's no address and she's not working. She's basically off the grid."

Roxy sighed, not surprised. "She's been off the grid for years. For all I know, she could be dead. Can you get me Edward Cardell's address?"

"Roxy." Steve's voice held a steely warning. "I have your cell phone number. I'll call you with any information I get."

"Fine. Whatever." She whirled on her heels, grateful that at least with her back to him he couldn't see the tears that once again burned in her eyes.

She left the police station, got into her car and sat, unsure where she should go or what she should do but knowing she needed to do something. She couldn't just go home and twiddle her thumbs while Aunt Liz was missing. She also wasn't ready to share with her sisters what she'd found out, not until she knew more about this Edward Cardell.

Steve had called her a control freak. For crying out loud, of course she was a control freak. Otherwise she couldn't manage a successful business, take care of herself and her sisters and stay sane. The first seven years of her life had been so wildly out of control that she now clung to control and refused to relinquish it for anything or anyone.

Her aunt was missing, and her entire world was turned upside down. She'd lost control of things, and she'd do whatever it took to find Aunt Liz and make her world right once again.

With this thought in mind, she started the car and pulled out of the parking space. She'd check in at the Dollhouse, where the lunch rush would be in full swing, and while she was there she'd check the phone book. Surely Edward Cardell would be listed, and along with his phone number there would be an address.

Unless he didn't have a landline. If that was the case, then Roxy would get on her laptop to find him, or she'd walk the streets and ask people if they knew Edward and where he lived. The town wasn't so big that somebody wouldn't know him, especially if he had retired from the post office.

She didn't need to be with Steve Kincaid to investigate. She could do it on her own.

Unfortunately, when she reached the Dollhouse she found things in chaos. One of the waitresses that Josie had called in to help cover Roxy's absence hadn't showed up, and although Josie was doing the best she could with the staff on hand, it wasn't enough.

Roxy grabbed an apron and got to work. The afternoon passed in a haze, with Roxy alternating between the kitchen and the customers. Each time her cell phone rang she fumbled in her pocket to retrieve it, hoping it would be Steve calling to tell her he'd found her aunt with Edward Cardell and she was fine.

Instead, each call was from concerned friends or her sisters, checking in to see if there was anything new. By the time the restaurant closed at five, Roxy was exhausted and yet filled with a frustration that required some sort of action. She'd heard nothing from Steve all afternoon.

"Roxy, sorry about the mess this afternoon," Josie said as Roxy pulled an old thin phone book off a shelf.

"It's not your fault. You couldn't know that Allie would get sick half an hour before she was due to show up. We managed just fine," she said absently as she flipped through the phone book to the *c*'s.

"I haven't seen you eat all day," Josie said. "Have you eaten anything?"

Roxy frowned and looked at Josie. "Actually, I haven't." She looked back down at the phone book, a small edge of triumph yelling inside her as she found Edward Cardell. She memorized the address, then placed the phone book back on the shelf and looked at the clock on the wall.

It was five-thirty. Why hadn't she heard from Steve by now? Surely he'd been to Edward Cardell's place and had learned something.

"Roxy, you really need to eat," Josie said in concern.

"I don't have time now. I have someplace I need to be. I'll grab something on the way." There was no way she intended to call Steve for the answers she wanted. She'd just go find them out herself.

With Edward Cardell's address burned in her brain, she took off her apron, grabbed her car keys and headed outside. She knew the general area where Cardell's house was located, although it was on the opposite side of town and not exactly familiar stomping grounds.

Even though she knew Steve wouldn't be happy if he found out what she was doing, she felt compelled to speak to the man who had apparently been a part of her aunt's life for the past year…a secret part.

What other secrets might her aunt have? Secrets that might have brought some kind of danger into her life? Had she seen other men before Edward? Did she have an ex-lover who might want to hurt her? The very idea of her aunt having any lovers boggled her mind.

It took Roxy twenty minutes to find Edward Cardell's home, an older two-story that appeared to be in pristine condition. The front yard sported a huge pine tree, and the lawn looked neat and tended.

She was surprised to feel a wave of nerves sweep through her as she parked in the driveway and approached the front door. Surely Steve had already been there, and since he hadn't called her, there must have been nothing to report.

Still, she felt compelled to follow through. Drawing in a deep breath, she knocked firmly on the door. There was no response. She knocked again, this time harder. When there was still no reply, she left the porch and peeked into the garage door windows.

No vehicle.

Apparently nobody was home. Was that why Steve hadn't given her an update? Because when he'd come by, nobody was there?

Roxy got back into her car and stared at the house. Her stomach growled, reminding her that she hadn't eaten all day. Sooner or later Edward Cardell would have to come home, and she intended to be there when he did.

She backed out of the driveway, knowing what she had to do. She'd seen enough movies to know that the only way to assure she was there when Edward returned was to conduct her own private stakeout.

Half an hour later she parked on the opposite side of the street with Edward's house two driveways down the block. A quick stop at the nearest grocery store had set her up with enough food and beverages to last the entire night if necessary.

Who needs Detective Steve Kincaid? she thought. She'd take care of things herself, just like she always had and always would. She unscrewed the cap of a bottle of apple juice, grabbed a string cheese from the package and settled back to wait for the man who might have the answers to where Aunt Liz was.

Steve typed in the last of his report on the interviews he'd conducted throughout the afternoon, interviews that had given him nothing to work with in the case of the missing woman. He'd gone by Edward Cardell's place and found nobody at home. He'd tried to call the house several times throughout the afternoon but continued to get an answering machine.

He'd left no message. If the man was somehow responsible for Liz's disappearance, then he certainly didn't want Cardell to have a heads-up that he was potentially being looked at as a person of interest.

Liz's cell phone records had yielded nothing. Most of the incoming calls had been from Marlene, Sheri, Roxy or women friends, and there had been no incoming or outgoing calls on the morning she'd disappeared.

"Want to get a drink when you finish up?" Jimmy asked from his desk.

"I'm in," Frank replied. He leaned back in his chair and released a weary sigh. "Between trying to find some sign of Ramona Marcoli any place on the face of the earth and checking Liz Marcoli's finances, I'm beat."

"What did you find out about her finances?" Steve asked.

"Nothing worthwhile. Her bank account has had no activity for the last week. She isn't worth a ton of money. She owns her home and has some money in savings, but nothing to warrant a kidnapping for ransom."

"So if she has been kidnapped, we know the motive probably wasn't money." Jimmy got up and stretched.

"We still don't know that a kidnapping took place," Steve reminded them both. "Although I have to admit, the longer she stays missing, the more I believe that foul play was involved."

"She's only been officially gone for one night. It just feels early in the game for us to jump to the conclusion that she's in any kind of trouble," Jimmy said.

"Try telling that to Roxy," Steve noted drily. She'd been on his mind all afternoon, mostly because he couldn't guess what she might be up to, but he knew she probably wasn't consoling her sisters or taking a nap. If he was to guess, she was up to her ears in something that could either cause trouble for him or for herself.

He hadn't called her because he hadn't had anything to report. He looked at his watch, surprised to discover it was after seven. "About that drink, I think I'll pass," he said. Maybe he should check up on Roxy and see exactly what she might be up to.

"Are you sure? It's Saturday night. The Wolf's Head Tavern will be jumping with hot women and half price beers," Frank said, as if sure that Steve couldn't resist the temptation.

The three of them often spent their Saturday nights at the bar just down the street from the police station.

Rustic and without pretense, it was a popular place on weekends.

"Actually, I need to check in with Roxy and make sure she's staying out of trouble," Steve admitted.

Jimmy grinned. "So you plan on spending the night wrestling with a wildcat."

"Something like that," Steve said. "I'll see you two Monday morning. Don't do anything tonight that I wouldn't do."

"Ha. I'd like to get the chance to do something that you would do," Frank replied.

Minutes later Steve was in his car and headed toward the Dollhouse, where he hoped to find Roxy curled up in a chair in her living quarters with her sisters by her side.

He'd tried to call Edward Cardell again and still had gotten no answer. He had no idea if that indicated anything or if it was just a coincidence.

He turned down the alley that would take him to the back of the Dollhouse, where he knew Roxy parked her car. The back of the establishment not only had parking for the staff and a large Dumpster for trash, but also a flagstone patio with a couple of umbrella tables that people sat at when the weather was particularly nice.

When he reached the area, he was somehow not surprised to find Roxy's car missing. *Damn.* He parked and pulled out his cell phone, calling first Marlene and then Sheri, neither of whom had any idea where Roxy might be.

Double damn. Steve frowned and tried to crawl into Roxy's brain and figure out where she might be and what she was doing.

He was unsurprised to discover that it was impossible to crawl into her brain, but he knew what he would do in a situation like this if he was as determined as Roxy at finding answers.

He backed his car out of the lot and headed in the direction of Edward Cardell's house. It was the only lead Roxy knew about, the only lead that had yet to be checked out because the whereabouts of Edward Cardell were, at the moment, unknown.

By the time he reached Edward's street, twilight had begun to sweep over the area. He immediately spied Roxy's car parked ahead of him. *Surprise, surprise,* he thought, not surprised at all.

He pulled to a stop, cut his engine and got out of his car. He approached her vehicle, irritated that she was there, yet understanding why she was.

He peered into the passenger window. She was slumped back in the driver's seat, sound asleep, and the passenger side was littered with string cheese wrappers and two juice bottles, one empty and one full. There was also a bag of ready-to-eat celery, a couple of protein bars and two apples.

She looked as if she was settled in for a long night. She also looked stunning in sleep, with her lovely features relaxed in a way he'd never seen them and with her curly black hair in its usual disarray.

It was the first time he'd seen her without movement, without that defensive cast to her shoulders, the readiness for a fight in her eyes. It was also the first time he embraced how she physically drew him in a way no woman had in a very long time.

She was beautiful, and she definitely inspired a healthy dose of lust inside him, but she was also drama, unbridled emotion and unpredictability, and he'd already been there, done that and would never do it again.

Jeez. She was sound asleep and her doors weren't even locked. He opened the passenger door and she jerked up, her gaze hazy, as if for a moment she didn't know where she was or what was happening.

He swept the items off the passenger seat and to the floor, then slid inside. "I always knew you were a messy girl," he said.

She blinked as if to clear the sleep from her head. "What are you doing here?"

"I'd say the real question of the hour is what are *you* doing here?"

She sat up straighter in her seat, her eyes clearing. "I'm on a stakeout."

He looked down at the packaged food at his feet. "Impossible. This can't be a real stakeout. The food is all wrong."

She glanced down at the packaged food and wrappers at his feet. "What are you talking about?"

He leaned his seat back as if settling in for a long night, and, despite the falling darkness outside the windows, he saw her eyes narrow. "If you want to do a stakeout right, then you have to have a sack of greasy burgers and a couple bags of potato chips. You want donuts and cupcakes and about a case of soda on ice."

"You're going to die before you're forty if that's the way you eat all the time."

"And you're going to get yourself in a lot of trouble if you keep interfering with an official investigation," he replied.

"I'm not interfering in anything," she said coolly.

"I'm just parked on a city street. Last I heard there was no law about that."

"You're playing with fire, Roxy. What if Edward Cardell is a serial killer or the sexual deviant you said he might be? Haven't you considered how dangerous it might be for you to confront him here all alone?"

Their conversation halted as a car pulled into the driveway at the house next door to Edward's. Steve was out of the car in an instant. He'd tried several times throughout the day to contact one of Edward's neighbors but had found nobody home.

He was vaguely aware of Roxy also getting out of the car as he raced across the street and down the sidewalk to catch up with the man who had just exited his car.

"Sir," he called as he fumbled for his identification. "Detective Steve Kincaid. Can I ask you a few questions?"

The man, who appeared to be in his forties, frowned with a touch of concern in his eyes. "Am I in trouble for something? Is my family okay?"

"As far as I know, your family is fine," Steve assured him. "And, no, you aren't in trouble. This isn't about you. It's about your neighbor, Edward Cardell." By that time, Roxy had joined Steve's side.

"Eddie? What about him?"

"Do you know where he is?" Roxy asked.

"Pretend she isn't here," Steve said with a quick stern glance of aggravation at the woman next to him. Couldn't she just let him do his job? "Do you know where Eddie is?"

"He left Friday to go up in the mountains to a friend's cabin."

"Do you know the name of his friend?" Roxy asked.

The young man looked helplessly from Roxy to Steve. Steve stifled a sigh, knowing that it was impossible to rein in Roxy. He nodded to give permission to answer her question.

"Sorry, I don't. I think it belongs to somebody he used to work with at the post office, or maybe an old army buddy. I know the guy who owns it doesn't live here in town."

"Does Eddie go to the cabin frequently?" Steve asked.

The man shrugged. "Maybe once a month or so, when the weather permits."

"And how long does he usually stay gone?"

"Anywhere from three to five days."

"When was the last time you saw him?" Roxy asked. The energy that vibrated from her was a physical entity pressing against Steve.

The neighbor frowned thoughtfully. "It would have been Thursday night. He always comes by and asks me to keep an eye on his place while he's gone. I imagine he got up before the crack of dawn to leave for the cabin on Friday. What's this about? Is he in some kind of trouble?"

"Did he mention taking a woman with him to the cabin?" Roxy took a step closer to the man. Steve grabbed her by her arm and pulled her back.

"He didn't mention anything about a woman, but we weren't real buddies like that. I mean, we're good neighbors and chat occasionally but not much about personal stuff. I'm not expecting him back before Monday or Tuesday."

"And there's nothing else you can tell us about the location of the cabin?" Steve asked.

He shook his head. "Sorry. I really have no idea where it's at other than someplace up in the mountains. I know it's not too far, less than an hour, and Eddie has mentioned that he likes the isolation of the place."

A perfect place for romance...or murder, Steve thought. As he took down the contact information of the neighbor, Rex Donner, he could only guess what thoughts were shifting through Roxy's head.

He took her arm to lead her back to her car. When they reached it, he opened the driver's door and she got inside. "There's no point in a stakeout tonight," he told her.

Her eyes were filled with emotion in the illumination from a nearby streetlamp. "I have to do something, but I don't know what to do."

Steve hesitated a moment. "Why don't we go back to your place and you can make us some coffee? Meanwhile I'll contact the appropriate authorities to find out what kind of vehicle Edward drives, and we'll get a BOLO out on it."

"A BOLO?"

"Be on the lookout," he explained. "If the vehicle is spotted by any law enforcement, it will be stopped and he'll be detained. I'll follow you to your place," he said and closed her door before she could protest.

He shouldn't be following her home. He shouldn't be spending any time with her whatsoever. She couldn't help advance the investigation—in truth, she could only screw things up acting as a lone wolf without any direction.

However, he felt her need to be a part of it. He understood her desire not to be at home alone, where horrible thoughts might intrude and the unknown could create all kinds of terrifying scenarios.

Been there, done that.

She shouldn't be left alone. Why wasn't she with her sisters? Why wasn't her family gathered together to gain strength from each other and wait for whatever answers might come?

This was the time when family support was vital. Steve would have never survived his own personal heartache if not for his parents' support two years ago. There were still days he wasn't sure he'd completely survived.

He parked behind Roxy at the rear of the restaurant and joined her at the back door as she unlocked it and gestured him inside. Once in, she locked the door behind them.

"Why aren't you with your sisters?" he asked curiously.

"Because I'm not." Her tone indicated she didn't want to pursue that particular topic of conversation.

He was surprised when, instead of leading him into one of the public dining areas, she took him up two flights of stairs to her personal living quarters.

As they passed the second floor, he glanced in the open doorway and saw that it was a storage area, a jumbled mess filled with boxes and bins and extra tables and chairs. He assumed Roxy's living space would mirror the Victorian flare of the dining rooms and was surprised when he stepped into the sleek, contemporary space.

He knew instinctively that the cool, almost Spartan,

surroundings were a glimpse of the real Roxy—controlled, without clutter or too many personal effects.

"Have a seat," she said and gestured him toward the sofa. "I'll put on the coffee and be right back."

As she disappeared from his sight, he fought a need to check and make sure she wasn't crawling out a window to escape him and continue her personal crusade to find her aunt. He reminded himself that they were on the third floor of the building; there was no way she could escape through a window.

While she was gone, he called the station and spoke to the lieutenant on duty to set in motion finding out the make and model of Edward Cardell's vehicle and to put out the BOLO on the vehicle.

First thing in the morning he'd try to hunt up friends of Cardell to see if anyone knew where the cabin was located.

There was still no evidence that Liz was with Cardell, either willingly or by force. There was no solid proof that any kind of crime had taken place.

But with each hour that passed without word from Liz, a knot pressed harder in the pit of Steve's stomach that made him believe something criminal might have occurred in that kitchen.

He hoped like hell that Liz was on some romantic getaway and had uncharacteristically decided to stay incommunicado with her family.

As he waited for Roxy to return, he looked around the room more closely, noting the bits and pieces that spoke of the woman who lived there. A black bookcase held a small flat-screen television, several cookbooks by famous chefs and a handful of framed photos of Roxy and her sisters and aunt.

He'd like to take a peek into her bedroom, to see what he could glean about her from the way it was furnished, the things she chose to surround her. But he didn't want to snoop, and, besides, he didn't care who she was in her heart because it didn't matter. Once Liz was found, he'd go back to being a customer at her restaurant and nothing more.

He frowned and gazed toward the kitchen. It seemed to be taking a long time to make coffee, and he heard no rattle of cups, nothing to indicate she was even there.

A fire escape. Hadn't he noticed an iron fire escape leading from the top floor to the ground level on the outside of the building?

Damn, had she escaped with some other scheme in mind? He jumped up off the sofa and raced into the kitchen. He screeched to a halt in the doorway when he saw her, seated at a black wooden table, her head down and her shoulders shaking as she silently cried into the cradle of her arms.

Chapter 6

She'd been just fine as she'd fixed the coffee and pulled two light blue mugs from the cabinet. She'd been completely under control as she'd gotten out the sugar and creamer, unable to remember how Steve drank his coffee.

But as the fragrant brew had begun to drip into the awaiting carafe and she'd thought about her sisters and missing aunt, she'd lost it.

She'd lost it in a way she never had before. She'd always been so strong. She'd always made things right for her sisters. Tears had always been alien to her. Until she'd lost Aunt Liz. Unable to stop the sobs that racked through her entire body, she'd made her way to the table and lowered her head.

Knowing Steve was in the next room, she'd wept as quietly as possible. She didn't want him to see her this way. She didn't want anyone to see her like this… so weak and vulnerable.

She had to pull it together, to be the tough Roxy that everyone knew, that everyone depended on, but she'd found it impossible to staunch the weeping that felt as if it had been bottled up inside her for a hundred years.

She jerked upward when she felt the soft touch on her shoulder. Her watery gaze met Steve's, whose eyes held nothing but soft concern.

"Roxy," he said as she quickly swiped her cheeks, horrified that he'd come into the kitchen, that he'd seen her like this.

"I'm sorry. I'm fine," she said quickly. "What are you doing in here?"

He sat across from her at the small table. "It seemed to be taking a long time for the coffee to be ready. I was afraid you might have used the fire escape to run out on me."

She knew he was trying to make her smile, but tears continued to leak from her eyes.

"Roxy, why are you going through this all alone? Why aren't you and your sisters together? This should be a time when you're drawing support from each other."

"Sheri and Marlene probably are together," she managed to say as she finally got control of her tears. "I can't see them right now. I can't see them until everything is right again, until Aunt Liz is back home safe and sound."

"Why not?"

She sighed impatiently, thinking that he should somehow understand and yet knowing it was unfair to expect him to. He couldn't know the role she'd taken on so long ago, the role of protector as the older sister. "I promised them I'd fix things, and things aren't fixed yet."

She got up to pour the coffee, aware of his gaze lingering on her. When she'd filled the two mugs, she returned to the table and set one of them in front of him.

She sat back down and curled her fingers around her mug, seeking the heat to warm the spaces inside her that had been icy cold since she'd realized her aunt was missing.

He took a sip of coffee, his gaze locked on her over the rim of his cup. "Have you always been the one who takes care of things for your sisters?"

"Yes, ever since I was seven years old and Ramona dropped off three-year-old Marlene and me at my aunt's house, and then a year later dropped off Sheri, who was just a couple weeks old."

"So your mother considered her older sister's home a safe house to drop off the children she had whom she couldn't take care of?"

"I felt like we were more like UPS deliveries, but yes." As Roxy thought of the mother who she'd spent the first seven years of her life with, a hard knot of anger fisted in her chest. "I helped raise Marlene and Sheri, and I was always grateful that they didn't remember what life was like before Aunt Liz's house."

"Because you remember." His eyes held a gentle appeal she found unsettling because she wanted to fall into those blue depths and not have the conversation that was happening.

She sighed and took a sip of her coffee. "Yes, I

remember life with Ramona, and it was the scariest place a child could ever be."

She wanted to run from the horrible memories, hide from the pain and the trauma of those first years. Aunt Liz had saved her, had humanized her when she'd been little more than an animal just trying to survive.

"I think I've always been closer to Aunt Liz. I've always appreciated her more than Sheri and Marlene because of the first seven years of my life." She forced herself to go there, back in time. She wasn't sure why she needed Steve to understand where she had come from, but she thought it might make him realize just how much she needed her aunt to be found.

As if Steve knew how difficult the conversation was for her, he reached out and covered one of her hands with his. "Talk to me, Roxy," he said gently.

Although she knew she should pull her hand from his, she didn't. The simple connection made her feel safe, at least for the moment, and she relished the feeling.

"My first real memory is of me sitting on Ramona's lap after she'd shot up heroin and had nodded off. I was probably three or so, and I couldn't figure out why she wouldn't wake up. We were in some sort of abandoned building with a bunch of other dope addicts, and I was scared and hungry."

She paused to take another drink as his hand tightened over hers. "That was pretty much the sum of my life with Ramona…abandoned buildings or crack houses, running from a landlord or an abusive boyfriend and living like an animal. I think she finally dropped me off at Aunt Liz's house when her newest boyfriend showed more of an interest in me than in her."

"Jeez, Roxy, I'm so sorry." Gone was the usual flirtatious spark in his eyes, replaced by the light of compassion.

"Men were my mother's downfall. She always chose their wants, their needs over her own, and they always wound up being creeps and abusers. Anyway, I survived, but I have to admit, Aunt Liz had her hands full with me. I hoarded food in an old backpack just in case Ramona came back to get me. I had no manners, no understanding of what normal was, but Aunt Liz never lost patience with me. She loved me like I'd never been loved before."

She squeezed Steve's hand painfully tight. "And don't you see? That's why we have to find her. She saved me, and now I'm so afraid she's in trouble and I need to save her." She released his hand and got to her feet, frantically seeking something to do, somewhere to go to find the missing woman.

"Roxy, come back and sit down and finish your coffee," Steve said. "There's nothing that can be done tonight. I've set in motion everything I can to find Cardell and the cabin where he's gone."

"What if she isn't with him? What if she's someplace else?" She returned to the table and once again sank down in the chair.

"Then we'll do everything we can to find her, and by *we* I don't mean you and me. I mean the police department." He took another sip of his coffee and then leaned back in his chair and eyed her thoughtfully.

"If you want to do something to help, then I suggest you get together with your sisters and make some posters to hang around town. Keep talking to her friends. Check out the places she would go in town. See if you can find out if anyone saw her Friday morning when she should have been delivering the baked goods to your shop."

"I've already done that," she said, thinking of all the people she'd called on Friday afternoon and evening.

"Then walk the streets and ask more questions. There are a lot of people in this town, some who might have a relationship with your aunt that you know nothing about. You didn't know anything about Edward Cardell. It's possible there are other things you don't know."

She wanted to protest, to declare that Liz didn't keep secrets from the women she considered her daughters, but that obviously wasn't true. Edward Cardell had been a secret, and it frightened Roxy to think there could be more things she didn't know about Liz.

"Roxy, I'm sure your sisters don't expect you to personally find your aunt. You all need to band together, to help each other through this trying time."

"You don't understand." Once again she felt the burn of tears in her eyes. God, for somebody who had prided herself on never crying, she seemed to be doing it a lot lately. "I am their strength, and right now I don't feel strong. I can't let them see me so afraid. It will only frighten them more than they already are."

"And you think I'm arrogant," he said with a lift of one of his blond eyebrows.

"I do," she said without apology. "But what does that have to do with me?"

"You're so arrogant, you don't think anyone else can be strong but you. You don't believe you might be able to draw some strength from your sisters, that they might be able to help you as much as you can help them."

"You just don't understand," she repeated, irritated by his assessment. She wasn't arrogant; she just knew what was best for the people she loved. He knew nothing about her or her family dynamics.

"Maybe I don't understand," he conceded. "But I will tell you this—you can't keep up this pace. We don't know when we'll find your aunt, and the best thing you can do right now is go about your life as normal as possible." Once again his hand covered hers, as if trying to comfort her.

"Roxy, I know the adrenaline that's coursing through you that makes you need to move, to take action, to do something, anything within your power to solve this. I understand the heartache and fear that you're experiencing right now, but eventually that adrenaline is going to pass and you'll have to get back to your life no matter how hard it is."

"I just want Aunt Liz found before the adrenaline crash," she said with a touch of anger.

"I know, and I hope that happens." He pulled his hand back from hers, and she was surprised to realize it was as if he removed any warmth that might have built up inside her.

He drained his coffee cup and stood, and she knew he was about to leave. She had the crazy impulse to wrap herself around his knees, keep him with her as she faced another long, dark night ahead.

You don't need anyone, a little voice whispered

inside her head. *You especially don't need Steve Kincaid to make you feel warm and fuzzy. You don't do warm and fuzzy.*

She got to her feet, as well, fighting against a new well of tears that threatened to escape. "I'll walk you down," she said, appalled that her voice was filled with the tears she refused to allow release.

They were silent as they descended to the back door. It was only then he turned and looked at her, his blue eyes glowing almost electric in the safety lights that dimly lit the kitchen.

"No more stakeouts," he said. "Promise me."

She sighed. "I promise," she said reluctantly.

"I'll let you know when we know something." He studied her for a long moment and then pulled his little notepad and pen from his pocket. He scribbled something down and then tore off the piece of paper and handed it to her. "It's my personal phone number that rings through on my cell phone," he explained. "I always answer. There are only a few important people who have that number."

She eyed the paper dubiously. He'd made it fairly clear that so far she'd been a pain in his behind. The number would probably ring in some bar or an old pay phone still standing on some highway on an old mountain road.

He released a low laugh, as if he'd read her thoughts. He motioned toward the landline on a table nearby. "Go ahead—call it."

She did exactly that and felt slightly embarrassed when the phone in his pocket rang. She hung up and moved closer to where he stood by the door.

He raised a hand and placed it on her cheek. "Don't you trust anyone?"

Her heart stopped in her chest at the warmth of his hand on her cheek. "Just my aunt, my sisters and myself," she said softly.

"Then we're going to have to see what we can do to change that." He dropped his hand, turned on his heels and went out the door.

She closed and locked the door behind him, her face burning from his touch. For just a moment as he'd stood so close, as his hand had been so gentle against her skin, she'd wanted to lean into him and feel his arms embrace her.

For just a moment she'd felt as if she *needed* him, and that scared her almost as much as her aunt's vanishing.

No matter how old he got, Steve always felt a sense of homecoming when he entered the space where his mother lived, and Sunday afternoon was no different. Even though this condo was not the place where he had grown up, in the past seven months it had begun to feel like home to him.

Maybe it was because there was nothing but silence and grief in his own house, he thought as he entered the condo, carrying with him the cake that Roxy had given him the day before.

"Mom?" he called.

"In the kitchen," she replied.

"Mmm, something smells good," he said. He entered the kitchen to see his blond-haired, youthful-looking mother pulling a browned turkey breast from the oven.

"Turkey and stuffing, mashed potatoes and a cranberry salad," she said as she placed the baking pan on the counter and then beamed at him. "I felt like Thanksgiving in April, and you're right on time for a change."

"I'm always on time," he protested.

"No, you aren't. You're usually late, but I always forgive you because I love you."

He grinned. "I'm not only on time, but I also come bearing dessert."

"Where did that come from?"

"It was part of a potential crime scene," he told her, delighted when his mother's blue eyes widened and her dainty nose wrinkled in distaste.

He laughed and sat down at the table, then proceeded to explain to her about his latest case and how he'd been spending his time.

His mother, Rebecca, was not only a good listener; she was a good judge of people, and although she'd only had a high school education, she was one of the wisest people Steve had ever known.

By the time he'd finished filling her in on the missing Liz Marcoli and how he'd come to possess the cake he'd brought, she had the food on the table.

"The Dollhouse? I've driven by it a hundred times but have never gone inside. It looks quite charming from the outside."

"The food is great. Jimmy, Frank and I eat breakfast there about three mornings a week."

"Tell me more about this Roxy."

He couldn't tell his mother about how badly he'd wanted to hold Roxy last night or confess how much he'd wanted to kiss her when they'd stood at the back door.

"She's strong and unpredictable, emotional and has a bit of a temper," he replied.

"Sounds like the exact kind of woman you should stay away from," Rebecca said with a lift of one of her perfectly arched brows.

Steve knew it was a warning for him not to repeat any past mistakes. "Don't worry, Mom. I'm not about to get involved with Roxy or any woman."

"Funny, that's not what I've heard about my son." Rebecca stabbed a piece of turkey with her fork, and Steve braced himself for what was about to come.

"And what have you heard?" he asked, even though he was fairly certain he didn't want to know.

"I've heard that you're a real Romeo and you have a revolving door policy with women. That you are an outrageous flirt and leave a string of broken hearts behind you."

Steve laughed. "The gossipmongers have been busy. Unfortunately, my reputation far exceeds the truth of my romantic life."

"Then what is the truth about your romantic life?"

He sighed, wondering how the conversation had become so uncomfortable. "I flirt and occasionally take a woman out to dinner, but that's about it. That's all it will ever be."

"I certainly don't want you to be the kind of man you're rumored to be, but at some point you do need to move on, Steve," his mother said gently. "I want to see you happily married and with children to parent."

"That's not going to happen," he said firmly. "I can't have a future until I find my past."

"And there's been no word? No leads for you to follow?"

"Nothing. I got a call from Tanner Cage earlier today, and he basically told me that he felt bad taking my money considering he hadn't come up with any results." Tanner Cage was the private investigator Steve had hired nine months ago.

Steve tried to shove away the hollowness in his heart. "So tell me what you've been up to all week," he said. He stared his mother in the eyes, daring her to continue to discuss the current topic of conversation.

She took the hint and they finished the meal pleasantly, with his mother talking about the meeting of her Red Hat group, the latest gossip making the rounds in town and a particular purse she'd like for her upcoming birthday.

As she chattered, Steve thought of all the things he hadn't told his mother about Roxy. He hadn't mentioned that she had a good sense of humor or that she was loyal to a fault. He hadn't told her that Roxy's hair was curls of black silk or that her expressive eyes displayed every emotion she felt. Not that any of that mattered.

It didn't make a difference if his mother liked Roxy or not because Steve knew that Roxy would never have a place in his life. No woman would.

He was stuck in a place of pain that he hid with a glib, slick shell to protect himself. He would never allow any woman to pierce through that shell, not even hot Foxy Roxy.

They lingered over the dessert and coffee, talking about memories of Steve's father, the weather and Steve's work.

"Why would a woman who was dating a man for a year keep it a secret from the women she considered her daughters?" he asked, hoping his mother might have a slant he hadn't considered.

Rebecca frowned thoughtfully. "I can think of two reasons right off the top of my head," she replied. "The first might be because there's something about the man she thinks her daughters wouldn't like or wouldn't approve of."

Steve nodded. "And the second idea?"

"Maybe the relationship just wasn't serious enough for her to mention to her family."

"According to her friend, they were seriously dating," Steve said.

Rebecca grinned. "According to my neighbors, my son is the local Lothario."

"Point taken," he said easily and then frowned. "I just hope Liz Marcoli turns up alive and well, and the sooner the better."

"She's been gone since Friday morning and nobody has heard anything from her." Rebecca's forehead wrinkled in concern. "On the surface, it doesn't look good."

"I know." He released a deep sigh and felt the need to head into the station and do something, anything that might help find the missing woman. "I'm going to head into work and see if anything has popped on the case since last night."

He got up from the table, and his mother did the same. "You know Sundays are supposed to be your day off," she chided as she walked him to the door.

"There's nothing and nobody waiting for me at home. I've got no hobbies. My work is what keeps me sane."

"I know, and I just wish—"

Steve kissed her gently on the forehead. "I know, Mom. So do I." With a wave of his hand, he stepped out into the beautiful spring late afternoon.

As he drove from his mother's house to the police station, he tried to put their conversation out of his head. Since his father's death, his mother had subtly pushed harder for Steve to find a nice woman and settle down.

He knew she wanted grandchildren to spoil and to fill her home with giggles and fun. She wanted a daughter-in-law who she could lunch with, enjoy spending time with, but no matter how much Steve wanted to please his mother, he couldn't do what she wanted.

It didn't take him long at the station to find out that nothing was new on Liz's case. He'd assigned several uniforms to check with shopkeepers and people on the streets to ask if anyone had seen Liz at any point on Friday morning. Unfortunately, nobody had.

Whatever had happened to her had most likely happened before she left her house on Friday morning. Was it criminal, or was it some sort of a crazy misunderstanding?

He hoped Roxy would follow his suggestion that they get posters up. It was the best way for somebody whom they had yet to contact to come forward with information that might help.

The sun was just beginning to sink as he headed home. Home was a three-bedroom cabin built into the mountain. At one time it had been his dream house. He'd overseen every detail of the building, from the floor-to-ceiling windows in the living room that overlooked the woods and a small stream in the back, to the handmade wooden railings that led up to the three bedrooms.

When he got to the cabin, the first thing he did was snag a beer from the fridge, and then he climbed the stairs to the master suite. The bedroom was large, with French doors that led out to an intimate deck. The larger deck was below, just outside a door in the kitchen.

He opened the French doors, stepped outside and sank down in one of the two lounge chairs. This was the best time of the day to be out on the deck, when the trees took on the golden hue of twilight and shadows began to chase around their bases.

When he'd built this place six years ago he'd never envisioned he'd be here all alone, and for a while he hadn't been.

He popped the top of his beer and took a long drink, trying to shove memories of the past away. He sipped his beer, breathing in the sweet, fresh mountain air and vowed that tonight he would not go into the bedroom at the end of the hallway.

He'd enjoy the view, finish his beer and then go to bed early and hit the case of the missing Liz hard in the morning. But he would not go into that bedroom that was filled with broken dreams, crushing heartbreak and a rage that knew no bounds.

He froze as he saw a doe and her fawn in the woods, moving with breathtaking grace as they approached the small stream. Unexpectedly a thick, painful emotion pressed against his chest.

Even after the doe and fawn had disappeared from sight, the emotion remained. He finished his beer, threw the bottle in the trash and went back into his bedroom.

He went into the adjoining bathroom, stripped off his clothes and got beneath a hot shower. The bathroom not only had a shower, but also a jetted tub big enough for two people to enjoy at the same time.

As the steamy needles of water played across his shoulders, he tried not to think about how soft Roxy's cheek had been to the touch.

Her breakdown in the kitchen had shocked him, as had the glimpse he'd gotten into her early childhood. He couldn't imagine the kind of horrors she'd endured before landing at Liz's house.

Was it any wonder she was emotional? Had a temper? Felt the need to control everything and everyone around her? He felt as if she'd given him a glimpse of the woman beneath the fresh mouth and hard edge.

He had a feeling that if she dropped her defenses he might like her, but he also had a feeling that she never allowed anyone too close.

Which was just fine with him, he reminded himself as he shut off the water. He had no space in his heart for anyone.

He dried off, pulled on a pair of boxers and then headed for the king-size bed. He was just about to climb beneath the sheet when he realized he couldn't do it. He had to make his nightly pilgrimage to the room that held both sweet memories and a yawning grief.

His feet began to drag as he left his bedroom and approached the closed door at the end of the hallway, his heart thudding the slow rhythm of dread. The doorknob felt cold beneath his hand as he grabbed it and turned.

The door opened to a bedroom, with a twin bed covered in a navy spread with dancing and rearing horses in black and brown and white. A bookcase against the wall held storybooks and a collection of hand-sized plastic horses in a variety of poses. On the nightstand a lamp was turned on; the base was a cowboy boot in black and gold.

Steve changed the lightbulb in that lamp once a week to ensure that the light never stopped burning. Like a candle in a window, it awaited the return of the beloved person who belonged there.

He sank down on the bed and grabbed the stuffed horse that had been a favorite snuggle buddy for the first five years of Tommy's life.

Tommy. Steve's heart cried out as he thought of the towheaded little boy who had loved all things horses and chocolate ice cream with raspberry sprinkles and pretending to be a cowboy.

How many times had Tommy crawled up on Steve's back, punching Steve's ribs with his small heels as he cried, "Giddy-up, Daddy"? And like a dutiful horse, Steve had crawled around the house as Tommy's giggles had ridden the air until they'd both collapsed.

It had been two years since Steve had seen him. Two long, agonizing years. Once a year Steve went out and bought clothes in a larger size, so the closet would hold the apparel he assumed would fit a growing boy—so the clothes would be ready when Tommy finally came home.

The room held its breath as Steve had done for the past two years, ever since the day that his former girlfriend, Tommy's mother, had kidnapped him and disappeared.

He pulled the stuffed horse up to his nose, hoping for a lingering scent of the little boy he'd loved more than anything or anyone else on the face of the earth.

He finally placed the stuffed horse back on the pillow and stood. This was madness, this nightly torture he forced himself to endure.

How could he hope to find Liz Marcoli when in the past two years, with the help of a seasoned and intelligent private investigator and all the resources he had at his fingertips, he couldn't even find his own son?

Chapter 7

Roxy had taken Steve's advice and spent part of Sunday with her sisters at Sheri's house. They'd eaten dinner together and then had worked on a mock-up of a poster that Marlene would take to the printers the next day and have a hundred copies made.

Roxy had forced herself to stay upbeat, indicating more than once that she believed their aunt had gone off on some crazy romantic mini-vacation with the mysterious Edward Cardell.

It had taken very little persuasion for Marlene and Sheri to embrace the idea, which was far less frightening than any other possibility.

Still, the posters were made with the unspoken knowledge that if Liz wasn't with Edward, then they'd need everyone in town helping them to find her or coming forward with some kind of information that would aid the investigation.

Roxy had left Sheri's at nine that evening, and to her surprise had gone home and straight to bed, where she had immediately fallen asleep. She'd slept hard, without dreams, as if her body needed to make up for the previous nights of too little sleep.

She awakened before dawn and went about her usual routine, trying to keep her mind off the fear that simmered inside her.

Monday morning and still no word from Aunt Liz. She knew in her heart, in her very soul, that Liz hadn't gone off somewhere with a man without making any phone calls to check in with the people she knew would worry about her absence. With each hour that had passed she'd become less convinced that Liz was with Edward Cardell.

The plan for the day was for Roxy to work in the Dollhouse and keep business as usual, then at six that evening she was meeting Sheri and Marlene at their store, the Roadside Stop, and they would split up to hang posters all over town.

It felt odd to be working a day like everything was normal, but Steve had been right when he'd told her the best thing they could all do was try to stick to their routines as much as possible.

She didn't doubt that he would call her when he had information to impart, and she could always call him to check in when the fear got to be too much for her to handle alone. She'd memorized his cell phone number after he'd given it to her. Oddly enough, the number in her brain was comforting.

But she wasn't in a big rush to speak to him after

her embarrassing breakdown on Saturday. Aunt Liz used to tell her that it was healthy to cry, but Roxy had always seen tears as a sign of weakness.

She had a distinct memory of crying only once during the years she had spent with Ramona, and she'd gotten the beating of her life from Ramona's current boyfriend for making a scene. She'd never really cried again…until Saturday with Steve.

It was just after six when she went downstairs to find Josie already prepping in the kitchen and Gregory out in one of the dining rooms making sure the tables were set and ready to go for the day's business.

The room smelled of freshly cooked chicken and savory breads and the sweetness of pastries and cakes. "Marlene has already been here?" she asked when she saw the goodies still in their containers on one of the prep tables.

"You just missed her. She said to tell you she'd see you this evening," Josie replied. Roxy nodded and grabbed her apron from a hook.

"Are you working here all day?" Josie asked curiously.

"It's back to business as usual," Roxy said. "I can't do anything to help find Aunt Liz, and I can't just sit around doing nothing, so I'm back to my routine."

"That's probably the best thing for you to do," Josie said, a hint of compassion in her voice.

"Best thing or not, it's the only thing I know to do at the moment. Has Isaaic Zooker made a delivery yet?"

"Not yet, but he should be here anytime." Josie began to slice a steaming roast, and Gregory returned to the kitchen to begin making the specialty chicken salad.

Gregory Stillwell was a tall, thin and silent man. Roxy didn't know much about his personal life, but she knew what she needed to about him—that he was dependable, had a terrific palate and worked seamlessly with Josie.

Roxy got busy cutting the vegetables that would be added to a variety of dishes for the day. She was halfway through the task when a soft knock fell on the back door.

She opened it to see Isaaic Zooker. "I've brought your cheese," he said, his gaze not quite meeting hers.

"And what have you brought for me today?" she asked. She knew the middle-aged Amish man didn't particularly like her, that he thought her brash and outspoken. But she also had a feeling Isaaic, known in his community by the nickname Cheese Man, found working with the English a necessary evil.

"I brought you cheddar, Colby white, the horseradish cheddar and bacon Swiss." He plunked a large woven bag on the counter and unloaded the chunks of cheese.

Roxy took the invoice he offered and paid him. Then, in the blink of an eye, he was gone.

"He's the most unpleasant man," Josie said as she placed one of the chunks of cheese on the electric slicer.

"I imagine he's quite nice when he's at home among his own community," Roxy replied. "He just seems to be uncomfortable conducting business. Right now he's one of my favorite people for bringing that horseradish cheddar. It will be awesome on a sandwich with the roast beef."

At precisely seven she opened the restaurant, slightly

disappointed that Steve, Jimmy and Frank weren't there to begin their day. She told herself she should be glad they weren't having breakfast, that hopefully they were all busy working to find Aunt Liz.

The day flew by, and Roxy stopped at every table to ask the patrons if they had seen Liz since last Friday. A lot of the diners didn't even know Liz, and those who did know her hadn't seen her recently.

Other than phone calls from Sheri and Marlene to firm up their plans, her phone didn't ring. Apparently Steve had nothing to share with her, and she could only assume from his silence that Edward Cardell was still missing, as well.

There was no time for a break; patrons filled the place throughout the day. She saw the faces of both new customers and familiar ones. Roxy was grateful for the business, not only because it meant money coming in, but more so because it made it easier for her to put her worries about Liz on the back burner.

It wasn't until the last patron had left and she'd flipped the Open sign to Closed that the near-crippling worry came slamming back. She could only hope that the posters would help yield results of some kind.

"Aren't you supposed to meet your sisters?" Josie asked at five-thirty as she worked next to Roxy, cleaning up the kitchen.

"It only takes me fifteen minutes to get from here to the Roadside Stop," Roxy replied.

"Go on—get out of here. Gregory and Gus and I can finish the cleanup and lock the doors. Take fifteen minutes to go upstairs and change your shirt. You have mustard on the sleeve of the one you have on."

Roxy looked at her shirtsleeve, surprised to see the

yellow-brown smear. "Okay, I'll leave this all up to you and I'll see you in the morning."

She raced up the stairs with a new purpose as she thought of working with her sisters to do something positive in the search effort.

Minutes later she'd changed into a clean bright yellow T-shirt and jeans and headed out to meet her sisters at the store. As she drove along the highway to reach their place, she noted the wildflowers that spread their beauty along the sides of the asphalt.

Aunt Liz loved spring. It had always been her favorite season. She'd spend hours planting flowers in the gardens in the front of her house and in the back. She'd water and weed, and she loved the feel of the warming earth beneath her fingers. She put in a nice garden each year, but she had yet to get to it this spring. Hopefully she'd be home in time to get it done this year.

Roxy clutched her steering wheel tighter. They had to find her. The four days that she'd been missing felt like a year…like an agonizing eternity.

Once Roxy left the outskirts of Wolf Creek, she turned onto the major highway that would lead toward Harrisburg. She only had to drive about ten miles before she spied the large, low wooden building that boasted a big sign indicating it was the Roadside Stop.

She pulled in and parked. In the distance the Amish settlement was in view, with silos rising up and large barns in pristine white. The houses were modest, surrounded by rich green farmland and pastures. She could see the men working, old and young, their wide-brimmed hats a familiar sight.

The community and Sheri and Marlene's store were

symbiotic; the Amish people provided much of the goods that Sheri and Marlene sold. Signs along the building advertised Amish cheese and furniture, butters and relishes. The store also sold Wolf Creek souvenirs and travelers' needs and had so far been more successful than Sheri had ever dreamed it would be when she'd bought the old building three years before.

She and Marlene had planned to own and run the place together, and then Marlene had eloped and moved to Pittsburgh. It had only been since Marlene's return a year ago that the two had become partners as they'd once planned.

Roxy got out of the car and entered the store, embraced by the scents of fresh-cut wood and herbs, of foodstuff and lemon cleanser.

She ran her hand across the smooth, polished wood of a rocking chair she was sure Abraham Zooker had crafted, and then smiled as she saw Sheri behind the counter.

There was almost nine years' difference in age between Roxy and her youngest sister, and Roxy definitely felt a maternal kind of love for Sheri.

Maybe part of it was that Sheri was small and dainty, sweet-natured to a fault and never had a bad word to say about anyone. Most of the people from the Amish settlement often stopped in just to visit with Sheri, finding her to be a woman who embraced many of their values, particularly about personal vanity. Sheri rarely wore makeup, unlike Marlene, who always looked as if she was ready to attend a movie premiere.

Sheri smiled at the sight of her and hurried around the counter to give her a quick hug. "Marlene just went to the back room to get the posters and some hammers and nails."

"Can you get away for a couple of hours?" Roxy asked.

Sheri nodded, her long chestnut brown hair swaying with the movement. "Abe should be here anytime, and he's going to close up for me tonight."

Marlene came out of the back room, her arms filled with posters and everything they'd need to hang them. She laid everything on the counter, and for a moment the three of them looked at one of the posters of Liz.

Liz Marcoli was an attractive woman, with brown hair that only went to her ears. It was just beginning to show strands of silver, and her dark eyes always appeared to hold both wisdom and humor.

They'd chosen a photo of her laughing, because that's how people thought of Liz…always happy, always finding something to laugh about. Roxy desperately hoped she was laughing now. She needed to believe that wherever Liz was at the moment, she was happy and healthy.

"Somebody will find her, won't they, Roxy?" Sheri asked, her whiskey-brown eyes so solemn, so trusting that Roxy would have the right answer.

"Of course somebody is going to find her. Maybe she hit her head or something and is suffering from some kind of amnesia, wandering around without knowing who she is or where she belongs," Marlene offered.

"And if that's the case, it's possible she ended up by the highway where somebody picked her up and took her to a hospital not around here," Sheri added.

"And that means somebody will see our posters

and call my cell phone to tell me where she was last seen or where she was taken to, and then we'll just all go get her," Roxy said with a conviction she hoped was convincing.

"We...we j-just need to get her back where she belongs," Sheri replied. The faint stutter broke Roxy's heart as she realized Sheri was obviously more stressed and upset than she appeared.

"We'll get her back where she belongs, but right now we need to get as many of these posters up as possible before dark," Marlene said.

They all turned as Abe Windslow came through the door. He was a bear of a man, tall and broad with shoulders as wide as a mountain. Four years ago, at the age of fifty-six, he'd lost his wife, and his two children lived out of state. He'd taken the job of helping Sheri and Marlene at the store to stave off the loneliness of his little cabin in the woods.

He greeted them all and then gazed at the posters with a somber expression. "I hope you get some results," he said, his gaze lingering on the picture of Liz. "She's a nice woman. I asked her out once." He smiled and shook his head. "Turned me down flat, she did."

"When was this?" Roxy asked in surprise.

His broad shoulders moved up and down in a shrug. "About a year ago. It was no big deal. She'd come in here for a jar of mint jelly, and I asked her if she wanted to have dinner with me sometime. She told me she liked to dine alone, and then the next day brought me a chocolate cake as a consolation prize." He rubbed his stomach. "I've got to say, it was a good consolation prize."

At any other time the sisters might have laughed,

but instead Sheri gave him quick instructions for finishing up the night and then the three women walked outside.

They agreed that the best way to get as many posters hung as possible before dark was to split up. Roxy would take the area around the Dollhouse and the east side of Main Street, Sheri would take the west side of Main Street and Marlene would head into Hershey and hang as many signs as possible there.

They'd have a good two and a half hours before the darkness of another night descended. They divided up the posters, hammers and nails, and then they each got into their cars and headed in different directions.

As Roxy headed back toward the Dollhouse, she thought about Marlene. She knew Aunt Liz had been worried about Marlene since she'd returned to Wolf Creek after her divorce.

It had been bad enough when Marlene had eloped with a man none of them knew very well, and even worse when he'd taken her to live in Pittsburgh. During her two-year marriage she'd only spoken to her family sporadically, and then one day she'd come home, telling them all that she was divorced and didn't want to speak about her husband or her marriage ever again.

They'd all respected her wishes, but they also saw the changes that had occurred in Marlene. There was a depth of sadness in her beautiful blue eyes that had never been there before.

Roxy just wished her sister would talk to one of them and let them know what had placed that grief in her eyes. She wished Marlene trusted them enough to share whatever heartbreak she carried.

The Dollhouse was surrounded by other businesses, and Roxy parked on the street and began the task of nailing posters on posts, walking into stores and asking if a poster could be placed in the window and then working her way down the block.

Maybe Marlene was right. Maybe there had been some kind of accident, and Aunt Liz had hit her head and was suffering some sort of amnesia.

Then why hadn't she been taken to a hospital here in Wolf Creek or in Hershey? Roxy had called all the local hospitals and urgent care centers and had come up with nothing. Maybe she had been taken to a hospital farther away.

She wondered if Steve and his partners had checked the hospitals all over the county. If she heard nothing from him tonight, then she'd call him first thing in the morning. She'd been patient all day and had used all the self-control she possessed not to call him.

But tomorrow all bets were off. She needed to know what the detectives and other lawmen were doing, how they were moving the investigation forward. She wanted to know that everything under the moon and sun that could be done was being done.

He would know tomorrow that she and her sisters had done as he suggested when he saw the posters everywhere in town. He might not be too happy that she'd used her own cell phone number as a contact on the posters, but she hadn't known what other number to use. Besides, she certainly intended to share with him any tips that might come in from the poster blitz.

By eight o'clock her hand and arm ached from the hammering her body was unaccustomed to, and there was no point in stopping in at the shops, as most of them were in the process of being closed for the night.

By the time another half an hour had passed, the shadows of night had begun to fall. Roxy quickened her pace, wanting to get as many posters up as possible before complete nightfall.

Another night of people not being where they were supposed to be. Another night of no answers, a night filled with more fear and anxiety. It was completely dark when Roxy pulled into her driveway, disheartened emotionally and wearied physically.

As she entered the back door and stepped into the kitchen, the first thing she saw was that the large black trash can hadn't been emptied into the big Dumpster at the back of the lot outside.

She was tempted just to leave it, but she knew it was full of food that would stink in the morning, and she'd much rather start the day with the trash can empty.

Making a mental note to herself to remind Gus for the hundredth time that this was part of his nightly duties, she grabbed the heavy container and carried it out the back door.

With some effort, she managed to dump the trash into the large bin and then headed back to the house with the empty can. She hated nights. She never had before, but since her aunt wasn't home where she belonged, Roxy had come to hate the darkness of the nighttime hours.

She'd just reached the back door when she felt something fly by her head and heard a loud *thwack* in the door woodwork. She barely turned her head and gasped when she saw a knife buried deep into the wood, its odd, cross-shaped hilt shimmering in the light spilling out of the open kitchen door.

What? Her brain refused to work, to make any sense of it. *A knife?* Where had it come from? Before her mind could fully comprehend it, another knife slammed into the door frame on the other side of her.

She dropped the trash can and fell to the ground in a crouch. Her heart beat so hard she couldn't draw a breath. Somebody was throwing knives at her! Who? And why?

Tentatively she reached up and twisted the doorknob and opened the door. She crashed inside the restaurant, slammed the door closed and locked it, and then scurried around the corner of the walk-in freezer where nobody could see her if they peered into the window in the door.

Somebody had thrown knives at her, with near-deadly results. Somebody had just tried to kill her. As she remained on the floor, stunned, she waited to hear the breaking of the glass in the door that would indicate whoever was outside was coming in to complete the murder attempt that had been botched by a mere inch.

Steve was just about to get into his car to head home, disheartened by the lack of leads in Liz Marcoli's whereabouts, when his cell phone rang.

It took him a moment to recognize that the frantic, half-comprehensible woman on the other end of the line was Roxy.

"Roxy, slow down. I can't understand what you're saying," he exclaimed.

"There were knives.... Somebody tried to kill me.

I'm in the kitchen. You have to come now. Please hurry. Come to the back door and be careful—there's a killer out there. Somebody just tried to kill me."

Before he could get any more information out of her, she hung up. Heart thudding, he jumped into his car and took off, wondering what in the hell was going on at the Dollhouse.

A killer? Knives? Was Roxy just overreacting to some crazy situation, or was something terribly wrong? She'd said something about the kitchen and knives.... What in the hell did that mean?

He blew out of his parking space like the devil was chasing him, and within minutes he pulled up next to her car in the back parking area of the Dollhouse.

He instantly drew his gun, unsure what to expect but remembering Roxy's warning that there was a killer somewhere out there.

He got out of his car, closed the door and crouched down, making himself a smaller target for anyone who might be out there with him. He narrowed his gaze and moved it from the left to the right, seeking a source of danger.

The Dumpster made an effective cover for somebody to hide behind, but there was really nothing else that impeded his view of the general area.

Heart pumping, still unsure of what the situation was, he began to make his way toward the Dumpster, needing to clear the area before he advanced into the building.

Though what he wanted to do was rush inside and assure himself that Roxy was okay, he reminded himself that she'd made the phone call, so she had to be all right. He needed to think like a cop, not like somebody who might care for the woman inside.

He was grateful for the nearby street lamp that illuminated the back of the large Dumpster. Although the light was faint, it was enough for him to see that there was nobody there, no threat, no killer waiting to pounce—nothing.

He circled the Dumpster and then headed toward the house, his gun firmly in his hand, his heart still thudding a quickened rhythm.

The back door was locked, and a large trash can lay on its side nearby. He looked back over his shoulder and then rapped on the door. "Roxy, it's me. It's Steve. Open the door."

She appeared at the window of the door like a wraith, her face blanched of color and her eyes wide and dark with fear. She fumbled with the lock but finally got it open and stepped back, as if afraid that danger might somehow follow him inside.

"Did you see them?" she asked, her voice breathy and higher in pitch than usual.

"See who?" he asked as he holstered his gun.

"Not who—what. The knives. Didn't you see the knives in the door frame?"

He gazed at her in confusion, feeling as if he'd suddenly entered the *Twilight Zone*. He turned and flipped on the overhead light, wanting to see her face with more illumination than the security lights in the kitchen provided. "Roxy, what are you talking about?"

"Somebody threw knives at me as I started to enter the back door." Her voice trembled, and her eyes remained huge.

Steve opened the door and looked out. "Roxy, there are no knives in the door frame."

She flew to the door, her face even more pale as she looked at the wood around the door. "They were there. I didn't imagine them. I swear I saw them. I heard them." She ran her fingers over the frame and stopped. "Here," she said and then turned to the other side and lightly touched the wood. "And here."

Steve checked the areas she indicated, stunned as he felt the deep gouges that would be consistent with very sharp knives thrown into the wood and then obviously removed.

He pulled her back into the kitchen and closed and locked the door behind him. He led her to the small square table shoved against a wall in the kitchen and motioned for her to sit.

"Tell me exactly what happened." He took the chair opposite hers.

"Marlene and Sheri and I spent the evening hanging posters around town, and it was dark when I got back here. When I got inside I noticed that Gus hadn't taken out the garbage, so I carried it out to the Dumpster and emptied the can."

She placed her hands flat on the table, and he couldn't help but notice that her fingers trembled. At least some of the color had returned to her cheeks, and her skin no longer looked pasty and pale.

"I'd just reached the back door when I felt something fly past my head and heard the sound of something slamming into the wood next to me. I turned my head and saw the hilt of the knife sticking out, and at that moment another one flew and hit the wood on the other side of me. Less than an inch… They were both less than an inch from slamming into my head."

She took a moment and drew a deep breath, as if to steady herself. "You believe me, don't you? You believe me, Steve?" A touch of higher color filled her cheeks as her chin shot up.

He thought of the gouges he'd felt, slashes in the wood that would be more apparent in the light of day. "Don't lift that chin at me," he said. "I believe you." Not only had he felt the gouges, but he couldn't imagine what reason on earth she would have to lie about what had happened.

A shudder stole over her. "Whoever it was, while I was cowering by the walk-in, he must have come right up to the door and taken his knives with him." She tilted her head sideways and eyed him curiously. "Do you think this has something to do with Aunt Liz?"

Steve raked a hand through his hair, wishing he had a definitive answer for her. "I don't know," he finally replied. "My gut says it isn't related, and that would beg the question of who you might have ticked off lately." He pulled his pad and pen from his pocket.

She gave a weak laugh. "You're probably going to need a bigger notebook if you really want me to answer that question. You might as well write Gus down as the first name because I intend to give him all kinds of hell first thing in the morning for not taking out the trash earlier tonight."

"I'll definitely need more paper if you're going to start with the names of the people you intend to tick off in the future," he said.

Although he kept his tone light, his concern over what had just happened had his nerves nearly jumping out of his skin. An inch or so in either direction with those knives, and Roxy could have been badly hurt or killed.

And even though she had attempted a joke, her hands had yet to stop trembling and her eyes still held the horror of the close encounter with death.

"I know I make a lot of people mad," she admitted. "I'm brusque and don't always hide my temper. I want what I want when I want it. I expect people to work as hard as I do. I—"

"Roxy." He placed a calming hand over one of hers, knowing instinctively that she was about to go off the rails and into an emotional tailspin. "We'll figure this out."

"Like we've found Aunt Liz?" The instant she said the words, she pulled her hand from beneath his and slapped it over her mouth as her eyes widened. He saw the sheen of sudden tears. "I'm sorry, I didn't mean that." She dropped her hand back to the table. "That's what I'm saying—my mouth gets ahead of my brain too much of the time."

He didn't even try to deny what she'd said about herself because they both knew it was true. "Okay, so I really need to know if in the last couple of days your mouth has worked overtime to make somebody mad enough to want to hurt you."

"You mean besides you?"

He couldn't help but admire her spirit, but if he was going to get to the bottom of this newest mystery, he had to keep her on track. "Besides me," he replied, his gaze somber and his lips unsmiling.

"I know this is serious," she said. "But you don't have to look so mean." Her lower lip trembled ominously.

The last thing he wanted was to make her cry. "I'm not trying to look mean, but we need to stay focused on the fact that you could have been seriously hurt."

"Or killed," she added. "But honestly, I can't think of anyone who I've been ugly with lately. Of course, the last four days I've been pretty much focused on finding Aunt Liz."

"What about staff here? Anyone who might have a grudge against you?"

"No, I've got a great staff here, but there are people at the Golden Daffodil restaurant who hate my guts."

Steve raised an eyebrow. "Why?"

"I was working there as head cook before I opened the Dollhouse. When I left, I took my secret personal recipes with me, and the owner of the Golden Daffodil tried to tell me that the recipes were hers. She also wasn't thrilled when she realized I intended to open here and become her competition."

"Is the restaurant business so competitive that she'd try to kill you?" he asked incredulously.

"I've been open here for almost four years. If Rita Whitehead was going to kill me, I imagine she would have done it right after I left the Golden Daffodil."

"Think harder. There has to be somebody. Those knives didn't magically appear. They were thrown specifically at you," he said, surprised by how his heart jumped at the thought of anything happening to her.

Roxy was nothing more to him than an occasional waitress, a woman searching for her missing aunt and now the near victim of a crime. She was nothing more to him than a job, so there was no reason his heart should do anything whenever she was around.

"I need to call Jimmy and Frank and get them over here to take a look around outside and see if they can find something the person might have dropped or inadvertently left behind. I did a cursory search around the Dumpster, but we need to do a more thorough search."

He grabbed his phone from his pocket and contacted both of his partners. It took only a couple of minutes to explain the situation to them.

"They should be here in the next few minutes," he said after hanging up.

"I'll make some coffee." She jumped up from the table as if grateful for something to do. "Do you think I should make some sandwiches?"

"No, coffee is just fine."

As she prepared the coffee, neither of them spoke. Why would somebody want to harm Roxy? Granted, she was outspoken, brash and a firecracker that probably exploded too often. But the price for that shouldn't be death.

Had she stirred somebody up with her questions about Liz? Had she somehow gotten too close to someone and now was perceived as a threat?

He'd be a fool not to think that this was a viable possibility. "I may have been wrong and spoken too soon," he said.

She turned around from where she'd been pulling mugs from a cabinet and gazed at him curiously. "About what?"

"About whether this is tied to your aunt's disappearance or not. Maybe it isn't about you personally, but maybe you made contact with somebody who had something to do with Liz's disappearance, and that person now sees you as some kind of a threat."

She set four mugs on the table, fear once again emanating from her eyes. "If that's the case, then I'll never be able to figure out who threw those knives. I've probably talked to a hundred people since Aunt Liz disappeared, and I don't remember hearing anything from anyone that would make me a risk. How on earth will I know where danger might come from again?"

Her entire body trembled, and she slammed her hands down on the table, as if embracing anger rather than the fear that was obviously overwhelming her. The shine of tears in her eyes grew more visible.

Steve had no idea what she might do next. She could scream in frustration, throw a cup across the room or crumble into a weeping mess.

Not knowing for sure what was about to happen, he did the only thing he knew to stop any of it. He stepped up to her, wrapped her in his arms and kissed her.

Chapter 8

Roxy's initial instinct was to shove him away, to ask him what the heck he thought he was doing just grabbing her and kissing her without her consent, without any warning at all. But his lips were so warm against hers and his arms were so tight, making her feel safe and secure.

The night had been filled with such horror, and rather than stopping the kiss, she opened her mouth to him. As their tongues danced together, all thoughts of knives and death momentarily fled from her head and she simply fell into the pleasure of kissing Steve.

She wasn't even sure she liked Detective Steve Kincaid, but right now she clung to him as if he were a solid rock in a wind-tossed sea, an anchor that kept her from drifting into an emotional storm she feared she'd never leave.

She might not have decided yet if she liked him as a person, but she definitely liked the way he kissed… soft but with a faint hint of demand.

Allowing herself to melt into him, she realized that she could like being held in Steve's arms, enjoy kissing him and still not be sure that she liked *him*.

She knew she didn't approve of what she'd heard about his personal life, but that didn't matter, not now, not with his mouth plying hers with a heat that warmed the icy chill that had suffused her since the moment she'd seen the knives in the door.

His hands swept up and down her back as the kiss continued, and she pressed herself more tightly against him, certain at that moment that his embrace was the safest place in the world, falling deeper into a sensual haze that allowed all rational thought to leave her mind.

A knock on the kitchen door made them jump apart. Roxy watched in a stunned daze as Steve walked to the door and opened it to admit Jimmy and Frank.

Both of them looked at her with concern. "Roxy, are you okay?" Jimmy, the younger of the two, walked over to her and gently touched her shoulder. His brown eyes held a genuine concern.

She smiled at him. She'd always thought that Jimmy, as the youngest of the three detectives, was the least jaded and the nicest. "I'm fine, especially now that you all are here."

She didn't look at Steve. Her lips still burned with the heat of his kiss, and she was afraid that if she looked at him his partners would guess something about the brief intimacy they'd just shared. She'd told

Jimmy she was fine, but she wasn't fine. Her aunt was missing, somebody had thrown knives at her and Steve's kiss had just confused the heck out of her.

She noticed that Frank carried a medium-size black bag with him that she assumed was a crime scene evidence-processing kit. He looked stern and distinguished, with the hint of premature silver strands at his temples.

Frank was the quietest of the three, always extremely polite but with a distance in his cool blue eyes that reminded her of the way her sister had come home after her divorce.

"Jimmy and I will head outside and see what we can find," Frank said.

Roxy sank down at the table as Steve showed the two men the gouges in the door frame; then Jimmy and Frank disappeared into the night, leaving her and Steve alone once again.

"You shouldn't have kissed me," she said with a touch of censure in her voice.

"Probably not, but I thought you were about to lose it and it just seemed like the appropriate thing to do at the time," he replied easily, as if the kiss had meant nothing, as if he hadn't felt the instant chemistry that had soared between them.

"You could at least warn me next time of your intention," she said, surprised to find herself irritated by his obvious lack of response to the kiss.

She'd officially lost her mind. She had a missing loved one and somebody crazy throwing knives at her from the dark, and all she could think about was how Steve's kiss had rocked her to her very core.

She didn't want to like Steve's kisses. She didn't

want to like anybody's kisses. Kisses led to other things, to relationships and expectations and ultimately heartbreak. Kisses involved men, and her mother's men had destroyed her life.

With the adrenaline rush that had screamed through her in the minutes before Steve had arrived now ebbing away, she was left with a bone-weary exhaustion. She got up and poured herself a cup of coffee and one for Steve, as well, then returned to the table.

Once again he sat across from her, his features sober and his eyes darkened as if deep in thought. "We have to work this two ways," he finally said. "There are two possibilities. The first is that this is somehow tied to your aunt's disappearance. The second is that it has nothing to do with Liz's disappearance and is just about you."

"So what happens next?"

"We wait to see if Jimmy and Frank come up with anything, and by sometime tomorrow I want a list from you of people you have regular contact with and anyone from your past who might have a reason to want to hurt you."

The very idea made Roxy's head hurt. "I don't want my sisters to know about what happened here tonight. It would only frighten them more than they already are about Aunt Liz."

"Roxy, at some point you're going to have to realize that your sisters are grown women and don't need you to protect them from life."

"Now isn't the time," she said firmly. Of course he couldn't understand her need to shield her sisters from all things bad.

"Do you have siblings?" she asked.

"Nope, I'm an only child," he replied.

She nodded. "That explains a lot."

He leaned back in his chair. "Like what?"

"Like your natural arrogance, your sense of entitlement. You were probably shamelessly spoiled."

His lips curved up in that slow, lazy grin that both maddened and charmed her. "Spoiled completely rotten," he agreed.

The smile fell, and once again his eyes darkened. "But by no means have I lived the charmed life I suspect you think I have. We all have issues, Roxy. Right now I need to stay focused on what issue might have made somebody want to throw knives at you tonight."

She cupped her hands around her coffee cup. "I feel like I've fallen into somebody else's nightmare."

"Unfortunately, it's yours, and we've got to figure out who the boogeyman is before you fall into another nightmare."

She looked at him sharply. "You think something else could happen to me?"

He took a sip of coffee, as if giving himself a chance to figure out how he intended to answer her question.

She leaned forward. "Steve, you have to be honest with me. We need to make a pact that we'll be completely open and honest with each other until all of this madness is over."

"Then my honest answer to you is that I don't know. It's possible those knives were thrown with such precision so that they wouldn't hit you, or it's possible the person intended for them to hit you and their aim was slightly off."

"In which case, if the desire is to kill me, then the

job isn't finished yet," she replied. She fought off a new shiver of fear as she wondered from where a new danger might come and what form it would take.

Jimmy and Frank remained outside for nearly an hour. When they came inside, Roxy poured them each a cup of coffee, and the four of them sat at the table.

"We checked all around the area and found nothing to link to anyone, then took measurements of the gouges in the wood," Frank said. "By the slant of the gouges, I would guess that whoever threw the knives was hiding someplace by the Dumpster. Whoever threw them had to be strong to get them as far as they flew and as deep as they hit."

"They had strange hilts, like big ornate crosses," she said, suddenly remembering the odd shape of the handles.

"Sounds like professional throwing knives," Jimmy said. He shrugged as both Frank and Steve looked at him. "What can I tell you? I went through a ninja phase when I was younger, and one of the things I learned was about throwing knives and stars."

"Should we be calling you Ninja Jimmy?" Roxy asked, trying desperately to alleviate her fear and the sober atmosphere that had taken over her kitchen.

He shot her a quick grin. "Nah, I like being a detective better than a ninja." His smile fell. "But if we can identify what kind of throwing knives they were, then we might be able to chase down the owner. Why don't you come into the station sometime tomorrow, and we'll go through some pictures and see if you can specifically identify the hilts."

She nodded. "Did you find anything else out there?"

"Nothing," Frank replied. "Whoever was out there didn't drop or leave anything behind that we could find."

"And my concern is that I don't know if this attack tonight is somehow tied to Liz Marcoli's disappearance or if it's something completely different," Steve said.

"We need to investigate it both ways," Frank said.

Steve nodded. "That's what I told Roxy." He looked at her. "When you come in tomorrow to check out Jimmy's pictures of throwing knives, I want you to bring me a list of anyone and everyone you work with, that you interact with on a daily or weekly basis."

"I know—anyone who might have a problem with my scintillating personality," Roxy said wryly. It was easy for her to feel safe now, with three detectives seated in her kitchen.

She didn't want them to leave while darkness still remained outside. She'd like to keep them right where they were until dawn stretched across the sky. Nothing was as frightening in the daytime as it was in the dark.

But all too soon Jimmy and Frank finished their coffee, made arrangements for Roxy to come into the station around two the next afternoon and then left.

Steve remained sitting at the table, as if sensing her dread of being all alone. She wasn't sure that she liked the fact that he apparently was starting to know her well enough to read her emotions. But she supposed fear was an easy emotion to read, and he'd probably been through nights like this with plenty of other crime victims.

"Are you sure you don't want to call one of your

sisters to come and stay here with you for the rest of the night?" he asked.

"Positive."

"You have a friend you can call?"

She stared at him, realizing for the first time that she had her sisters and she had her staff, but she really didn't have any friends. There had never been time for friends.

"No, not really." She got up from the table and carried the empty cups to the sink, deciding she'd wash them by hand rather than load them into the industrial-size dishwasher.

When she turned back around Steve was on his feet, and for the first time she noted the exhaustion that paled his eyes and deepened the laugh lines that gave character to his handsome features.

"Are you going to be okay for the rest of the night?" he asked.

She wanted to tell him that she wouldn't be, that she wanted him to stay and make sure whoever had thrown those knives didn't come back to try to harm her again. She wanted to tell him that she needed him to stay with her, that he made her feel safe as no man had ever done before, but she didn't.

She glanced at the large clock on the wall. "It's almost two. Surely bad guys have to sleep. I'll be fine. I've got a dead bolt on my apartment door upstairs." She straightened her shoulders, digging for the inner strength and independence that had always been her best friends.

He hesitated, as if torn with the decision whether to go or to stay.

"Go home, Steve. Get some sleep. It sounds like we're going to have a long day tomorrow."

"I'll make sure the patrol guys do drive-bys here every half hour or so for the rest of the night."

She nodded and walked with him to the door, needing to be strong when all she wanted to do was throw her arms around his neck and beg him to stay.

He opened the back door, looked outside and then turned back to her. "I'm just a phone call away, Roxy. I can be back here within ten minutes if you need me."

"I'm sure the drama is over now." She believed that. She really didn't expect anything more to happen for what remained of the night.

He lifted a hand, as if to touch her cheek or stroke her hair, and then apparently thought better of it and dropped his arm back to his side. "Then unless something else happens or new information comes in, I'll see you tomorrow afternoon in the office at two."

It was only after she'd closed and locked the door after him that she realized how much she wished he would have touched her…stroked her face or run his fingers through her hair. And if she looked deep inside herself, she recognized that her wanting him close had nothing to do with fear.

Kissing Steve had shaken her, creating a desire for him that was unwanted, that would only complicate their lives.

It had been over a year since Roxy had tried a relationship with a man, and she'd found the experience frustrating, unpleasant and ultimately not worth the effort. Gary Holzman had fooled her, professing to admire and adore her, yet trying to change everything about her.

Fantasizing about a relationship with Steve Kincaid was a fool's dream, and Roxy was no fool. She quickly washed the cups and placed them back in the cabinet, then turned out the lights in the kitchen and headed upstairs to her living quarters.

Once inside, she checked to make sure the door was locked with the dead bolt and then sank down on the sofa. As exhausted as she was, she was too wired to sleep.

Where was Aunt Liz? Who had thrown those knives at her? Were the two related, or did Roxy have a deadly enemy she didn't know about?

She chewed her thumbnail as thoughts whirled in a dizzy spin in her head. While she had no reason to believe any danger would come at her for the rest of the night, what kept her awake was the idea of what might happen in the future.

It was just before noon the next day when Steve got word from an officer he had sitting on the Cardell residence that Edward had just pulled into his driveway.

He considered calling Roxy but immediately cast the idea out of his head. He'd call her after he checked out Edward. It would make things easier on everyone.

Frank rode with him, as Jimmy was busy preparing a showcase of throwing knives on the computer to show Roxy later in the day.

"Have you spoken with Roxy this morning?" Frank asked.

Steve nodded. "I called her just before the restaurant was due to open. I just wanted to check in to make sure she'd gotten through the night okay."

"She's a tough cookie."

"She's one of the most aggravating women I've ever met," Steve replied.

Frank smiled. "You like her."

Steve thought about the past couple of days and released a sigh. "Yeah, I do," he admitted reluctantly. "But that doesn't mean it's going anywhere. She has no interest in a relationship with me or anyone else. And you know how I feel about getting serious again with any woman."

"We're on the same page where that's concerned," Frank said.

The two fell silent. As Steve drove, he thought about his partner, who had been married for two years and had come home one day to find his wife dead, having committed suicide. Frank had been devastated. While he knew his wife suffered from some depression, he'd had no idea how desperate and miserable she'd become.

Frank blamed himself for not seeing clearly, for not taking action to save the woman he'd loved. He and Steve shared the common bond of love gone terribly wrong and the determination never to go there again.

As Steve approached Cardell's street, he shoved all thoughts of love and Roxy out of his mind. He hoped Liz was with Cardell, that the two of them had sneaked away for a romantic couple of days and hadn't realized the frantic worry they'd left behind. He hoped they'd been thoughtless and rude, not criminal, in their actions.

A white panel van sat in the driveway, and Steve pulled up next to it and parked. He hadn't told Roxy that Edward owned a panel van, the perfect vehicle for camping—or for kidnapping.

The air crackled with a new intensity as the two detectives got out of the car and approached the front door. From the information gathered from people they'd contacted about Edward, he had a reputation for being an affable guy, but Steve knew more than anyone how people might wear facades, and when those masks slipped there were sometimes monsters beneath.

Steve knocked on the door, and Frank stood just off to the side of the porch with his hand on the butt of his gun. Although neither of them were anticipating trouble, they were prepared for it in case it reared its ugly head.

The door opened and a tall, older man dressed in a pair of jeans and a T-shirt that read Gone Fishin' gave them a quizzical but pleasant smile. His hair was a thick salt and pepper, and his blue eyes appeared guileless. "Can I help you folks?" he asked, looking first at Steve and then at Frank.

His pleasant expression grew worried when he saw Frank's gun. Steve quickly introduced them. "Mind if we come in and ask you some questions?"

Edward appeared both confused and concerned at the same time. "Sure," he agreed and opened the door to allow them inside.

A large duffel bag, along with a grocery bag, sat just inside the door. "Sorry about that," Edward said as Steve stepped over it. "I just got back from the mountains and haven't had a chance to get things put away." He frowned. "Is there a problem?"

"Was Liz Marcoli with you at the cabin in the mountains?" Steve asked.

Edward's frown deepened. "Liz? No. The mountains aren't Liz's thing, and the cabin is definitely too primitive. I'd never take her there. Why?"

"When was the last time you saw or spoke to Liz?" Frank asked as Steve fought off a wave of discouragement. He'd been so hopeful that this was all some misunderstanding, that Liz had taken off with Edward and simply forgotten to tell Roxy and her sisters her plans.

"Thursday evening. I called her to tell her goodbye before I headed out early on Friday morning." Edward gestured them toward the sofa. "Please, have a seat and tell me what this is all about."

Steve exchanged a glance with Frank, and the two sat on the sofa while Edward sank down in a chair opposite them, his features still radiating confusion and concern. "What's all this about Liz? Is she okay?"

"We don't know. Nobody has seen or heard from her since Thursday night, although we know she was at her house early on Friday morning." Steve watched Edward intently, looking for any signs of deception in facial expression or body language. "Did you and Liz have a fight?"

"Of course not. Liz and I don't fight. The girls haven't seen or heard from her?" Once again he looked from Steve to Frank. "Nobody has seen her since Thursday?" It was as if he couldn't wrap his brain around it.

"She apparently worked Friday morning to prepare some baked goods to take to Roxy at the Dollhouse, but she never made it there. The baked goods and her purse were still on the kitchen counter when Roxy insisted I do a well check on her."

Roxy... Steve couldn't think about her now, about

how the fragile hope she'd held that her aunt was with Edward would be shattered.

A flare of panic lit Edward's eyes. "And nobody knows what's happened to her?"

"We hoped she might be with you," Frank said.

"No, Liz never had any interest in going to the cabin with me. She knew that I enjoyed the solitude, and she preferred sticking around town. God, I wish she would have been with me. What could have happened to her?" Edward sat forward on his chair, as if ready to spring into action to find the woman he obviously cared about.

"Would you mind if we take a look in the back of your panel van?" Steve asked.

The question stunned Edward. His mouth opened and closed as his eyes widened. "You think maybe I…?" His voice trailed off. "Of course, you can look wherever you want. I'll even give you directions and the key to the cabin if you need to check it out. Why on earth would you think I'd want to hurt Liz? I care deeply about her."

"We heard that the two of you weren't exactly on the same page about some things," Steve said. "We heard you were irritated that she wouldn't introduce you to her family."

Edward leaned back in his chair and sighed. "I wasn't irritated about that, and we certainly didn't fight about it. Sure, I wanted it to happen, but Liz wasn't ready for that so I accepted her wishes that we keep things as they are."

"And exactly how are things between you?" Steve asked.

"Our relationship has been a slow build over the

past year. We met at bingo, sat next to each other for the evening, and after the games were finished I invited her to lunch the next day."

The blue of his eyes softened. "That was the beginning of a lot of lunches and occasional dinners together. We were both lonely and we fit well together, but Liz wanted to take things slowly and that was fine with me. I just enjoyed her company. Then about three months ago we took the relationship to a deeper level. She spent the night here occasionally, usually on Saturday nights when she didn't have to get up and bake the next morning. Check wherever and whatever you want, just please find her for me…for her girls."

Minutes later Steve and Frank were outside looking in the back of the panel van and finding only the kinds of things an outdoorsman would normally carry—fishing poles and tackle boxes nestled next to a sleeping bag and a stack of precut firewood.

What they didn't find was any evidence that Liz or her body had ever been in the back of the van. They left thirty minutes later with the location of the cabin and the key, although there wasn't time to check it out before they were to meet with Roxy at the station to look at the computer show of throwing knives that Jimmy had spent the morning preparing.

"What did you think?" Frank asked when they were back in the car and headed to the station.

"My gut is telling me he didn't have anything to do with Liz's disappearance, but my gut has been wrong before." Steve gripped the steering wheel as he thought of the last time his gut had given him false information—and the result had been the loss of his child.

"I say we check in with Roxy at the station, and then you and I drive up to that cabin and check it out," Frank said. "According to Edward, it's less than an hour's drive. We could be there and back before dark."

"Sounds like a plan to me." It was a plan he wouldn't mention to Roxy, and hopefully she wouldn't think about the need to check out the cabin. It was bad enough he had to tell her that, at least on the surface, Edward appeared genuinely perplexed and worried about Liz's absence.

"She's going to be so upset that Liz wasn't with Edward," Steve said, more to himself than to his partner.

"This definitely moves Liz's disappearance into a different light," Frank replied. "Even though her kitchen showed no signs of foul play, it's been four days and it's definitely time to step up the investigation process and consider this a real crime."

"I've been investigating it like it's a real crime since the beginning," Steve said. "I never truly embraced the idea that Liz went willingly with Edward, that she'd just up and left with him without letting any of her family members know her plans. She's too close to Roxy, Marlene and Sheri to stay incommunicado."

"So maybe she went with Edward unwillingly," Frank speculated. "That panel van would have made it easy for him to somehow overtake her, stash her back there and drive her to the mountain cabin. Maybe he killed her up there and buried her someplace in the woods."

"Possible, but there's one basic element lacking— what's the motive? Why would Edward want to kill Liz?" Steve always liked to approach solving crimes by looking for the motive.

"Maybe Edward really was ticked off that Liz didn't want him introduced to her family," Frank offered.

"So ticked off that he drove her halfway up the mountain, killed her and then buried her body? Sorry, buddy, but that motive doesn't have many teeth as far as I'm concerned."

Frank nodded. "Especially since, from everything we could find out about Edward, he has no history of violence at all. The man doesn't even have a speeding ticket on his record."

"We'll still check out the cabin, see if there's anything there. Roxy is supposed to be at the station at two to look at some knives. I doubt that will take too long, so we might be able to take off for the mountain around three."

"Should I contact Jed Wilson and have him bring a couple of dogs?" Frank asked.

Jed Wilson worked search and rescue and had dogs that were trained to find people who were alive and people who were dead. "Maybe it wouldn't be a bad idea to have a couple of his dogs sniff around and see if they get a hit in the area," Steve replied. "I'll need something of Liz's for them to have a scent to follow. I'll get something from Roxy and get back to you."

"If the dogs don't catch a scent on the van, then maybe it's pointless to search the cabin," Frank pointed out.

"But they will get her scent in the van. I'm sure during the course of Edward and Liz's relationship, she's ridden in his van."

Steve pulled into the parking space near the police station, unsurprised to see Roxy's car in a nearby space even though it was only one-thirty.

Of course she'd be early, and now he had the heart-breaking task of telling her that Edward Cardell had returned home and Liz Marcoli hadn't been with him.

It was a conversation he didn't want to have with her because he knew he'd see the fear, the frightening uncertainty crawling into the depths of her lovely eyes. He also knew when that happened he'd want to pull her close and kiss her trembling lips in an effort to staunch her fears.

He shouldn't have kissed her before. He'd known that kissing Roxy would be hot and sexy and imminently addictive. The problem was that he wanted to kiss her again…and often, and that wouldn't be fair to either of them.

She was like a shining beacon seated in front of Jimmy's desk as Steve and Frank entered the room. She was clad in a bright pink T-shirt and black jeans, with her hair a riot of dark curls and her energy filling the entire room. The mere sight of her hitched his heart.

Her smile was somber and reminded him of what she'd been through the night before. He walked over to where she sat and, unable to help himself, lightly touched her shoulder.

"You're early," he said and noticed the slight shadows that clung to the skin beneath her eyes. "Did you get any sleep at all last night?"

"Not much," she admitted. "But Jimmy found the knives I'm pretty sure were thrown at me."

"Well, that's something," he said and pulled up a chair next to her. Apparently she didn't know yet that Edward Cardell had returned and Liz hadn't been with him.

He wasn't about to bring it up right now. He wanted to focus on the threat that had occurred last night. "So what did you find?"

Jimmy swung his computer around and pointed to where the screen displayed a pair of throwing knives that had ornate cross hilts. They looked both beautiful and deadly, and Steve's heart stuttered as he thought of how close those blades had come to Roxy's head.

"There's good news," Roxy said, her eyes holding an overbright, frantic light that Steve knew could only mean bad news. "They're called Vampire Cross Throwing Knives, so all we have to do now is identify any vampires in town and bring them in for questioning."

Chapter 9

Roxy desperately tried to find humor in the situation, but she certainly wasn't laughing as she stared at the photo of the knives that had nearly pierced through her the night before.

"So anyone who is wearing a cross or has garlic hanging in their windows probably shouldn't be on our suspect list," she said.

Steve fought the impulse to touch her again as he sensed the disquiet that threatened to erupt into a roar inside her. "Roxy, I have it on good authority that we don't have to worry about any vampires here in Wolf Creek. I'll have Jimmy chase down any place in town that carries those kinds of knives, and maybe we'll get lucky."

Steve looked at Jimmy for confirmation. "Sure, I already know a couple places here in town and in

Hershey that specialize in martial-arts weaponry. I'll start checking them out right now and see what I can find out about the buyers." He got up from his desk and looked at Steve. "I'll give you a call and let you know what I find out later this evening."

Roxy stared at him and braced herself against the back of the chair. She sensed he knew information he hadn't shared, information she probably didn't want to hear. "What?"

He pulled his chair closer to hers and started to reach for her hands, but she refused to allow him to grab them. "I know you have something to tell me, so just spit it out."

"Edward Cardell came back from the cabin earlier today."

She'd half risen from the chair before he grabbed her by the arm and pulled her back down. "Liz wasn't with him," he said.

She stared at the shaggy-haired surfer dude she'd come to rely on, the man who had somehow transformed from a flirting, buzzing, irritating fly to a solid, hardworking rock she wanted to cling to.

"What did he say?" Her voice sounded hollow, and she realized at that moment how desperately she'd hoped that her aunt was with Edward, that she'd thrown caution to the wind and gone off for four days with her secret lover.

"That the last time he spoke to her was Thursday night, to tell her goodbye before his trip to the cabin."

"And you believed him?" Roxy was acutely aware of his hand still on her arm and she welcomed it, for the place where he touched was the only warmth her body possessed.

He hesitated. "He appeared to be genuinely upset by the fact that nobody has seen or heard from her since Friday. We checked his van and found no evidence that your aunt was in there. But to be sure, Frank and I are heading up to the cabin to check things there."

"Frank and you and me," she replied.

"Roxy—"

"Don't even think about leaving me behind," she exclaimed. "Have you forgotten that a vampire tried to kill me last night? I need my aunt, and if she's in that cabin then I intend to be with you when you find her."

"We don't know what we'll find there, Roxy. Maybe nothing, or maybe—"

"I know," she interrupted, not wanting to hear him say anything more. For the first time she realized the possibility that she might never see her aunt again, the possibility that whoever threw the knives at her the night before might be the same person who had done something horrible to Aunt Liz.

She moved so that his hand no longer touched her arm and straightened her back. She had to be strong. "I have to go with you, Steve. If you find something bad there, then I need to know before my sisters so I can be the one to tell them."

His gaze lingered on her, as if assessing whether she was truly strong enough to survive whatever might be ahead. She raised her chin a notch, despite the fact that every internal organ trembled with the fear that before the night was over they'd find out her beloved aunt was dead.

"Okay, even though I know this is probably a mistake, you can come with us. But you have to stay out of our way and let us do our job," he finally said.

"I promise."

It was exactly three o'clock when Roxie sat in the backseat of Steve's car, Steve behind the wheel and Frank riding shotgun. In her lap she held Liz's favorite soft pink cardigan sweater. Liz kept it hanging by the back door and often pulled it on during this time of year.

Roxie anxiously chewed what was left of her thumbnail as they reached the curving mountain road that would twist and wind them to the cabin. Both Marlene and Sheri had called that morning to check in with her, but she'd had no news to share with them, only the promise that she'd let them know if any information came to light.

It had been five days since anyone had seen or heard from Liz. Roxy realized with each day that passed that the odds of finding her alive were growing slim.

When she heard the two in the front seat talking about Jed showing up with his dogs, she knew they were not only looking for an alive Liz, but a dead one, as well.

She tried to hang on to a piece of fragile hope, but given the circumstances, it was becoming more and more difficult. She simply couldn't imagine her life without the woman who had saved her from her mother, the woman who had taught her how to be human, how to love and be loved.

She stared at the back of Steve's head as she dropped her hand from her mouth to her lap. He confused her. If he was the womanizer rumors made him out to be, there had certainly been no signs of that in the past five days.

Not only was she intensely physically drawn to him, but she'd found him to be tender and caring and definitely patient with her.

Not many men had the patience to be around her for any length of time. Gary certainly hadn't been able to deal with her volatile personality long-term. He'd spent most of their relationship trying to change her, not simply embracing who she was and loving her.

The truth was that she knew she was difficult to love, that her past had made her defensive and wary, prickly and controlling.

Her own mother hadn't loved her enough to keep her. The only people who had ever truly loved Roxy were Aunt Liz and her sisters, and the idea of no longer having her aunt in her life pressed a tight weight of frantic grief into her chest.

She sat up straighter as they turned off the main road and onto a rutted mountain pass that was little more than a trail. The newly leafed trees slapped against the roof of the car as thick brush rubbed the undercarriage.

Roxy checked the clock on the dashboard and buried her hands in the softness of the sweater in her lap. They had to be getting close to the cabin where Edward had spent the past four days. Had he kidnapped Liz and brought her up there? Had they fought and something snapped inside him—had he killed her and buried her someplace out in the woods?

Roxy's thumbnail found its way back to her teeth, and she nibbled as wave after wave of nervous tension filled her. Would this be the end of their search?

Or would they leave the cabin with more questions than answers?

Steve met her gaze in the rearview mirror, and in his eyes she saw the depth of his concern, not just for her, but for the victim they sought.

"We should be getting close," Frank said. "The turnoff for the cabin should be on the left someplace in the next couple of miles or so."

They were deep in the woods now, with trees and brush nearly choking off the trail. The idea that her aunt could be in the woods, wandering around lost and alone, or dead, made drawing normal breaths nearly impossible for Roxy.

"There," Frank said and pointed to a turnoff just ahead.

Steve took the turn, and after driving half a mile the first thing they all saw was Jed's bright red pickup parked in front of a wooden cabin that appeared as if a strong gust of wind might blow it down.

As they pulled up behind Jed's truck, the two dogs in the back began to bark. Jed got out of the truck, and with a sharp command the dogs fell silent.

They all got out of the car and Roxy stared at the cabin, which was obviously intended to be a hunting or fishing shelter as opposed to a vacation destination.

Roxy hugged the sweater to her chest as they all greeted each other. Jed was a nice-looking guy in his early thirties who lived on a farm not far from the Amish settlement. He had a respectable business training working dogs and was a frequent breakfast visitor at the Dollhouse.

With the greetings out of the way, Roxy followed Steve and Frank up the rickety stairs that led to the cabin door. Steve used a key to open the door, and the three of them stepped inside the one-room structure.

"There's no way Aunt Liz would come here on her own," Roxy said, trying to hide her disgust as she looked around the dingy room that was lit only by the sunlight drifting through a dirty window.

There was a single cot shoved against one wall and a small counter with two cabinets above it. A rickety two-top table sat in front of another wall, and that was the sum of the amenities.

"No electricity, no running water. I'd say this is definitely not a hot spot for a romantic getaway," Frank said.

Steve walked around the small room, his gaze appearing to take in every minute detail. Was he looking for bloodstains? Splatter on the walls?

Roxy needed to get out. The very idea that her aunt might have been brought to this hellhole was too much for her to handle.

She stepped outside and drew in a deep breath of the fresh mountain air and hugged Aunt Liz's sweater closer against her chest. It smelled of her aunt's favorite scent, a combination of lilac and vanilla.

Jed had gotten back into the cab of his pickup, and Roxy was grateful not to have to make small talk. She stepped off the porch onto a path that apparently led toward the back of the cabin.

She'd done what Steve had asked of her last night and spent most of the morning in her own little kitchen upstairs, writing down the names of anyone and everyone she could think of who might want to hurt her.

But right now she couldn't think about her own brush with death. Right now her thoughts were only about Aunt Liz. It had been easy for Roxy to fill a page with people who might not like her, but it had been impossible to come up with the names of anyone who might want to harm Liz Marcoli.

If they didn't find some trace of her here, if Edward Cardell was truly innocent of any involvement in her disappearance, then Roxy didn't know what the next move would be.

She'd received half a dozen calls resulting from the posters they'd hung, each call nuttier than the next. She tried to pull her thoughts together as Steve and Frank left the cabin, and Steve approached her while Frank went to speak to Jed.

"I need that sweater now," Steve said gently. She nodded, and after a final hug of the soft material that smelled like Liz, she handed it to him.

She watched as Jed got the dogs from the back of the truck and held the sweater beneath each of their noses. It was like watching a movie. Somehow she'd emotionally detached from everything that was happening around her.

After Jed's shouted command, the dogs took off, one heading toward the open door of the cabin and the other shooting off into the woods. The dog that had run into the cabin came right back out and continued sniffing the ground; then he, too, headed toward the wooded surroundings.

Jed followed the dogs while Steve and Frank leaned against the pickup. Several times Steve looked at her, as if willing her to join them, but she remained alone, trapped in a daytime nightmare that felt surreal.

The scent of pines surrounded her as the dogs barked and suddenly she was thrust back in time, back to a seedy motel room that smelled of pine cleanser and sweat. A big man was in the room with a pit bull on a chain, and the man was yelling at Ramona about money.

Roxy was curled up on the floor at the foot of the bed, terrified that the man would release the snarling, hot-breathed dog, afraid that the dog would eat her and that the man would kill her mother.

Ramona had ordered Roxy outside and had taken care of the problem with the man with the only commodity Ramona had. Roxy had sat just outside the door in the darkness of the night and had sworn that she would never be dependent on anyone else for the rest of her life. Men had destroyed her mother, and Roxy would never follow in her mother's footsteps.

She jumped as Steve touched her on the shoulder, pulling her from a past nightmare to the present one. "The dogs didn't pick up any scent," he said and handed her back Liz's sweater.

"So she wasn't here?"

"According to the dogs, she wasn't here."

Roxy nodded and headed back to the car. She should be relieved Aunt Liz wasn't there. But there was no relief, for there were no leads anywhere.

She'd checked out. Steve glanced in the rearview mirror at Roxy, who hadn't spoken a word since he'd told her the dogs hadn't picked up any scent of Liz.

She sat still as a statue, her head turned to peer out the window. He was worried about her. She seemed shut down in a way he'd never seen before. The internal fire was doused, leaving only a shell.

When they reached the station, Frank went inside

the building and Steve stopped Roxy as she started to head to her car. "Do you have a list of names for me?" he asked.

She nodded and pulled a piece of paper out of her jeans pocket. "I listed everyone I could think of who might have a reason to dislike me. It even shocked me that it was such a long list."

She spoke the words without emotion, her tone flat and her eyes still holding an emptiness that was very un-Roxy-like. The knives the night before…the cabin today…the absence of the rock in her life—it was apparently all too much.

"Why don't you come with me to my place for dinner?" he asked. "I've got a couple of steaks I can throw on the grill and enough fixings for a salad."

She shrugged, as if it didn't matter where she went or what she did. "Okay."

He wanted to grab her by the shoulders and shake her until flames lit the depths of her empty eyes. He wanted to demand that she return from wherever she'd run to in her mind.

He led her to his car and opened the passenger door. She said nothing as she shoved his latest car trash off the seat and onto the floor. Once she was seated, he shut the door and hurried around to the driver side.

He remembered this. He remembered crawling into himself in the weeks after Tommy had disappeared. It had been when the fear and the anger could no longer be sustained, and all he'd wanted was to be left alone to wallow in his own misery. He couldn't let her go there, not now and definitely not alone.

"Are you hungry?" he asked.

"A little," she replied, not looking at him as her fingers dug deeper into the pink sweater on her lap. She kept her gaze out the passenger window, disconnected not just from him, but apparently everything.

He didn't try to have any more conversation with her. He hoped when he got her to his place, she would come around and be as okay as she could be under the circumstances.

As he drove up the mountain road that led to his home, her silence broke his heart just a little bit. Roxy wasn't made to be silent. She wasn't meant to have dark hollowness in her eyes, her lush lips slightly downturned.

Before the night was over he intended to figure out a way to bring her back to life, even though she still faced a missing loved one and a potential threat.

She roused herself as he pulled into his driveway. "This is your house?"

"All mine," he replied.

"It's beautiful."

"I worked with a friend who's a contractor to get it just right so that we disturbed as little of the surrounding forest as possible. He framed it in, and then Frank and Jimmy and I worked during our off time on the inside until it finally all came together."

They both got out of the car, and Roxy continued to gaze at the front of the home. "It looks like something out of a magazine."

They walked up the steps that led to the front door. "You're actually the first woman who has ever been here, other than my mother, so I'll be interested to hear what you think."

She eyed him dubiously. "I'm the first woman

who has ever been here? Tell me another funny story, Detective Flirt."

There was the spark of life Steve had wanted to see, shining from the depths of her dark eyes. He grinned and then turned to open the door before looking back at her. "Detective Flirt, hmm, I like it. But it's the truth, Roxy. I've never brought a woman here before."

She searched his features, as if looking for a lie. "Then I'm honored," she finally said.

As they stepped into the entry her gaze went everywhere, and he wasn't sure if she was admiring the woodwork and high ceilings or looking for some woman's frilly panties hanging from the ceiling fan or peeking out from a couch cushion.

She placed Liz's sweater on the back of the sofa. "Do I get the full tour?"

"Sure," he replied, although there was one room upstairs he had no intention of showing her.

As he led her around the lower level, which consisted of the great room, the kitchen and a bathroom, he noticed that she was beginning to show more life. He was grateful that whatever fog had struck her at the cabin and on the way home appeared to be dissipating.

While they were in the large kitchen, he grabbed a package of steaks out of the freezer. "I've got a grill on the deck." He pointed out the kitchen door to a deck with an umbrella table and a barbecue grill. "We'll just toss these on when we're ready, and they shouldn't take too long. If it's still warm enough, we can eat outside. Otherwise we'll eat in here."

"Sounds fine. It would be nice to eat outside. The weather has been so pretty."

He nodded. "But once the sun goes down, it still

gets pretty cool. Come on, and I'll show you the up-stairs."

He wasn't sure why, but he was eager to show her the master suite, with the deck overlooking the stream and the bathroom with the jetted tub big enough for two.

As she climbed the stairs, her hand caressed the smooth banister and Steve fought off thoughts of what her hands would feel like stroking his chest.

He mentally smacked himself. The last thing he needed to think about now was how much he'd like to kiss her again, how strong his desire was grow-ing for her.

They reached the top of the stairs, and he ushered her into the large room that was his, grateful that he'd actually made his bed that morning and that there were no stray boxers or briefs anywhere in sight.

"It's nothing like what I expected of you," she said.

He grinned. "You were maybe expecting a round black velvet bed that revolved to music and mood lighting?"

Her lips curved upward, and he breathed a sigh of relief. "Something like that," she replied. She walked to the French doors that led out to the upper deck and peered outside, where the golden rays of the setting sun painted the forest in a rich glow. "What a stun-ning view."

"I spend a lot of evenings sitting on the deck when the weather is nice," he said.

She gasped in delight as she entered the adjoin-ing bathroom with its big tub and the skylight above.

"A bubble bath and a sky full of stars," she said,

more to herself than to him. She turned to look at him. "This is all so lovely."

He hadn't realized that her opinion really mattered until now, and pride filled him as he led her to the next room. "This is where my mother stays when she decides to spend the night here."

It was a pleasant guest room decorated in shades of pinks and mauves with a double bed and a dresser with a pretty fake floral arrangement adorning the top.

"Does your mother stay here a lot?" she asked.

"Maybe once every couple of months or so," he replied. "And then only if I insist. She likes her own bed in her own condo."

He wouldn't tell her that there had been a time when his mother had spent the night often, when this house hadn't breathed of the grief it now contained.

He walked to the window and stared out, remembering when his mother and father had both spent so much time there, when laughter had filled every corner and love had been alive and well.

He turned his head and realized that Roxy had left the room. He hurried into the hallway and saw her at the closed door at the end of the hall.

"Roxy!" he said at the same time she turned the knob and opened the door.

Steve froze, as did Roxy as she stared into the room. She turned and looked at him, her gaze curious. "And who belongs in this room?"

Steve's chest expanded with a heavy weight, and as always the guilt and grief he felt when he thought of Tommy was nearly overwhelming.

"That's Tommy's room," he finally answered, vaguely surprised that his voice sounded raspy.

"Tommy?"

"Tommy is my son. His mother kidnapped him two years ago, and I haven't seen him since." The grief that was never far from the surface fought to consume him, but he battled against it.

He had brought Roxy there in an effort to assuage her emotional turmoil, not to air his own, but by opening that door she'd opened Pandora's box, and now no matter how hard he tried he couldn't stuff his grief back inside.

He forced a smile. "Come on, let's head downstairs and see about some dinner."

Chapter 10

The steaks were on the grill, and Steve stood next to Roxy as they worked on making a salad together. She was still stunned by the news that he'd had a son.

"Why doesn't anyone else in town know about Tommy?" she asked. "I mean, I've never heard any gossip at all about you having a son."

He hesitated a moment, obviously reluctant to talk about it. "There aren't very many people who knew about Tommy. His mother, Stacy, lived in Hershey. We met and dated mostly there. We'd been dating about six months when she told me she was pregnant," he said as he tore up the lettuce. "I was surprised, but I immediately asked her to marry me. I was willing to make a go of it, of building a family unit together, but she turned me down."

"That must have been a shock." Roxy paused with

her paring knife in the air and the green pepper she'd been slicing on a cutting board in front of her. "I mean, most women want to marry the father of their child."

"Stacy wasn't most women." He tore up the last of the lettuce with more force than necessary. "We continued to see each other through the pregnancy and for about a year after Tommy was born. Then she told me that while she wanted me to continue to be a presence in Tommy's life, she didn't want me to be a presence in hers."

"And you were okay with that?" Roxy finished slicing the peppers and dumped them in the bowl of lettuce. She knew she was pushing him, but it was easier to focus on his trauma than her own, and besides, she couldn't help the fact that she was curious, that she cared about what had gone into making him the man he was now.

"I had to be okay with it. Things had gotten strained between us, and I realized we weren't meant to be a couple. I was never really in love with her, but I did love her as the mother of my child." He shrugged and picked up a tomato. "I figured lots of people have children and share custody, and I loved Tommy more than anything else on the face of the earth. I was determined to make it work."

She saw it there, shining from his eyes—pure, unadulterated love—and for a moment she wished she saw that in somebody's eyes, she wished somebody felt that kind of love for her. She grabbed the tomato from him, irritated by her own thoughts.

"And so the two of you shared custody?" she asked, wanting to focus only on the topic at hand and not her growing feelings for Steve.

He nodded and grabbed one of the bottles of beer he'd pulled out of the fridge for them before they'd started making the salad. "And for the first couple of years it worked out just fine. Stacy kept him during the week, and he spent his weekends here with me. Tommy was about four when I started noticing troubling changes."

He paused and took a long sip of his beer, and Roxy felt his growing agitation as darkness filled his blue eyes. "When I'd go to Stacy's apartment to pick him up, there were people hanging out there who didn't look like they were solid citizens, and Tommy was usually dirty and unkempt, often hungry as a wolf. I suspected Stacy had fallen into drugs and a bad lifestyle that I certainly didn't want for Tommy. So around that time I petitioned the court and was granted full custody of him."

"How did Stacy handle it?"

"Stacy had always been overly dramatic, driven by emotions, and at first she was livid. But I think she was also secretly relieved, and I promised her that she could come here whenever she wanted to visit with him."

Happy memories leaped into his eyes. "I loved having Tommy here, waking up in the mornings with him jumping on my bed, getting him dressed and ready for the school bus. My mom was here to greet him when he got home, and then when I'd get home from work it would just be me and Tommy."

The light of memories faded from his eyes, and Roxy's heart ached once again as she saw the hollow grief that deepened their color. "Stacy came by occasionally to see him, but not often, and when she did show up she was usually high or just plain crazy. Although I didn't like her hanging around, I also didn't want to deprive Tommy of an opportunity to have some sort of a relationship with his mother. It was the worst mistake I ever made. I trusted her."

"So what happened?" Roxy grabbed her beer and took a drink to fortify herself for the story of his broken heart.

"One day my mom was here waiting for Tommy to come home from school, and as the bus lumbered up the hill she realized Stacy was parked along the street. Before my mom could get outside, Stacy was gone with Tommy, and I haven't heard anything from them in the last two years."

Roxy set down the bottle she'd been holding, her need to comfort him suddenly overwhelming as she saw the raw emotion in his eyes. But before she could move close enough to embrace him, he headed for the door.

"I need to check on the steaks," he said and disappeared outside.

She finished cutting up the tomato and sliced a cucumber as she waited for him to come back inside. Her entire impression of him had been wrong. Just like Roxy used her anger and her frankness as a guard to keep people from getting too close, Steve used his flirting and easygoing attitude to hide what had to be a near-devastating heartache.

Two years. Two long years of not knowing where his son was, of what was happening to him or how he was living. Her heart positively ached for him. How did he survive each day? Her aunt had only been missing for a matter of days, and she was a basket case.

FREE Merchandise is 'in the Cards' for you!

Dear Reader,

We're giving away FREE MERCHANDISE!

Seriously, we'd like to reward you for reading this novel by giving you **FREE MERCHANDISE** worth over $20. And no purchase is necessary!

You see the Jack of Hearts sticker above? Paste that sticker in the box on the Free Merchandise Voucher inside. Return the Voucher promptly...and we'll send you valuable Free Merchandise!

Thanks again for reading one of our novels—and enjoy your Free Merchandise with our compliments!

Pam Powers

Pam Powers

P.S. Look inside to see what Free Merchandise is **"in the cards"** for you!

H-RS-12/13-FM-13

He came back through the door with the steaks still sizzling on a plate. He set it on the counter next to her. "I'll grab some plates and silverware, and we need to eat these while they're still good and hot."

It was obvious he'd gotten his emotions under control, and he was ready to move on to a new topic of conversation. As he set the table, Roxy tossed and dressed the salad, and then together they sat down to eat.

They didn't talk about Tommy or Liz; they didn't speak of Vampire knives or crime of any kind. For the first time in a very long time, Roxy tried to entertain a man.

She found herself telling him about the humorous trials and tribulations of establishing the Dollhouse, of recipes gone horribly wrong and the crazy people who had applied for jobs there over the years.

She was satisfied that his eyes had lightened, and he laughed with her as she stretched her tales to make each one of them funnier and more outrageous than the last.

When they'd finished with the meal, he reached across the table for her hand and she curled her fingers with his. "Thank you," he said simply.

"For what?"

"For bringing laughter back into this house, for pulling me back from the edge of an abyss."

"I'm just returning the favor," she replied. They released their joined hands and she leaned back in her chair. "When we left the cabin this evening, I had already plunged into the abyss and you somehow managed to pull me out of it."

She got up, fighting against the press of anxiety

in her chest as she thought of her missing aunt. She grabbed their two empty plates as he stood and collected the glasses and silverware they'd used.

They were both quiet as they quickly rinsed and placed in the dishwasher everything they'd used for the meal. "How about some after-dinner coffee?" he asked.

It was getting dark outside and she knew she should go home, but she found herself nodding instead. "That sounds good," she agreed.

"Why don't you go relax in the living room, and I'll get the coffee."

Roxy went into the living room, where again she was vaguely surprised by how warm and inviting it was. It wasn't the living room of a single, superficial man; rather, it was a living room that belonged to a family.

The sofa was a comfortable overstuffed one in a chocolate-brown color. A matching chair sat nearby with a reading lamp behind it. A flat-screen television was mounted on the wall above a beautiful stone fireplace, and bookshelves held an array of books, photos, puzzles and games that caused Roxy's heart to flinch with pain for Steve and the child he'd lost.

She'd had years and years with her Aunt Liz, but Steve had really only had one year to fully parent and enjoy his son. What kind of woman stole her son from his father? What kind of person stole a woman like Aunt Liz from her loved ones?

She smiled as Steve came into the room with a small tray that contained their coffee and a platter of store-bought cookies. "I can't get over how beautiful your home is," she said as she settled back in the sofa cushions with her coffee cup in hand.

He sat next to her. "Thanks. I bought the land on the day Tommy was born. Before that I'd been living in a bachelor apartment, and when I saw that baby I knew my life had changed forever." He looked across the room to the bookshelves where the puzzles were stored. "Tommy was the best son, and I tried to be the best father possible for him. He loved horses and cowboys and wanted to own a ranch when he grew up."

She took a sip of her coffee and eyed him over the rim of her cup. When she was finished, she set the cup back on the tray and leaned toward him. "Don't you ever think about trying it again? Falling in love, getting married and maybe having more children?"

"That's what my mother wants for me, but I'm not interested."

"How do you do it? How have you survived the last two years without knowing where he is?"

"I didn't think I would survive the first week," he admitted. "I went more than a little crazy. I went to Hershey and searched everywhere I thought Stacy might be, talked to every creep she'd ever known, but nobody knew where she had gone. I didn't eat. I didn't sleep. I was possessed with the need to do something, to make something happen that would bring Tommy back to me." He offered her a soft smile. "Sound familiar?"

"Painfully so," she admitted. "Are you still looking for them?"

"I'll never stop," he replied fervently. "I've hired private investigators, have police officers in a dozen other counties and cities keeping an eye out for them, and I do a monthly check on Stacy's social security number to see if I can find a place where she's working. Frank and Jimmy help me with checking schools to see if we can find one where Tommy is enrolled. It's an ongoing process that will never stop until he's back with me where he belongs."

He took a drink of his coffee and then set the cup on the tray as she had. He scooted closer to her and leaned forward, bringing with him the scent of barbecue smoke and his sandalwood cologne.

"That's why I told you how important it was—it *is*— that you stay on a normal routine as much as possible, that you don't allow the missing to completely destroy you."

"But how do you do that?" Roxy asked.

"One day at a time. When Tommy was taken, I never dreamed that two years later I'd still be looking for him. I never dreamed that the sun would come up each morning and the moon would appear each night, that life would go on despite my desire to make my world right again. And now I want to make your world right again, and I'm not sure how quickly we're going to do that."

She wasn't sure if he reached for her or she reached for him, but suddenly she was in his arms and his lips were kissing hers with an intensity that made everything else melt away.

It was as if they were the only people on the face of the earth, the only two who mourned the missing in their lives, who understood the heartache of the other.

Then the kiss transformed into something deeper, something different. It was no longer that of two people sharing the same life trauma; it was filled with lust and want that had nothing to do with loss.

She found herself stretched out on the sofa, his body against hers as the kiss deepened and her desire for him spiraled higher.

She wanted him. Somewhere in the back of her mind, as he filled her with heat, with fire, she was astonished to realize she wanted to make love to the surfer dude detective she'd once found so irritating.

It was the recognition of her overwhelming desire for him that forced her back up to a sitting position. He immediately sat up, as well, eyeing her questioningly.

"I forgot— I was supposed to warn you before I kissed you again," he said.

"I think maybe it's best if you take me home before we both do something we might regret," she replied, surprised by the tremor in her voice.

"Okay," he said, his voice sounding huskier than usual.

Within minutes, they were in his car and he was driving her back to the police station, where Roxy's car was parked. As she got into her car, he stood at her driver door. "We aren't finished, Roxy. We're going to find your aunt."

She desperately wanted to believe him, but as they said their goodbyes and she headed back to the Dollhouse, she couldn't help but think that he had more motivation to find his own son than he'd ever have to find Liz, and so far he hadn't been able to find Tommy.

She instantly told herself it wasn't fair to compare the two. Liz was a grown woman who had left the footprints of her life all around town. Tommy had been a little boy who hadn't had the chance to make footprints.

She could only pray that some day he would find his son, but at the moment she also prayed that he would find her aunt. At least they knew now that Edward Cardell had told the truth, that he hadn't absconded with her to that dreadful cabin.

She trusted that Steve and his partners would continue to look for leads, would do everything in their power to find Liz, and she also knew he was right. She had to try to keep her life as normal as possible while she waited for Liz to be returned to where she belonged.

As she pulled into her parking place at the Dollhouse, she sat for a moment with her headlights on full beam, checking out the area to see if there was anyone lurking around.

Before she got out of the car, she saw a police car slowly driving down the alley behind where she was parked. She remained in her car as the patrol vehicle pulled to a stop and Joe Jamison got out.

His big frame was a comfort as he ambled to her door. She got out of the car to greet him.

"Evening, Roxy."

"Hey, Joe. What are you doing hanging around in the back alleys of town?"

"Steve knew I was on patrol and called me and wanted to make sure you got inside safe and sound."

Her heart warmed as she thought of Steve making the call to ensure that she got inside her place without any danger. "Thanks, Joe. I appreciate you and Steve having my back."

Joe laughed, the sound a pleasant rumble in the otherwise still night. "Heck, I can't let anything happen to you. You're the only one who makes me that special omelet stuffed with all kinds of mysterious goodies."

"It's nice to know I'm good for something, and there's somebody who wants to keep me safe," she replied.

"I'd say Detective Kincaid seems to have a desire to keep you safe and sound, since he's the one who made the call to me."

Roxy was grateful for the darkness of the night as she felt her cheeks flame with color. "In any case, I appreciate the special escort." She got the key to the kitchen door in hand. "Good night, Joe, and thanks again."

"No problem." He remained standing by her car as she hurried up the walkway, confident that there would be no knives thrown at her with Officer Jamison on hand.

She unlocked the door and then turned to wave at Joe. He returned the wave and headed back to his car. She closed the door and locked it, then placed her purse on a nearby cutting block, deciding that she'd pull out of the freezer a turkey that needed to defrost in the fridge for a day or two.

As she opened the double-door walk-in freezer, the light inside blinked on, displaying an array of frozen items. Although she always tried to use the freshest ingredients possible, there were times when frozen had to be used.

She shivered with the cold and could see her breaths as they created short clouds of condensation. She'd just grabbed hold of the turkey when the doors to the freezer slammed shut and the light blinked off.

She muttered a curse, grabbed the blasted cold bird and headed for the door.

She turned and used her back to push the doors open, but nothing happened. She tried again, and still the doors didn't open.

In the utter darkness, she placed the turkey on the floor at her feet, her heart beating so hard she heard it in her ears, resounding in the small frozen area.

She shoved on the door, hoping that it was just a case of the vacuum seal sticking, but there was a tiny bit of give and no more.

Frantic now, she used her shoulder to slam into it, putting all her force behind the hit. She smashed into the door again and again, until her lungs ached from breathing in the freezing air.

She finally sank down to the floor.

Trapped.

Somehow she knew that something had been done to the door so that she couldn't open it.

There was no lock on it, but there had been dozens of times she'd been in there when both of the heavy doors had slammed shut behind her, and she'd easily shoved them back open.

This time was different.

She'd been so focused on Aunt Liz all day, she'd almost forgotten that somebody wanted to hurt her. She'd felt so safe at Steve's home and then with Joe in the driveway, she'd never considered anyone might already be in her house.

She'd made it easy for them. She'd left her purse with her cell phone on the table outside the freezer. There was nobody else in the house, and there was no way for her to call for help.

Josie would come in to work around six in the morning, but by then Roxy would be dead of hypothermia. With this thought, she rose to her feet once again and slammed into the door with the hope of somehow saving herself.

Still the doors refused to yield. She sank down to the floor again and wrapped her arms around her shoulders, already starting to feel the beginnings of the freeze taking over her body.

She shivered, goose bumps rose on her skin and her lungs burned. She should have stayed at Steve's. She should have never stopped their kissing and just let things progress in a natural way between them.

If she'd allowed it, she knew right now she'd be in Steve's bed, warmed by his naked body, flaming with his intimate caresses.

And afterward she might have run a tub full of hot water and sank down in the steaming heat with her head tipped up to view the stars through the skylight.

Maybe for a single night she wouldn't have thought about her missing aunt, and just maybe with her being there with him, he wouldn't have thought about the little boy's bedroom that lacked a little boy. Maybe for just a little while, he would have found some peace in her arms.

If she'd just let herself go, followed through on her desires, she wouldn't be locked in her freezer, slowly dying.

Chapter 11

Steve finished cleaning up the kitchen, and as he placed their coffee cups in the dishwasher his head remained full of Roxy. He'd been with a couple of women since he and Stacy had broken up, but nobody had stirred him in the way that Roxy had; nobody had made him want more than he had when they'd been on the sofa kissing.

His heart had nearly stopped when she'd opened the door to Tommy's room, and he'd known he'd have to explain. It had been a long time since he'd talked to anyone about Tommy. It hurt too much, and yet with Roxy it had been easier than he'd expected.

He'd felt her compassion, but she hadn't offered meaningless platitudes. She'd asked questions, but he hadn't found them intrusive or offensive.

Although he carried the grief of the loss of his son

in his heart, along with the guilt that he hadn't realized just how crazy Stacy really was, he also held a tiny seed of hope that eventually Tommy would be back where he belonged.

He'd also recognized how hard Roxy had worked to make him laugh as they'd eaten dinner. She'd been charming and delightful, and he felt as if she'd given him a gift as she'd taken his mind off Tommy and that particular pain.

As he left the living room, the first thing he saw was Liz's pink sweater on the back of the sofa. Roxy had forgotten to take it with her when she'd left.

He glanced at his watch. It was just a few minutes after nine, not so late that he couldn't run the sweater back to her. He picked up his phone to call her, but then tucked it into his pocket, deciding not to bother.

As he picked up Liz's sweater and grabbed his car keys, he realized part of the reason he didn't want to call was because she might say she'd pick it up the next day, and the truth was he entertained a little bit of hope that he'd get the opportunity to kiss her once again, to hold her in his arms one more time before the day officially ended.

He wanted her, and he knew from the way she'd responded to him that she wanted him, too. He'd sensed her reluctance when she'd called a halt to their kissing, and there was a part of him that hoped when he returned the sweater they might take up where they'd left off.

There was nothing that said they had to make any commitments to each other, but there was also nothing that said they couldn't spend the night together, make love with each other as consenting adults. She'd made it clear that she wasn't looking for any kind of a long-term relationship, and he certainly felt the same way, but one night of passion explored was a long way from a relationship.

As he parked beside her car in the back of the Dollhouse, he also knew that there was every possibility that she would take the sweater from him, thank him and then send him back on his way.

As he walked toward the back door, he noticed that no lights shone from the windows on the third floor. Odd, he wouldn't have expected her to already be in bed. It hadn't been that long since she'd left his house.

The kitchen light was on. Maybe she'd decided to get a cup of tea or a snack before going upstairs to bed. He knocked on the back door, expecting to see her peer around the corner of the kitchen to the door.

When he didn't see her, he knocked once again, this time harder. He also pushed the doorbell next to the door that he knew would ring throughout the house, including in her private quarters. When he still didn't get an answer, he pulled out his cell phone and punched in the numbers to her phone.

He immediately heard the ring of her cell phone coming from just inside the door, and he noticed her purse on the table nearest the door.

Why would she leave her purse there instead of carrying it upstairs with her? And why wasn't she answering his knocks?

A discordant *clang* went off inside his head. Something wasn't right. He quickly punched in the numbers to connect him with Joe Jamison.

"Jamison," the big man's voice barked.

"Joe, it's Steve. Were you here when Roxy got home?"

"Pulled up right behind her in the alley. We spoke for a minute or two, and then I waited until she got safely inside before I left. Is there a problem?"

"I don't know. I'm at her place now, and I can't get her to answer my knocking or the doorbell." Steve tried to tamp down the anxiety that grew exponentially with each moment that passed.

"Want me to swing by?" Joe asked.

Steve hesitated. "Yeah, if you don't mind," he said. "If she's in trouble I might need backup, and if I break this window to gain access and she's not in trouble, then you can keep her from killing me."

"On my way." Joe clicked off.

Once again Steve knocked and rang the bell, praying that she'd answer, that everything was okay. Dammit, he'd allowed the search of the cabin and memories of Tommy to cloud his mind, to make him forget that somebody had attacked Roxy, as well.

He still had the piece of paper she'd handed him earlier in the day, on which she'd listed people who might have a problem with her.

Instead of lusting after her and inviting her to dinner, he should have been doing his job and protecting her.

Thankfully it took only minutes for Joe to arrive on the scene.

He got out of his car and joined Steve. "Still haven't been able to rouse her?" he asked.

"I've been knocking and ringing the bell, and nothing."

Joe shone his flashlight on the door. "I know she got inside okay."

"But you couldn't have known if anybody was inside waiting for her." Steve's heart felt as if it were about to pound out of his chest. He pulled his gun from the holster and motioned at Joe to hit the window in the door with his flashlight.

Joe used the back end of the light and tapped out a hole big enough for him to get his hand inside and unlock the door. Once that was done, Joe drew his weapon, as well.

With a nod of his head Steve opened the door and stepped inside, Joe just behind him. A quick glance in the kitchen let them know Roxy wasn't there, so they moved forward.

"Roxy!" Steve yelled. He placed Liz's sweater on the back of a chair as he and Joe looked around the mauve dining room. They turned on lights as they went through each room until the bottom floor had all been cleared.

Steve started up the stairs, his heart banging painfully hard, making it difficult to draw a deep breath. Where was she? He yelled her name again. Why didn't she answer? Why couldn't she answer?

He turned the light on in the second-floor storage room, wanting to clear every area before advancing upward. The room was crowded with tables and chairs, boxes and crates of miscellaneous dishes and such. He and Joe silently moved to look in every corner, check each and every shadow. It took several minutes to make sure that she wasn't anywhere on the second floor.

Finally they climbed the stairs to her private rooms.

The door was unlocked, and as Steve pushed it open he prayed that they'd find her asleep in bed, or standing under the spray of a shower, unaware that they were searching for her.

But there was no sound of water running, and it didn't take long for the two lawmen to realize she wasn't anywhere in the rooms.

Gone.

Just like Liz Marcoli.

Vanished into thin air.

Steve's heart crashed against his ribs as panic rose up the back of his throat. "Maybe she went out with a friend," Joe offered as they started back down the stairs.

"And left her purse here?" Steve asked, remembering when Roxy had asked him the same question concerning her aunt.

"It's possible. Maybe one of her sisters came by."

"I need to check her cell phone and see if anyone called her around the time she would have gotten home." Roxy leaving the house at this time of night just didn't feel right, especially after the long day they'd had. Nothing about this felt right.

Steve reached the bottom floor and went into the kitchen to retrieve Roxy's phone from her purse. A faint thump sounded. He looked at Joe. "Did you hear that?"

The noise came again, a dull thud. "Roxy?" Steve yelled once again. As he reentered the kitchen, he noticed the mop that was between the two handles on the double door freezer, and it was from the freezer that the thuds came.

"Roxy!" Steve grabbed the head of the mop and

pulled it out of the handles, then swung open the doors. His heart nearly burst out of his chest when he saw her curled into the corner, her teeth chattering and her body quivering uncontrollably. Her pale skin made her dark eyes look enormous as she gazed up at him in an obvious daze.

"Joe, find some blankets or something," he said as he raced to Roxy's side and scooped her up in his arms. Her body was cold...so cold.

"You're going to be fine," he said as he hugged her to him, hoping his body heat would warm her.

"Turkey salad with green grapes," she replied, her voice slurring as if she were drunk.

"Sounds delicious," he muttered as he gently placed her on the floor and began to briskly rub his hands up and down her arms.

By that time Joe had returned with a black-and-white bedspread he suspected the man had pulled straight from Roxy's bed. Steve wrapped it around her, and she closed her eyes and released a sigh of pleasure.

"Cold...so cold," she stuttered.

"Make some hot tea," Steve said to Joe as he continued to cradle Roxy against him.

Joe opened and closed cabinets, finally finding tea bags, then quickly nuked a cup of water and dunked the bag. The cup looked dainty in his big fist as he carefully carried it to where Steve and Roxy were on the floor.

Roxy snaked a hand from out of the blanket and took the cup from him, and Steve was grateful to see that the intense trembling of her body was gone.

She took a couple of sips of the warm drink and then leaned weakly back against Steve's chest.

"What are you doing here?" she asked. Her voice sounded stronger, more normal.

"I came to bring you back your aunt's sweater. You left it at my house earlier," Steve answered. "When you wouldn't respond to the doorbell or my knocking, I got worried so I called Joe. We broke your door window to get inside and searched the place, but we couldn't find you."

"I was having a moment in the freezer with a big bird." She took another sip of her tea. "And you're going to pay for that broken window."

It was at that moment that Steve knew she was going to be just fine. He got to his feet, and together he and Joe helped her up and off the floor.

"I guess the door stuck or something. All I know is I was in the freezer to get a turkey, and the door slammed shut and I couldn't get it back open."

"You couldn't get it open because somebody stuck a mop through the handles, making it impossible for you to get out," Steve explained.

She stared at him, and he thought it was impossible for her chocolate-brown eyes to grow any darker, but they did as she looked to the floor where the mop had landed when Steve had removed it.

She began to tremble again, and this time he knew it wasn't from an outside cold, but rather from an inward chill. "So somebody was waiting for me when I got home," she said softly.

"It would seem so. And now we're going to go upstairs, and you're going to pack a bag. I'm taking you back to my place for the rest of the night," Steve said.

He turned to Joe. "Would you give Frank and Jimmy a call and get them over here and help them process this kitchen as a crime scene? I want to get Roxy out of here as quickly as possible."

"Got it covered." Joe began to dial numbers on his phone while Steve and Roxy went upstairs to pack her a bag.

"It's just for one night," she said as she pulled a small overnight bag from the closet and set it on her bed. "Just for the rest of tonight—that's all."

"We'll see," Steve replied. He certainly wasn't eager to have her here alone for another night, for another attack that might take place.

It didn't take her long to pack what she needed, and by the time they went back downstairs, both Jimmy and Frank had arrived.

"Joe filled us in," Frank said. "We'll fingerprint the mop and the front of the freezer, check for the point of entry and anything else that might give us a clue as to the identity of the perp."

"Let me know what you find," Steve said. He could feel Roxy's anxiety and realized she couldn't wait to get out of there.

"Go on, we'll take care of this and touch base with you in the morning," Frank said.

Minutes later they were in his car and headed back to his house. "I thought I was going to die," she said, her voice softer than he'd ever heard it.

"I'm so sorry, Roxy. I should have known that it wasn't safe for you to be home alone, especially since somebody had already attacked you by throwing knives at you."

"You couldn't have known anyone would be in my house waiting for me tonight," she said.

"But I should have considered the possibility," he countered, a touch of anger in his voice as he remembered that horrible moment when he'd seen her curled up on the freezer floor.

He might not be able to find her aunt, he may forever grieve the loss of his son, but he'd be damned if he'd let anyone get close enough to Roxy to hurt her again.

Roxy paced the carpeting in Steve's guest room, unable to halt the shivering that overtook her every few minutes. As she thought of the time she'd spent in the freezer, she felt as if she'd never get warm again.

Who had been in the kitchen with her? Who had crept into her house in the dark of night and waited for her?

What would the person have done if she hadn't made it so easy by walking into the freezer? Would she have been stabbed by the knives that had missed her before?

And if somebody wanted to kill her, then why not just stab her with the knives? Why hadn't she been bashed over the head or stabbed or shot?

As a new shiver overtook her, all she could think about was Steve's bathtub and submersing herself in a tub full of hot jetted water.

She and Steve had said very little on the ride, and he'd immediately brought her up to the bedroom, given her a quick hug and told her good-night.

That had been about thirty minutes ago. Was he already asleep? Would he mind if she took a bath in his tub? She'd almost died tonight. Surely she deserved a bath.

She grabbed her nightgown and opened the bedroom door. Peering down the hall, she could see a light still on in Steve's bedroom.

Before she could change her mind, before she chickened out, she marched down the hall and lightly tapped on his half-open door. "Come in," he said.

She stepped in to find him propped up in bed, his bare chest a glory of smooth muscled skin that gleamed in the glow of the lamp on the nightstand.

"Roxy, is there something you need?" he asked, half rising out of the bed.

You. I need you. The words slammed into her head as she motioned for him to stay in bed. "Don't get up," she said hurriedly, wondering if he was naked beneath the sheet. "I was just wondering if you'd mind if I took a bath in your bathroom?"

"Knock yourself out," he replied. "Towels and washcloths are in the cabinet just to the left of the tub, and if you need me to scrub your back, just let me know." He gave her that slow, sexy grin that used to drive her insane—only now she realized that she'd missed seeing it over the past couple of days.

"In your dreams, buster," she quipped and went into the bathroom and closed the door behind her. She started the water in the tub and grabbed one of the thick bath sheets and a washcloth she found in the cabinet. She sat on the commode and waited for the huge tub to fill, the air around her growing steamy. A bar of soap sat in a white soap dish on the side of the tub.

A night-light was plugged into a nearby outlet and

she turned off the overhead light, knowing that this would allow the stars in the skylight to be more visible.

The night-light provided plenty of illumination, and once the water had filled to a point where it covered the jets in the sides of the tub, she undressed and eased down in the warmth.

She'd almost died. She turned on the jets, swirling the heat of the water around her as the tub finished filling. She turned off the water and lay her head back against the porcelain, staring up at the stars.

If Steve hadn't decided to return Liz's sweater tonight, she would have died in the freezer before Josie would have found her in the morning.

She sank lower in the water, submerging the tops of her shoulders. If she'd died, she would have died with a heart full of regrets. Her thoughts as she'd sat on the floor slowly freezing to death had been of her sisters and how, since Liz's disappearance, she'd isolated herself from them, afraid that they might see her weak and vulnerable.

She thought about the friends she hadn't made because she'd been too busy building the Dollhouse, making sure everything in her life was as perfect as possible.

Perfect was lonely, and while she didn't want a man in her life trying to make her something she wasn't, trying to mold her into his idea of a wife and forcing her to make bad decisions, she wouldn't mind having somebody to wrap her in his arms, somebody to make love to and feel a connection to for a brief time.

She thought of the man in the bed in the next room. While she'd been in the freezer, one of her regrets had been that she hadn't allowed their kissing to lead them into his bedroom. She'd been sorry that she'd stopped him from deepening their intimacy.

The stars twinkled down as the water warmed her, and yet she wanted more. She wanted Steve, and this time she recognized how short life might be. She didn't want to face death again with regrets.

"Steve?" She called his name before she could change her mind.

There was a moment of silence and then he answered, his voice just on the other side of the closed bathroom door. "Need something?"

She pulled her legs up to her chest, hiding most of her nakedness. "I think I'll take you up on the back wash after all."

Again there was silence; then the door crept open. He stepped inside, clad only in a pair of navy briefs. He looked amazing, his body perfectly proportioned with wide shoulders, slim hips and long, muscled legs.

It was his eyes, glittering with undeniable desire, that held her gaze, trapped her in a sensual warmth she wanted to fall into.

"My back," she finally managed to say and motioned to the washcloth on the side of the tub.

"My pleasure," he replied. He knelt down beside the tub, picked up the washcloth and dunked it in the water. He grabbed the soap and rubbed it on the wet cloth, then began to smooth it across the expanse of her back.

It was heaven. It was more than the smooth caresses down the length of her back; it was the faint scent of Steve that filled the room, the sight of his near nakedness so achingly close.

He caressed from her shoulders to her hips...up

and down as she sighed in pleasure and felt the stir of a different kind of heat curl in the pit of her stomach.

He slid his lips across the back of her neck, and in response she turned and grabbed him by the shoulders. Unbalanced, he fell into the tub with a respectable splash.

She laughed at his look of astonishment, but the laughter faded as he pulled her naked body against his and took possession of her mouth.

It was the most erotic experience Roxy had ever had, the feel of Steve's hands moving over her naked body coupled with the pulsing spray from the jets and Steve's hot mouth plundering hers.

He'd abandoned the washcloth and instead caressed her body as if he were blind and attempting to get a visual picture in his mind through his fingertips.

He finally broke the kiss, but only long enough to remove his briefs and toss them to the tiled floor next to the tub. Then she was back in his arms and his mouth and hands were everywhere, stirring a lust inside her that she'd never known before.

He was fully aroused, and she encircled his hardness with her hand beneath the water. "I've wanted you for a long time, Roxy," he whispered against her neck.

"I want you, too. But I don't want it to mean anything beyond right now, this moment in time." She felt the need to set boundaries, to let him know that she didn't want or need anything else from him.

"Just tonight," he agreed as he nuzzled her neck.

For the first time since she'd been pulled out of the freezer, Roxy was warm…heated from the inside out as he alternated his kisses from soft and tender to masterful and demanding. Their caresses grew more intimate, more fevered, until suddenly he stood and grabbed the towel she'd laid out on the nearby counter.

"I want you in my bed," he said.

She stood, her body trembling from what they'd already shared and the promise of more pleasure to come that shone from his eyes.

As she stepped out of the tub, he wrapped the big bath sheet around her and dried her as if she were a precious piece of china. Then he scooped her up in his arms and carried her to his bed.

Immediately his body covered hers, his mouth plying hers with fire as his hands cupped her breasts. Their tongues battled as he teased her nipples, making them taut with want. As he moved his lips down to capture the tip of one, a moan escaped her and she tangled her hands in his glorious hair.

"My Foxy Roxy," he murmured against her skin. For the first time she didn't mind the silly nickname, but rather loved the fact that he thought of her that way.

She was an active participant in their foreplay, running her fingers down his flat stomach and teasingly touching him on his inner thighs. He groaned at her tormenting avoidance of touching him where he most wanted her.

"Two can play at that game," he said with a husky laugh and ran his fingers down her stomach, across her hips and to and from her left inner thigh to her right. She arched, laughing in frustration and yet needing him to caress her where she most burned for his touch.

Then he was there, stroking her intimately, and a

rising tide inside her grew bigger and bigger and then drowned her in a sea of pleasure.

While she was still breathless, boneless, he moved on top of her and eased into her. Braced by his elbows on either side of her, he gazed down, his blue eyes like the ocean, drawing her back in, stirring new life, new desire inside her.

He moved his hips back and then deeper into her and she gripped his firm buttocks with her hands, wanting to pull him into her forever.

Their gazes remained locked as he moved faster against her, into her, and the room filled with their moans and sighs of desire.

Roxy felt him pulsating, and her own climax came at the same time as his. She felt as if they melted together, became one soul and one heart as he gasped her name and then collapsed to the side of her.

The only sound in the room was their efforts to regain normal breathing. "Please keep me in mind anytime you want your back washed," he finally said.

She laughed and turned on her side to face him, loving the way the light from the nightstand caressed his handsome features. "I must say, you do a very good job."

"I aim to please," he replied and lightly touched his finger to the tip of her nose.

She started to rise from the bed, but he caught her arm and pulled her back. "Stay here," he said. "Sleep here with me tonight. I'll sleep better knowing you're safe and sound in my arms."

His words stirred her on a level that both thrilled and frightened her, and yet she couldn't think of any place she'd rather be for the rest of the night.

"Let me get my nightgown," she said. She rolled from the bed and back into the bathroom, where she let the water out of the tub and then pulled her nightgown over her head.

She stood for a moment and stared at herself in the mirror. Her cheeks were flushed, and her lips were slightly swollen. She looked like a woman who had just been thoroughly loved.

Not loved, she corrected herself. *Sexed.* It had been nothing more than hot sex. And as wonderful as it had been, it would never happen again. It had nothing to do with any real feelings she had for Steve.

She didn't believe in love, and he'd told her time and time again that he wasn't looking for any long-term relationship. "Just sex," she whispered to the woman in the mirror and then turned and went back into the bedroom.

The bed was empty, but by the time she'd grabbed the towel off it and tossed it into the hamper in the bathroom, Steve came back into the room, clad in a fresh, dry pair of black briefs.

Together they pulled down the navy bedspread and got beneath the white sheets that smelled faintly of his cologne. He pulled her back into his arms, and she melted against him.

For just this one night she'd pretend it hadn't been just sex but something more. Roxy had never believed in fairy tales or magic, but for just this single night she wanted to believe that what she and Steve shared was magical.

The harsh light of dawn would bring her back to

reality, and the reality was that she and Steve meant nothing to each other, that her aunt was still missing and somebody wanted her dead.

Chapter 12

Steve awakened with Roxy's warm body cocooned against him. It was early; dawn wasn't even a thought in the eastern sky, but he felt rested and knew he wouldn't go back to sleep.

He remained in bed for a few minutes, remembering the pleasure of making love to Roxy. She'd been the kind of lover he'd expected her to be...impulsive, exciting and unbelievably sexy.

And somebody had tried to kill her last night.

It was this thought that drove him out of bed. He carefully disengaged from her, not wanting to awaken her, and slid from the bed. He grabbed a white terry-cloth robe from the back of the bathroom door, then the slacks he'd worn the night before, and quietly left the bedroom.

He hoped Roxy slept late. The past week had been

so filled with stress and turmoil for her, he hoped her body had crashed after their phenomenal sex and she got some extra rest before facing another day.

Barefoot, he padded down the stairs to the kitchen, where he fixed a pot of coffee and retrieved from his pants pocket the list of names Roxy had prepared for him the day before.

As the fragrant scent of fresh-brewed coffee filled the room, he checked his cell phone for any messages that might have been left. There was nothing from Frank or Jimmy or Joe, indicating to Steve that they'd probably found nothing at Roxy's place so important it couldn't wait until morning to discuss.

When the coffee was ready, he poured himself a cup and stood at the window, staring out into the darkness as he thought of the missing Liz, the night before and the woman who remained in his bed upstairs.

Even though the cabin Edward Cardell had stayed in had come up clean for evidence of Liz being there, that didn't automatically take him off the suspect list. Unfortunately, they had no real evidence to tie him to her disappearance or to get a search warrant for his home. And unfortunately he was the only lead they had to follow in the case of the missing woman. They were at a dead end where Liz Marcoli was concerned.

He carried his coffee to the kitchen table and sat down; the list of people that Roxy had written was folded in front of him. These were the people she thought might have a problem with her.

He opened the piece of paper to view her neat, pretty handwriting.

Isaaic Zooker—he thinks I'm a demon
Michael Arello—he stole from me and I fired his butt
Gary Holzman—past relationship, ended badly
Sarah Fisher—has the best herb garden in the state
William King—thinks I tried to seduce his son
Jason King—teenager with a Mrs. Robinson complex
Rita Whitehead—the witch who thinks I stole her recipes
Gus Greene—part-time worker who I yell at a lot
Josephine Landers—don't know what I'd do without her
Greg Stillwell—Josie's assistant—good guy

That's all I can think of right now, but I still can't imagine any of these people trying to kill me.

Steve smiled as he reread each of her side notes about the people she'd listed. His smile faded as he got to the name Gary Holzman. She'd indicated that he was a past relationship that had ended badly. How badly? And when had this relationship taken place? And why did a little tinge of jealousy streak through him at the thought of Roxy with any other man?

He would have to wait to get his questions answered until Roxy got up, and he didn't want to closely examine why he'd feel any jealousy about any relationship Roxy had in her past or in her future.

He found his thoughts drifting to Stacy. At first

he'd thought Roxy was a lot like his ex. There was no question that Roxy and Stacy shared some personality traits. Like Roxy, Stacy had a temper, but he could never imagine Roxy playing the passive-aggressive head games that Stacy used to play. He could never imagine Roxy holding a grudge for weeks after a fight.

Roxy aired her anger and then was done with it. She came at you head-on, and you never had to guess or worry what might happen next.

As always when he thought of Stacy, his head filled with thoughts of Tommy. Once again he picked up his coffee cup and carried it to the window, where the light of dawn was just beginning to peek over the sky.

In the reflection of the window he imagined his son the way he'd been the last time he'd seen him. Five years old, towheaded with Steve's blue eyes, his boy had already been amazing. Bright and funny and loving, he'd been Steve's entire world. He'd be seven now, and Steve hated all the moments of Tommy's life that he'd missed in the past two years.

For the first six months he'd been certain that he'd hear from Stacy, that she'd come crawling back to him wanting money or something, and Tommy would be returned to him.

He no longer had that hope. Too much time had passed. The tiny thread of hope of seeing his son again that he'd been able to maintain had become so fragile, and yet he clung desperately to it.

He couldn't survive unless he sustained the belief that he would see Tommy again, and he felt as if everything else in his life except for his work was tied up until Tommy was back. He was trapped in a box of the past and couldn't move forward with his heart so filled with pain.

Last night with Roxy had been amazing, but it would never be a bridge to anything else; she would never be invited into his life in any meaningful way, because there wasn't enough room in his heart for the pain and new love to coincide.

When the sun finally popped up in the sky and began to lighten it, Steve pulled a pound of bacon out of the refrigerator and placed a handful of strips in an awaiting skillet.

As the bacon began to sizzle, he thought again about the list Roxy had made. There were definitely people on there he intended to investigate, although nobody except her ex-boyfriend really jumped out at him.

Several of the names were of Amish people from the nearby settlement. Maybe it was time for a drive there to ask some questions, although there had never been any crime or criminal activity among the Amish in the past. Crime wasn't a part of who they were or what they believed.

Still, it wouldn't hurt to take a drive out there and check in with Bishop Tom Yoder, whom Steve had occasionally visited with in the past. He and his fellow lawmen wanted to keep the lines of communication and trust open between the Amish and the English for the good of everyone in the small town.

The bacon was cooked and in the microwave ready to reheat by the time Roxy made an appearance. She'd obviously showered and had dressed in her jeans and T-shirt from the day before.

She looked at the clock on the oven and gasped in surprise. "Almost seven-thirty. I never sleep this late."

"Your body must have needed it," he replied. "Sit." He pointed to the table. "This morning I'll fix your breakfast and wait on you for a change."

"Hmm, sounds like a plan." She cast him a smile that made him want to throw her across the table and make love to her again.

Instead he poured her a cup of coffee and set it in front of her. He turned to the fridge and pulled out a carton of eggs. "I've been going over the list of people that you wrote out for me," he said. "Tell me about Gary Holzman."

She frowned as if she found the question distasteful. "Gary Holzman…a controlling jerk who wanted to make me into somebody I wasn't." She took a sip of her coffee and then continued, "He owns a real estate business in Hershey, and I dated him for three months about a year ago."

Steve scrambled eggs in a bowl, along with a dollop of milk. "You wrote that it ended badly."

"We said some pretty nasty things to each other at the end," she admitted.

"Who broke up with whom?"

"It was pretty much mutual. We were ill-fated from the beginning. He thought I was too obsessed with my business and suggested I see a doctor for some sort of tranquilizer to calm me down. He thought I should wear dresses instead of jeans, that I talked too much, that I should be more demure in how I approached people. Like I said, he wanted me to do things I didn't want to do, to be somebody that I could never be."

"So why did you date him for three months?" Steve

poured the eggs into the skillet and then loaded the toaster with bread.

"I honestly don't know. I think I tried to make it work for Aunt Liz, who wanted to see me happy with somebody. But Gary was my last attempt at having it all."

"Having it all?"

"You know, the business, a husband and a family. But I realize now I'm not wife or family material, and that's why I don't do relationships. The last time I saw Gary, he told me I needed to see a psychiatrist, that I was probably bipolar, and I told him at least that was better than having no personality and asked him when he'd gotten his lobotomy."

A burst of laughter escaped Steve.

"It wasn't funny," she protested, but the corners of her lush lips curved upward.

"He was obviously an ass and not the right man for you."

Steve made the toast, reheated the bacon and put the eggs on a plate, and he didn't ask her anything else until they were seated at the table, facing each other, with breakfast served.

"I noticed you listed several people from the settlement. I thought maybe this morning we'd take a drive out there and have a little chat with Bishop Yoder, see if any of his young people are into throwing knives."

"Amish people don't commit crimes," she said.

"Generally speaking, that's true," he agreed. "But Amish people are also human beings, and it is always possible there's a rotten apple in the bunch."

"I find it hard to believe that anyone from the Amish community would want to hurt me."

"What about Michael Arello?"

"He's not Amish, but he's a nasty piece of work. He's twenty-two years old, lives here in town, and I gave him a job a couple of months ago as a kitchen helper and busboy. I caught him carrying out a whole ham one night and fired him on the spot." She frowned thoughtfully. "Maybe he's responsible for what's happened to me. He was pretty upset when I threw him out, and now that I really think about it, he mentioned that he took martial-arts lessons at Ling's Studio."

Steve loved the way the sun drifting through the window sparked off her dark curls, but tried to stay focused on the mini-interrogation that was taking place.

"What about Isaaic Zooker? You wrote that he thinks you're a demon."

She laughed and picked up a piece of her toast. "I exaggerated a bit. He's my cheese man, and every time he delivers cheese to me he looks at me as if I'm a worldly harlot who has no humility."

"And William King?"

"His son, Jason, is about seventeen and for a while, whenever he'd come to town he'd hang around the restaurant. He never came inside, but I'd occasionally take a break and talk to him. He's a nice young man, and it was obvious he had a bit of a crush on me, and I was just trying to be friendly. But his father caught him in front of my place one day and yanked him away. I could tell William was quite angry."

She set her toast back on her plate without taking a bite. "But I still say that I can't believe anyone from the settlement would try to hurt me. Violence just isn't the way they deal with things."

"Does this young Jason have a nice Amish girl-friend?"

"I have no idea. Why?"

"I just think, given the nature of the attacks on you, we can't rule out the potential that a woman is behind them. Just how close are you to Josie?"

He'd obviously caught her off guard, and she looked at him in surprise. "You're barking up the wrong tree. She's my right-hand woman, the person I depend on most in running the business. Josie loves the restaurant, and we're good friends." He could tell she was getting frustrated. "And how does any of this tie into Aunt Liz?"

"I'm not sure it does," he admitted. "Eat, Roxy. I have a feeling it's going to be a long day."

Roxy stood in her bedroom and looked at her clothes in her closet, aware that Steve was someplace downstairs in the restaurant waiting for her.

They had finished up breakfast at his place, and then he'd taken a quick shower and dressed and they'd headed here so she could change into fresh clothing before heading out to the settlement to speak to Bishop Yoder and request permission to talk to some of the other people living there.

With that particular destination in mind, Roxy decided to forgo her normal choice of jeans and a T-shirt and instead pulled a long dress from her closet. The top was buttercup yellow, and the skirt was denim and hung to her feet. Although her arms were bared, at least her legs would be covered.

It was only respectful if she was entering their world to do her best not to offend anyone. She pulled on the dress and then stepped into a pair of plain brown sandals. She fought the impulse to add the denim and yellow earrings that she'd specifically bought to wear with the dress, and with a final glance in the bathroom mirror she turned and headed back downstairs.

She found Steve seated at his usual table with Frank and another uniformed officer as company. Frank and the uniform were in the middle of their breakfast, and Steve had a cup of coffee before him.

They all greeted each other, and then Steve got up and within minutes they were in his car and headed out. "Frank said it might be a good idea for you to talk to your sisters." He slid her a sideways glance. "Apparently Sheri called him and said you weren't keeping them up-to-date with anything, and he said she sounded pretty angry."

"He didn't tell them about the attacks on me, did he?" she asked in a panic.

"No, I think he just told her he'd pass along the message that you needed to contact them. You can't hide things from them forever, Roxy."

"I know. I was just hoping that when I talked to them I'd have something good to tell them."

"We keep having this same conversation. They're grown women. You don't have to protect them anymore. And on another topic, I'm assuming you haven't gotten any calls about your posters that I should know about."

"Only if you want to know that Aunt Liz was abducted by aliens, burned as a witch at midnight or seen in a dream in an igloo in Alaska," she replied with disgust.

"I don't have to tell you that it was a bad idea to put your personal phone number on the posters," he said. "We could have set up a dedicated phone line for tips. Rarely does a tip line yield any real results. It just stirs up all the crazies who like to play on the phone."

She nodded, her thoughts still on her sisters, whom she had been avoiding. "Maybe we should stop at the Roadside Stop on the way to the settlement so I can check in with Sheri."

"I think maybe that's a good idea," he agreed.

It didn't take long for them to get to the Roadside Stop. As Steve browsed the aisles, Roxy faced her youngest sister.

"Nice of you to check in, especially since you haven't been answering either Marlene's calls or mine." It was obvious her sweet-natured little sister was irritated.

"I'm sorry. Things have been a little crazy lately." Roxy knew the excuse was lame.

"Frank told me there's been no news on Aunt Liz." Sheri's golden-brown eyes darkened. "It's been almost a whole week."

"I know, but nobody is giving up," Roxy said firmly. "The police are doing everything possible to find her."

Sheri nodded. "Marlene and I need to hear from you, Roxy. You shouldn't have to bear this burden alone." Sheri slid her gaze toward Steve. "Hopefully you aren't going through this all by yourself," she said with a hint of slyness.

Warmth swept into Roxy's cheeks, and she tried desperately to will it away. "Steve is working the case hard."

"By the blush on your cheeks, I'd say he's working you hard," Sheri noted.

"Sheri! He's not like that at all." Roxy was amazed to hear herself defending the man she'd once thought the consummate womanizer. "I misjudged his character before all this. He's a nice man."

Sheri pulled her into a hug. "Just don't forget that Marlene and I are here for you, too. We need to stick together until Aunt Liz is back where she belongs."

Roxy returned her petite sister's hug. "And we are going to get her back where she belongs." The two broke apart. "Steve and I are headed over to the settlement to ask a few questions."

Sheri frowned. "You think somebody from the settlement has something to do with Aunt Liz's disappearance?"

"Not really, but Steve wants to ask a couple of men a few questions. It's all part of a thorough investigation."

"Let me know if you find out anything."

"I promise," Roxy said and meant it. Maybe it was time she stopped trying to protect her sisters from life, from hurt and pain. As Steve had reminded her a hundred times, they were adults and surely could handle whatever the future held.

After speaking to Sheri, she went in search of Steve, who had disappeared. She found him just outside the store on his cell phone.

He held up a finger to let her know he'd be a minute and then finished the call. "That was Jimmy with a report about what they found last night…or what they didn't find."

"What do you mean?"

"They found no point of entry other than the window I broke to get inside. The mop had no fingerprints on the handle, and the freezer door also had been wiped clean of prints."

"If there was no evidence of a point of entry, then that means whoever was in there must have had a key." A shiver worked up her spine as she thought of the people who had keys to the business, the people she considered friends.

"Or is an expert at picking a lock," he said as they walked to his car.

They got back into the car to drive the few miles up the road. "I need to buy a gun," she said as Steve pulled out of the Roadside Stop parking lot.

He nearly snapped her neck with his fast stop. He turned in his seat and frowned at her. "You are not getting a gun. You can be anything you want in the world, but you can't be a gun owner. You'd wind up shooting a customer or yourself by accident."

"Or you," she said, knowing he was right.

"There's always that, too," he agreed.

"It sucks being a target of somebody and not knowing who they are or why they want to hurt me."

"It's odd that whoever it is hasn't succeeded yet. I mean, instead of just locking you in the freezer, why not stab you to death or beat you with something?"

"I know. I thought of that already."

He turned down the lane that was Amish land. "It makes me wonder again if maybe the attacker is a woman."

Roxy frowned. "I just can't imagine any woman who would want me hurt or dead." She turned and looked out the window, where young and old men in black trousers, long-sleeved white shirts and wide-brimmed straw hats worked in the fields.

Steve drove up to a modest white ranch house with a huge dairy barn behind it. "This is Tom Yoder's place. He's the bishop, and we need to check in with him before we speak to anyone else."

"While we're here I'd like to stop by the Fisher house and pick up some fresh herbs from Sarah." She pointed in the distance to another pristine white house.

"We can do that," he agreed. He pulled to a halt before the Yoder house and cut the engine. He unbuckled his seat belt and then turned to look at her. "And, Roxy, just for the record, you should never have to change a thing about yourself for any man. You're perfect just the way you are."

He didn't wait for a reply, but instead turned and got out of the car. It was at that moment Roxy realized she was more than a little bit in love with Detective Steve Kincaid.

Chapter 13

Tom Yoder was in his sixties. He had a wide face that wreathed in a smile as he greeted Steve and Roxy. "It's been a while, Detective Kincaid," he said as he opened the door to gesture the two inside his home.

They walked through a neat, functional living room and into the kitchen, where two younger women worked side by side making bread on a long table.

Both of them were dressed in traditional fashion, in long dresses and white aprons with their hair braided and coiled in a bun covered with a small white cap.

"Daughters-in-law, we have guests. Some refreshments for Detective Kincaid and his friend, Ms. Marcoli," Tom said.

"Thank you, but that isn't necessary," Steve replied. "Unfortunately I'm here on some business."

Tom glanced toward the two women. "Then let's

go take a walk," he said. He led them out a kitchen door, where a handful of little girls around the age of four were playing with a puppy.

"Do you mind if I go see the children?" Roxy asked, obviously sensing that it would be better if the two men talked alone.

Tom nodded. "They are my sons' children."

As Roxy left them, Tom turned to Steve with a frown. "Have one of us offended somebody in town?"

"No, nothing like that," Steve said hurriedly. "We have always had open communication and a spirit of support among our people. But there have been two crimes that I'm investigating that require I speak to several people here."

"And those people would be?"

"Isaaic Zooker and William King and his son, Jason."

"And the crimes you are investigating?"

"A potential kidnapping of one woman and an attempted murder of another."

Tom shook his head. "You won't find the guilty party here."

"In my heart I know that's true, but as a detective investigating the cases, I can't exclude your community in my questioning."

"Understood. I will walk with you to the Kings'. They are our nearest neighbor."

Steve walked over to where Roxy had the four girls playing ring-around-the-rosy with the puppy yipping with excitement in the center, and as he heard the little girls' laughter mingling with Roxy's, he realized that she would be a good mother.

Fiercely loyal and protective to a fault, she possessed all the qualities that would make her a good wife and a great mother, and yet she consciously chose to be alone for the rest of her life.

Steve knew it was his mother's wish that he find another woman, build a new family for himself. He knew she wanted him to love again, this time smarter and forever. But he didn't trust himself when it came to love. He'd made such a terrible mistake when he'd trusted and loved Stacy so many years ago.

He halted the games long enough to tell Roxy where they were headed and then hurried back to where Tom awaited. Steve would have much preferred to drive to the house in the distance, but as he and Tom walked, he was treated to the pleasant scents of spring in a farming community...rich earth turned and planted, wildflowers, horses and hay.

They spoke of mutual acquaintances as they walked and waved to the men in the distance working their fields. They also talked of the weather and the forecast for a wet spring, which was desperately needed.

"You said a kidnapped woman. You're talking about Liz Marcoli?" Tom asked. Steve looked at him in surprise, and Tom smiled. "Gossip even travels here by horse and buggy."

"She disappeared from her house Friday morning, and nobody has seen or heard from her since," Steve explained. "Roxy has also been attacked twice, and we don't know if the two incidents are related or not."

"And you think William and his son have something to do with these attacks?" Tom shook his head. "William is one of the deacons, a godly man who would never do anything to harm another human being."

"And his son?"

"A young man entranced with the English ways, but he remains devoted to the *Ordnung*," Tom replied. Steve knew the *Ordnung* was the rules of the church, strictly enforced by Tom as bishop. "However, I know Jason has been struggling since his mother's death a year ago. William needs a new wife, as he has not only Jason, but five other younger children, as well. Many burdens have fallen on William's and Jason's shoulders since the death of Mariah."

"Roxy does business with Isaaic Zooker, and she thinks he believes she's a demon."

Tom laughed and shook his head. "Cheese Man Zooker can be a bit intimidating, but he's a good man. Unfortunately right now he's ashamed to be a brother to Abraham Zooker, who is at the moment being shunned and is an embarrassment to his brother."

"Shunned for what?" Steve asked curiously.

"Community issues that I can promise you have nothing to do with your crimes or the person you seek."

Steve nodded, aware that the internal workings of the community were rarely shared with the outside world. He also knew that shunning could occur for anything as simple as the width of the brim on a hat or something more serious such as the use of forbidden technology.

"Sounds like we have similar jobs," Steve said. "You keep the order here, and I try to keep the order in town."

Tom smiled. "I think my job is much easier than

yours. The people who are here among us live a simple life and find happiness in observing the *Ordnung* and serving the community and family."

Over the next two and a half hours Steve and Tom spoke to William King and his son, Jason. They headed to Isaaic Zooker's house and spoke to him. As they walked between houses Tom introduced him to the fieldworkers, and they paused to speak to each of the older and young men.

It hadn't taken Steve long to realize he wouldn't get any answers here. While he'd found everyone co-operative and friendly, he also couldn't imagine any-one in this close-knit community—where traditional values reined and rules guided every aspect of their lives—culpable of having anything to do with Liz's disappearance or the attacks on Roxy.

By the time they returned to Tom's house, his wife, Elizabeth, told him that Roxy had walked to the Fisher house to visit with Sarah.

Tom pointed out the Fisher home, and with a warm goodbye, Steve got into his car and drove to the house, which looked much like all the others.

Steve heard Roxy the minute he got out of the car. Her laughter came from the side of the house. He rounded the house to find himself at the edge of an herb garden that filled the air with savory and sweet scents.

Roxy had a wooden basket in hand, and the woman he assumed to be Sarah Fisher stooped beside her, placing sprigs of this and that in the basket.

"Rosemary, you must have rosemary," Sarah said and added a handful of greenery to the basket.

"I think you are a good saleswoman, Sarah Fisher,"

Roxy said with a laugh. "All I needed was a little fresh basil, and look how you've filled my basket nearly to the brim."

Sarah straightened. She was a tall woman next to the short Roxy, and her face was lovely, bathed with a smile and a glow from within. "You know I'll give you a good bargain for the basketful."

Steve watched silently as the two haggled over price and arrived at one that had each of them smiling. It was only after Roxy pulled money from a pocket in her dress that she saw Steve.

"I wondered if you'd forgotten me," she said. "Sarah, this is Detective Kincaid. Steve, this is Sarah Fisher."

Sarah nodded and cast her eyes downward shyly. "It's nice to know you."

"Nice to meet you, too," he replied and then looked at Roxy. "Are you ready to go?"

Roxy nodded. "In a couple of days you might send some more fresh things with Isaaic when he brings the cheese to the restaurant."

"I'll do that," Sarah said.

Minutes later Steve and Roxy were in the car and headed back to town. "Did you learn anything you didn't know before we got here?" she asked.

"Not really." The entire interior of the car smelled of the herbs, and he drew a deep breath of the fragrance. "Although I did learn that Jason King doesn't have a girlfriend, so we can rule out a jealous Amish girl trying to hurt you."

She nodded and looked out the window. "Sometimes I think the Amish have the right idea about life.

No electricity, no internet or television. Entertainment is getting together with families and cooking. It just all seems so simple."

"But all is not simple anywhere," Steve replied. "I heard that Abraham Zooker is being shunned for some reason or another. Tom wasn't specific."

"Using too much water," Roxy said. "Sarah told me. He'll be shunned for another week. It's a great disgrace to be shunned. Nobody is allowed to speak to him, and he can't attend any of the church or community gatherings. It might not be too hard on Abraham. His house is the farthest away from all the others, on the edge of the Amish land, and he seems to be a man comfortable alone and making his beautiful furniture."

"I didn't even know they had water in the homes."

"The houses are traditional houses, with water and electric lights and all the modern conveniences," Roxy said. "They're built to today's standards for resale value. But from what Sarah has told me on my visits to her house, none of the homes are hooked up to the electricity, and while they use their bathrooms like normal people, they are allowed to shower or bathe only once a week with their water monitored."

"So maybe Abraham is taking a couple of showers each week instead of just one," Steve said. "I'm surprised they use city water at all."

"It was a decision made by Tom after much prayer, according to what Sarah told me. About a year ago, all the old outhouses were torn down and each home was hooked up to the water, but with a strict guideline for use. I don't pretend to understand all of their ways, but I do admire their sense of family and community."

Roxy fell silent, and Steve knew she was probably thinking about her aunt and perhaps the fact that she'd never really had a traditional family unit.

The only way he felt as if he could help ease some of that pain was for him to find her aunt, and he had no clues, only flimsy leads to follow and the terrible feeling that the older woman was long dead.

"I think you need to stay at my place for the time being," Steve said as he parked next to Roxy's car at the Dollhouse.

Roxy frowned at the back door of her establishment. "I don't want to do that." She turned and looked at him, fighting against the anger directed toward the person who had tried to hurt her and the fear that stirred once again in her heart. "I mean, I appreciate the offer, but I hate that I even have to think about it. I hate that somebody is running me out of my house. And what am I supposed to do about the Dollhouse business?"

Steve stared at the house in front of him and then looked at her once again. "I don't know why you can't keep things going here. I can drop you off in the mornings and then pick you up and take you to my place for the nights. I'll be honest, Roxy, nobody can assure your safety here when nobody else is around."

She thought of the knives…of the agony of being locked in the freezer. "I know."

"It won't be forever," he assured her. "I have other people to talk to, people who were on your list. Going to the settlement today was just the beginning of a real investigation into who is behind these attacks on you. I think it would be best if you get back to work here full-time, and I'll take you to my house to sleep."

"Okay," she finally said. She wanted to feel safe, and she knew she wouldn't feel safe here alone at night for a while.

"Hopefully you and your buddies will be able to figure all this out in the next couple of days." She swallowed against an unexpected emotion. "I want my life back, Steve. I want Aunt Liz found, and I want my life back."

"I know," he replied softly. "And I hope we can all do that for you, but in the meantime I just want to keep you safe."

She looked at her watch. It was slightly past two. She didn't even care who he was going to check out next. All she wanted to do now was get inside her business and work for the rest of the afternoon, to lose herself in the joy of making other people happy through food.

She turned and grabbed her basket of herbs and then opened the passenger door and started to step outside.

"Roxy, I'll be back here to pick you up around six. You make sure Josie or Greg hangs around with you until I arrive."

"Okay, then I'll see you later." She was aware of him watching her as she walked to the back door. Somebody had fixed the broken window in the door at some point during the previous night or day. It was only when she stepped inside and turned that she saw Steve drive away.

He'd probably seen to the replacement of the window, feeling responsible since they'd broken it. She'd make sure whoever paid for it was reimbursed. After all, it had been broken to save her life.

"Roxy!" Josie greeted her in surprise. "I've been wondering what happened to you today, but I figured you must be out doing something important since you weren't here."

"Steve and I drove out to the settlement. He had some people to question, and while I was there I got some herbs from Sarah." She set the basket on top of the nearby counter.

"Good. You were out of basil, and we were running low on parsley. Since you weren't here to plan a menu for the day, I've got hot roast-beef sandwiches and barbecue chicken for the afternoon."

"Sounds fine." Roxy began to put away the herbs, her thoughts as scattered as dandelion seeds in the wind. There had been no point of entry when somebody had shoved her in the freezer the night before. Josie had a key, as did Greg and Gus, the older man who came in for the evenings to help with cleanup.

Josie had been with her since the opening of the restaurant, and Greg had worked for her for the past two years. Gus was a fairly recent hire, a widower who had decided to work the evening hours to staunch the loneliness since his wife's death.

She'd often had to get tough with Gus, but surely she'd never been mean enough to him that he'd want to kill her. He was just absentminded and often forgot what he was hired to do.

Josie appeared to have everything under control in preparation for a late afternoon rush, so Roxy excused herself and went up to her private quarters. Once there she made phone calls to both Marlene and Sheri, just to let them know that there were still no leads in Liz's disappearance.

She continued to keep secret the two attacks on her, afraid that both of her sisters would freak out, afraid that they'd insist they move in with her or she move to their places, neither of which was viable in Roxy's mind.

Marlene lived in a small walk-up apartment above the Treasure Trove, and the apartment was meant for one person. Sheri's cabin in the woods was bigger and had plenty of room, but it was too far up the mountain for Roxy to travel back and forth to the Dollhouse.

There was no way she wanted either of her sisters here with her, where they could potentially be in danger just by being close to Roxy.

At least for now, Steve's idea of her spending each night with him was the most realistic plan. However, there would be no more shared baths beneath the stars, no more lovemaking between them.

He'd already managed to get beneath her defenses more than she wanted. She couldn't allow herself to get caught up in any silly fantasy where Steve was concerned.

Even if he wanted a woman in his life, she was all wrong for him. She was all wrong for anyone. After all, her own mother had kept her for seven years and had ultimately found her not worth keeping.

Liz Marcoli had no idea where she was, how long she'd been there or who was holding her captive. She couldn't remember how she'd gotten there and only knew that she'd awakened from what felt like a drugged sleep to find herself in some sort of bunker.

The sides were concrete and the ceiling was earthen, along with the back wall, and she guessed that she was someplace underground. There were no windows and only one door. Within the door was a doggie door. About twenty-four inches tall and equally as wide, it was still far too small for her to attempt to crawl through. It was also locked from the other side.

She'd initially had no idea if it was day or night, but she had recently discerned a timetable of sorts by what happened each day.

The sound of footsteps on wooden stairs always preceded the sound of the little doggie door being unlocked, and a tray of food would be shoved inside.

When the tray contained eggs and toast or a large bowl of oatmeal and coffee, she knew it must be morning. When the food was a sandwich, then she knew it must be around noon. Dinner was usually a large meal, with meat and vegetables and hot water and a tea bag of her favorite chai tea blend.

She'd been conscious for three days now, and a silent scream of fear had been her only companion. Why was she here? And where was here? And who was it who kept her captive? Delivered her food?

The last thing she remembered was standing in her kitchen in the early morning and getting things ready to leave to deliver her usual goodies to the Dollhouse. But she didn't remember getting into her car or anything after that.

Had she somehow been driving and had a stroke or suffered some sort of crazy amnesia that had her wandering on a mountain road? Had she wrecked the car and been picked up by some crazy man and brought here?

She had no physical injuries that would indicate she'd been in an accident, but no matter how hard she tried, she couldn't figure out how she had gotten to this place, wherever it was.

She wasn't sure why, but she had a feeling she was somewhere in the mountains, that perhaps this had been some crazy survivalist's hideaway at one time or another.

The room where she was being held was small, with a cot against one wall and empty wooden shelves along the other wall. There was a stool and a stall shower with a tiny stainless steel sink. There was also a comfortable chair with a standing lamp just behind it.

So far she'd spent most of her time sitting in the chair, trying to keep her mind off her current circumstances and focused instead on the women she'd raised, the memories she had of their childhoods and how proud she was of how they had grown and who they had become in adulthood.

Still, no matter how hard she tried to keep her mind busy with happy thoughts, she couldn't fight against the yawning fear that shivered inside her soul.

Why was she here? And who on earth was going to find her in this underground bunker?

Who had the keys to the door, and what did they ultimately intend to do to her? More than once she'd considered lying down on the floor to see if she could get a peek at the other person when one of the food trays was delivered or retrieved.

But she had yet to get up the nerve. As long as she didn't know who held her captive, then if she somehow managed to escape he'd believe he was safe. But she feared that the moment she saw who held her, the moment she knew his identity, he'd have no choice but to kill her.

And so she waited and prayed that somehow, someway, she'd be found and saved from whatever might happen next.

Chapter 14

Steve dropped Roxy off at the Dollhouse and then stopped by the police station to get the address of Michael Arello, the young man who had worked for her that she'd recently fired.

Frank was still working to try to find Ramona Marcoli, and Jimmy was out checking stores that sold martial-arts equipment. He'd also planned to stop in at Ling's Studio, the only martial-arts dojo in town.

Armed with the address of Michael's parents' home, where apparently the young man still lived, Steve left the station house.

He had about two hours before he would return to the Dollhouse to pick up Roxy and take her home with him. He was conflicted about having her at the house. There was a part of him that he knew was getting too close to her, allowing her too deeply into his heart. That was the part of him that wanted, needed to throw up all his defenses and keep his distance, and yet he wanted her safe and knew the only place he could truly be assured of her safety was with him.

Even if she'd agreed to go to one of her sisters' places or had invited one or both of them to stay with her at the Dollhouse, he wouldn't have been satisfied that it would keep her safe. Besides, the last thing he wanted to do was put either Sheri or Marlene in a danger zone.

A healthy dose of frustration rode with him in the car as he drove down the Arellos' street. They were no closer to figuring out what had happened to Liz Marcoli. He had no idea who might be trying to harm Roxy, and they couldn't even discern if the two crimes were related or not.

Spinning wheels, that's what he felt like they were doing. Spinning wheels while Roxy's life was at risk, while Liz Marcoli was still missing.

He'd told Roxy that investigations were processes, but he was already impatient with the process. He wanted Liz found, and he wanted whoever had tried to hurt Roxy behind bars.

At least no attempts had been made to hurt Sheri or Marlene, leaving him to believe that this wasn't about the family, but rather focused solely on Roxy and her aunt. If the crimes were connected, he reminded himself.

Yes, he wanted the perp or perps behind bars. And he wanted Tommy home where he belonged, but that didn't appear to be happening in the near future.

When he reached the Arello home, he got out of the car and slammed his door with more force than was necessary. His frustration only grew when he introduced himself to Mrs. Arello, who told him that her son wasn't home but was probably at the Wolf's Head Tavern with his no-count friends.

Once again Steve got back in the car and headed toward the tavern. He didn't have a photo of Michael to go by, but at this time of day the tavern shouldn't be too busy.

He parked in one of the empty spaces in front of the long, low building that was a favorite place among the locals and headed for the door.

Stepping inside, he waited a moment for his eyes to adjust from the bright sunshine outside to the semi-darkness of the interior.

The Wolf's Head was aptly named. Along with the dark booths, the long polished wooden bar with stools and the pool table area in the back, stuffed wolf heads were the major decor. They hung on the walls, snarling from their wooden mounts, making the place a favorite for visitors to the area, as well.

"Hey, Travis," Steve greeted the man who owned and operated the place. Travis Brooks was also an avid hunter and responsible for most of the heads that adorned the walls.

"What's up? You're in here early."

"Actually, I'm working, not drinking." It was easy for Steve to guess where Michael might be, as a small group of twentysomethings was gathered around the two pool tables, their voices slightly raucous.

"Michael Arello one of those guys?" Steve asked.

Travis nodded. "The tall dark-haired one in the red T-shirt with the big mouth."

"Thanks." Steve ambled toward the pool tables, his

gaze focused solely on the tall man in the red shirt. There were five young men gathered around the two tables. Michael was one of the players, a cue stick in his hand.

They all paused in the action as Steve closed in on them. He recognized a couple of the guys, but his gaze narrowed in on Michael. "Michael Arello?" he asked, although it was more a statement than a question.

"Yeah?"

"We need to have a talk." Steve flashed his badge and motioned toward one of the booths nearby.

Michael frowned and handed his cue stick to one of the men standing next to him, and then stalked over to the booth and sprawled on the seat. "Talk about what?" he asked as Steve slid into the booth across from him.

"Roxy Marcoli." Steve watched the play of emotions on the other man's face. Michael was a fairly good-looking kid, with hazel eyes and a chiseled jaw, but his lips definitely appeared accustomed to a sullen cast.

"What about her?"

"She fired you about a month ago?"

"Yeah, so? Big deal. It was a stupid-ass job anyway," he replied. "All she had me doing was busing tables."

"I'd say it was a stupid-ass move for you to steal from her," Steve noted.

Michael's cheeks dusted with ruddy color. "What, are you here to arrest me for trying to take off with a couple slices of ham? Aren't there other crimes in this town a little more important for you to take care of instead of hassling me?"

"That's why I'm here…to ask you about some more important crimes. Are you into martial arts?"

Michael frowned, his eyes narrowing warily. "I do a little tae kwon do at Master Ling's. What's that got to do with anything?"

"Just gathering some information." Steve leaned back against the booth. "Are you into throwing stars and breaking boards?"

Michael shrugged, his gaze still distrustful. "I've thrown a few stars, but I don't break boards. What's going on? Why are you asking me this stuff?"

"Somebody decided to throw some knives at Roxy the other night outside her place." Steve leaned forward. "And she told me you were pretty ticked off with her when she fired you."

The sullen cast of Michael's lips disappeared as his face became more animated. "Yeah, sure, I was mad when she fired me. I was a good worker, and she could have just given me a warning instead of throwing me out. But I didn't have anything to do with any knives thrown at her. That's crazy, man."

"Where were you last night around nine o'clock?"

"Last night?" Michael's eyes darted around wildly. "Here. I was here with my buddies playing pool. Since I lost my job that's what I've been doing…just hanging out."

"And your buddies will tell me that you were here last night at nine?" Steve glanced over to where the other four young men were standing in a group, whispering to each other.

"Yeah, sure. They'll tell you the same thing," Michael said.

Steve had a feeling his friends would say that the

moon was green if it kept their buddy out of trouble. "And Travis should remember that you were here last night."

"He should." Michael looked over at the man standing behind the bar. "But it was kinda busy last night so I don't know if he really noticed me or not."

Steve leaned forward. "If I find out you tried to hurt Roxy, you'll be finding new friends to hang out with in jail. If anything bad happens to Roxy, you're going to be the first person I come after." Steve got to his feet.

"But I'm totally innocent, and that's not fair. I swear I didn't have anything to do with whatever happened to Roxy," Michael protested.

Steve smiled humorlessly. "Then you've learned an important lesson in life today. Life's not fair." With Michael still sputtering his innocence, Steve walked away.

With a wave to Travis, he left the tavern and got back in his car, processing his initial feelings about any culpability on Michael Arello's part in the attacks on Roxy. He'd call Travis later, when Michael wasn't in the tavern, to check Michael's story that he'd been there the night before.

The verdict was undecided. Steve punched in Jimmy's cell phone number. "Where are you?" he asked when Jimmy answered.

"On my way to Ling's Studio. Why? What do you need?"

"Ask him if Michael Arello is proficient in throwing stars or knives."

"You have a lead?"

"It could be nothing. It could be something. It all

depends on what you find out at Ling's. Call me back when you have an answer."

"I've already checked two of the places here in town that sell throwing knives, and neither store carries the Vampire knives in question. Tomorrow I'm going to head into Hershey and see what I can find out there."

"Sounds like a plan. Call me when you know something for me about Arello."

When the two men disconnected, Steve checked his watch. It was just about five o'clock and time for him to head back to the Dollhouse.

Maybe they were making some headway in solving the question of who was after Roxy, but they were no closer to figuring out what had happened to Liz Marcoli.

He wished he was returning for Roxy with some definitive answers, but he had nothing concrete to share with her concerning the two cases.

All he could do at the moment was offer her a safe haven in his home until somehow, someway, they figured out what was going on.

And while he was offering her that safe haven, he had to maintain enough distance that he didn't sink into the trap of falling in love with a woman who had made it clear that she had no intention of loving him back.

Roxy couldn't help the way her heart lifted at the sight of Steve walking through the restaurant's back door just after five. She'd spent part of the afternoon packing a suitcase so that she'd be ready to leave with him when they were finished with the day's cleanup.

She had mixed feelings about the plan to stay with him, but there was no question that she was afraid to stay here by herself. The horrible sound of those knives hitting the wood so close to her head and the thought of the icy cold of the freezer were still too fresh in her mind for her to want to attempt to stay here alone for a single night.

She hated being chased out of her business, her home, but she would hate giving somebody another chance to kill her. She might be occasionally hot-headed. She might be too brash and controlling, but she wasn't a fool. She would be safe at Steve's, and at the moment that's all she wanted, a feeling of safety.

"Hey, you," she greeted him as he came into the kitchen, where she and Josie were finishing the cleanup while Gus and Greg were taking care of preparing the dining areas for the next morning.

"Hey, yourself," he replied. "Hi, Josie, how's it going?"

"Good. I keep telling Roxy she should just get away from here for a couple of weeks. Go someplace exotic and take a vacation or something. I can handle things perfectly well, and that would give you all time to figure out who's after her." Josie wiped her hands on a towel and shook her head. "But she's stubborn as the day is long and apparently doesn't trust me to be able to handle things without her."

"Josie, you know that I trust you, but it's my job to be here," Roxy exclaimed. "This is my business. It's what I do, and I'm not going to allow anyone to chase me away from here."

"I know, I know." Josie threw up her hands and grinned at Steve. "Stubborn."

He smiled. "Tell me something about her I don't know."

"No ganging up on me," Roxy protested. She waved a finger at Steve. "In fact, you should be thankful I'm coming home with you because I'm bringing the leftover homemade chicken potpie for dinner, along with some raspberry scones to have with coffee later."

"Why don't you two go ahead and head out," Josie said. "I can lock up here."

Roxy pointed to the suitcase she had ready to go. "If you want to grab that, I'll get our to-go bags." As Steve picked up her suitcase, Roxy grabbed the foam containers she'd prepared to take to his house.

"I'll see you in the morning," Josie said. "Whatever time you get in is fine."

"Thanks, Josie," Roxy replied, and then she and Steve left the restaurant.

"I had a little talk with Michael Arello this afternoon," Steve said once they were in the car and headed to his place.

"Did he confess under your harsh grilling?" she asked, attempting to be light despite the subject matter.

"Not exactly, but he did admit to taking some martial arts training at Ling's. I'm waiting for Jimmy to call me from there with any information Master Ling can give him about Michael's proficiency at knife or star throwing."

Roxy sat back in her seat. "Is it really possible he'd try to kill me because I fired him?"

"It might be possible he intended to scare you. If he's really good with knives, then maybe he missed you on purpose. Scaring you and tossing you into the freezer is adolescent and reckless, but maybe if he is the guilty party, he didn't want to actually hurt you."

"If he is responsible then I want him charged with attempted murder," she said firmly. "Adolescent or not, I would have died in that freezer if you hadn't decided to bring Aunt Liz's sweater back to me that night."

She sighed and stared out the window, then turned back to look at him. "And I guess there are still no leads on my aunt."

"I wish I could tell you different, but I can't. Frank is still trying to find your mother and hoping Liz is with her."

"If that was the case, then Liz's bank account would have been tapped. Wherever Ramona is, whatever the circumstances in her life, she would definitely get money from Aunt Liz, probably to help support her latest boyfriend." Roxy shook her head. "I don't think they're together. What scares me is that this afternoon, as I thought about that cabin where Edward Cardell stays, I wondered how many other cabins are up there in the mountains? How many places a woman could be kept against her will?"

"If she was kidnapped, then it's probable that she was taken by somebody she knows, and the odds are we'll find that person right here in town. It's too early for tourist season, so I don't believe she was arbitrarily targeted by a stranger," he replied.

"I just want my life back the way it was last Thursday," she said softly.

"I know. If I had my way, I'd go back in time two years ago and I'd pick Tommy up from school instead of letting him ride the bus home."

"We're quite a pair," she said with a sigh. "But thank you for allowing me to stay with you for a day or two."

"You're welcome, and we'll see how long you'll stay according to how the investigation moves forward." He pulled into his driveway.

For the next hour they focused on dinner. Roxy reheated the potpie in the microwave as Steve set the table and made them each a glass of iced tea. He'd just finished that when his cell phone rang.

He grabbed the phone from his pocket and answered. "Yeah…right. Okay. Find out who is the star student, and we'll see if it's somebody friendly with Michael Arello. Okay, see you in the morning unless something breaks."

He clicked off, and Roxy looked at him expectantly. "That was Jimmy. According to Master Ling, Michael couldn't throw stars or knives and hit the side of a barn if he was only three feet in front of it."

Roxy took the chicken potpie from the microwave and set it in the center of the table. "So he's ruled out as the knife thrower."

"But not ruled out as having a friend at the dojo who might be willing to do him a favor." Steve waited until Roxy sat, and then he took the chair across from her.

"How about we make it a rule at dinnertime that we only talk about pleasant things," she said, feeling as if her head were about to explode with all the theories and suppositions.

"I think that sounds like a great idea," he agreed.

There were several long moments of silence as they stared at each other. A giggle bubbled up inside

Roxy as the silence continued. The giggle expanded to full laughter and he joined her, shaking his head as he laughed.

"It's pathetic. Surely we can think of something good to talk about while we eat," he said.

"Tell me about your perfect childhood," she said as she dipped up servings of the savory pie first on his plate and then on her own.

"It was as close to perfect as anything could be," he admitted. "My mom and dad were terrific parents. They supported and encouraged me in everything I did. The only time we had a little blip in our great relationship was when they found out Stacy was pregnant with my child and we weren't going to get married. They eased up on me when they knew I'd asked and she'd declined."

He took a sip of his tea and then set his glass back down. "You never wanted kids?" he asked.

"If I could find a sperm donor who wanted nothing to do with me or the child for the rest of our lives, then I might have wanted a baby at one time. But having seen what men did to my mother, I've never really been interested in inviting one into my life on a permanent basis."

"When I saw you playing with those kids at the settlement, my first thought was that you'd make a wonderful mother," he said.

Roxy's heart squeezed with an unexpected pang. She tried not to think much about her choice to live her life alone, without a husband, without any children. But his words stirred a longing that was both unexpected and surprising.

"I've got the restaurant, and that's enough. In fact,

eventually I'd like to expand the hours and keep it open through dinner, maybe close at nine or so."

"And that way you'd assure yourself that you'd never have a personal life," he replied.

"But I'd make enough money that I could take care of Aunt Liz when she needed me, or if Sheri and Marlene got into a bind I could help them out. Besides, personal lives are overrated as far as I'm concerned."

"You sell yourself short, Roxy."

"I'm not finding this conversation particularly pleasant. Let's talk about something else."

He grinned. "I think you're the first woman I've ever met who doesn't want to spend an entire meal talking about herself."

She returned his smile. "There are so many more interesting things to talk about, like you."

"Ah, being the spoiled rotten child that I am, it's one of my favorite topics of conversation." He scooped himself a second helping of the chicken potpie.

"What made you decide to be a detective?"

"My dad had a best friend who was a cop here in town. He was at our house often when I was growing up. He was a great guy, and I decided I wanted to be a cop because of him. Then after I'd spent a year in uniform, I began to study to get a shield. I love what I do."

"And what happened to the man who inspired you?"

His expression tightened. "Unfortunately he and his wife were visiting Hershey, and a dopehead kid that he'd arrested here in town recognized him and shot him. He hung on for two days and then died."

"Oh, Steve, I'm so sorry." She shook her head. "Maybe it's time to finish this meal and call it a night. We can't seem to find pleasant topics between us right now."

He released a deep sigh and got up from the table. "I guess you're right. It's been a long day." His cell phone rang and he pulled it from his pocket, looked at the caller identification and then glanced at her. "Excuse me, I need to take this." He answered and quickly left the room.

Roxy got up and began to clear the dishes. Only one other time had he taken a call in private, and that had been when they had been at her aunt's place.

Was the person on the other end of the line the sexy blonde who worked with him? Maybe another woman who he had some sort of relationship with? She'd only been involved with Steve for the past five days. What did she really know about his personal life with other women besides what he'd told her? And how did she even know he'd been truthful with her?

She shook her head, appalled that she would have even a tiny seed of doubt as to what kind of man Steve was after all they'd been through together.

She leaned against the sink in surprise, stunned to realize that for just a moment she'd been thinking like a jealous lover. He owed her no explanation for secret phone calls. He didn't owe her anything, and she had to get a hold of herself and the tiny streak of jealousy that had suddenly raised its head.

Maybe staying here with him wasn't such a good idea after all. Unfortunately it was the only idea that was practical right now.

Chapter 15

The one-week anniversary of Liz Marcoli's disappearance had come and gone, and while Steve was satisfied that his current living arrangements with Roxy were keeping her safe, he felt as if he were slowly losing his mind.

They had fallen into an easy routine. Each morning he got up and drove her to the Dollhouse, and around six in the evenings he picked her back up. Most evenings she brought home dinner from the restaurant and they ate together, and then went into the living room to sit and talk about their days.

Her scent permeated the house; her presence filled it with laughter and life. Having her there was slowly chipping away at the armor around his heart.

When it was bedtime, she went to the guest room and he went into his own bedroom, and every night his desire for her grew deeper and stronger. Despite the fact that she showed no more interest in a bath for two or joining him in his bed, there were times when he felt the desire snapping in the air between them, when he caught a dark shine in her eyes that made him know she wanted him, too.

Sunday morning he got up just before dawn and fixed the coffee, then sat at the table while the silence of the house surrounded him. Instead of going to his mother's for lunch, he'd invited her there, and Roxy had insisted on cooking.

He and Roxy had spent an hour the night before in the grocery store as she picked up this and that to make homemade tomato sauce and vegetable lasagna. Four bags later, she'd declared that she had what she needed. They'd made a stop at the Dollhouse to gather pots and pans that he didn't own.

He knew she was nervous about meeting his mother, but she wasn't concerned about cooking for anyone. To be perfectly honest, he realized he was a bit nervous about his mother meeting Roxy, and he didn't understand the butterflies.

It shouldn't matter to him if his mother liked Roxy, and it shouldn't matter to him if Roxy liked Rebecca. It shouldn't matter, but for some reason it did.

He got up and refilled his cup, then returned to the table and tried to focus on everything that had taken place over the past couple of days. One of the first things he'd done was forward the phone number on the posters, Roxy's personal cell phone number, to a line to the police station.

Roxy had gotten a new phone number, and Officer Chelsea Loren was now in charge of fielding the calls that came in on the poster tip line. Unfortunately no viable tips had come in concerning Liz Marcoli and her whereabouts.

Jimmy had checked out all the places in town and in Hershey to see if anyone had sold a pair of Vampire throwing knives, but none of the stores he checked even carried them. Whoever owned them had probably ordered them off the internet, which made finding the owner nearly impossible.

Unfortunately, with Liz now missing ten days, it was becoming more and more of a cold case, although Steve would never tell Roxy that. They did have an unmarked car following Edward Cardell on the off chance that he'd been involved in whatever happened to Liz.

The more pressing issue at the moment was who was after Roxy. Michael Arello wasn't off his list of bad boys who might have wanted to pay her back for his firing. But, although Steve hadn't shared his thoughts with Roxy, he'd begun to wonder about Josie.

He'd done a little background search on Roxy's right-hand woman, and while she'd come up clean as far as any criminal record, he'd also discovered that she'd looked into buying the Dollhouse around the same time Roxy had.

Was it possible Josephine Landers didn't like working for Roxy, that she'd imagined herself the owner and operator of a restaurant and Roxy had foiled her plans?

If Roxy died, then it was quite possible that the restaurant would be put up for sale, and he had a feeling Josie Landers would be the first one standing in line to take it over.

But suspicion and proof were two different things, and he had no concrete proof that Josie was involved in any way in the attacks on Roxy.

He looked up as the object of his thoughts entered the kitchen. Clad in a pair of jean shorts and an old blue T-shirt, she looked crisp and clean and offered him a slightly nervous smile.

"Good morning," she said as she headed for the coffeepot.

"Same to you," he replied.

"Don't worry, I'm planning on changing clothes before your mom shows up. I tend to be a bit of a messy cook, so I'll change right after I've got the cooking thing under control."

"I wasn't worried," he said.

She poured herself a cup of brew and then sat in the chair next to his at the table. She took a sip from her cup, eyeing him over the rim. "What time is your mother going to be here today?" she asked as she lowered her cup.

"Around two."

"I've got to get my sauce going. It needs to cook a couple of hours in order to make the flavors all pop together." She frowned, as if mentally ticking things off in her head. "If I can get the lasagna in the oven by one, then while it cooks I can make a nice salad and at the last minute bake the garlic bread."

Instead of bringing her cup back to her mouth, she gnawed on a fingernail, letting him know she was nervous about the day.

He got up from his chair, leaned over her and pulled the finger from her mouth. He gave her a sound kiss and then straightened. "It's going to be fine, Roxy. Just be yourself, and the day will be fine."

She smiled up at him gratefully. "Thanks. I guess I needed to hear that."

"What? That everything is going to be okay?"

"No, that I just need to be myself," she replied.

He grabbed his cup for a refill. "I can't figure out why you would think I'd want you to be anything different."

She jumped up from the table. "No serious discussions when I'm about to start culinary magic."

He returned to the table and watched as she pulled out a big pot she'd brought with her from the Dollhouse the night before. As she began to gather ingredients on the counter and pulled out the cutting board, he knew he'd lost her. She had entered her own little world and was focused solely on her task, and he was content just to sit at the table, sip his coffee and watch her.

He found it charming how her forehead wrinkled slightly in concentration, how she occasionally mumbled to herself and worked with a graceful efficiency of movements. She used a knife with frightening speed to chop and slice, to dice and trim.

It wasn't long before the kitchen smelled of simmering garlic and onion, and Roxy wore a lovely smile.

When he finished his coffee, he placed the cup in the dishwasher and told her he was going to do a little computer work. She nodded absently and continued with her own work.

By one-thirty the house smelled like the finest Italian restaurant on the face of the earth. Roxy had changed into a pair of navy capris and a white-and-navy blouse, and seemed pleased with her preparations.

They set the table together, and when they were finished, she put the garlic bread into the oven and perched on one of the kitchen chairs as if awaiting her execution.

"Stop looking so worried," he said.

"I'm not," she automatically replied and then cast him a small smile. "Okay, maybe I am a little. I'm just not used to mothers, especially normal ones."

"What makes you think my mother is normal?" he asked with a laugh.

"Because you're so normal."

He laughed again. "And what makes you think I'm normal?"

"Because I've been here in the house with you for a long enough time that if you weren't normal, I'd know it by now. Trust me, I have a nose for abnormal. I spent the first seven years of my life in it."

At that moment Steve's doorbell rang, indicating that his mother had arrived.

Rebecca Kincaid was a petite, pretty blonde who Roxy could have picked out of a lineup as Steve's mom. They shared the same blue eyes, general coloring and overall shape to their faces.

She greeted Roxy warmly, telling her that she was looking forward to going to the Dollhouse for lunch one day soon, and then she kissed her son on his cheek and told him she hated his shirt.

At that moment Roxy knew she and Rebecca were going to get along just fine. To be honest, Roxy hated the shirt Steve had pulled on just before his mother's arrival. It was a short-sleeved floral that made him look like a tourist on a tropical vacation.

Dinner was delightful. Rebecca and Roxy monopolized the conversation, talking about recipes and the lasagna that Roxy had served. Roxy apologized about the store-bought cake they had for dessert with coffee.

"I can wrestle any kind of meat and vegetables into all kinds of savory dishes, but I've never mastered the art of baking," she explained. "My aunt Liz used to tell me it was because I was too impatient, that I tried to control yeast rising and chocolate melting. I finally gave up trying my hand at sweets."

"Steve has told me about your aunt," Rebecca said. "I'm assuming there's still no word?" Her gaze held a sympathy that closed up the back of Roxy's throat with emotion.

"We're still working all the angles," Steve replied.

The conversation changed to Steve's childhood, and soon Rebecca had Roxy laughing in delight at Steve's antics as a child.

"He told me he was a perfect child," Roxy exclaimed.

"Perfect in what world?" Rebecca asked with an arched eyebrow at her son. "Let's be real here, what perfect son would choose to wear that shirt?"

Roxy giggled as Steve got up from the table. "Okay, I bought it on a dare. I'll go change so I don't offend you both any longer."

He left the kitchen, and Roxy's laughter halted as she looked at Rebecca seriously. "To be honest, I don't know what I would have done without Steve over the last week and a half. He's gone above and beyond his duty to help me since my aunt has been missing."

Rebecca's blue eyes held Roxy's gaze. "Do you realize he's in love with you?"

A gasp of shock escaped Roxy. "Oh, no, no…he's not. He's just helping me out, that's all."

Rebecca smiled and shook her head. "I know my son, and I know he's in love with you. I'm only telling you this because I don't want you to break his heart. He's had enough heartbreak already to last a lifetime."

"I know. He told me about Tommy," Roxy said, still reeling from Rebecca's words.

"Which only confirms to me how much he cares about you." Rebecca leaned back in her chair and smiled at Roxy. "You're a lovely woman, but what I'm saying is that if you don't feel the same way about him, then make sure it's very clear to him. Don't break his heart, Roxy. Please don't break my son's heart."

The conversation halted as Steve came back into the room, this time wearing a button-down short-sleeved light blue shirt. "So much better," Rebecca exclaimed with a beaming smile at her son. She stood. "And now I'm going to help with the cleanup and then head back home."

"You don't have to help clean up," Roxy protested. "I've got all the rest of the evening to take care of it."

"I feel guilty enjoying such a wonderful meal and not helping afterward," Rebecca replied.

"Mom, trust me, you don't want to argue with Roxy. She's as bullheaded as you are and will wear you plain slick to get her way."

"Well, in that case, I guess I'll gracefully admit defeat." At the front door Roxy was surprised when Rebecca pulled her into her arms for a quick, warm hug. "Thank you for bringing laughter back to my son's life," she whispered in Roxy's ear before she released her.

Roxy nodded, surprised to find a choking emotion rising up the back of her throat. If she gave herself the chance, she could love Rebecca Kincaid, who appeared to be a straight shooter just like Roxy herself.

As Steve walked his mother out to her car, Roxy went back into the kitchen and sank down at the table, her thoughts flittering from Rebecca to Aunt Liz and finally to Steve.

Surely Rebecca was wrong about Steve's feelings for her. Steve himself had told her he wasn't interested in finding love again.

But Roxy thought about the tension that had been rife between then while she'd been there, a tension that screamed of desire. As she thought of how many times his gaze had lingered on her with a softness, how easily he touched her or gently kissed her, she thought maybe Rebecca could be right.

And if she was right, then Roxy needed to get away from there…away from him. The very last thing she would ever want to do was cause Steve any pain.

Because there was no way she intended to have any real relationship with him, and she was going to have to make sure that was crystal clear to him. Otherwise she needed to leave and put some distance between them.

"That went well," Steve said as he entered the kitchen. "Mom liked you. I told you she would."

"I like her, too." Roxy got up from the table to begin to clear the dishes, needing some sort of action to attempt to clear her head.

Steve jumped in to help, and it didn't take long before they were finished. They poured fresh coffee and then went out on the deck to sit before the air became too cool to be outside.

"You're suddenly very quiet," he observed.

She looked toward the sinking sun, feeling as if she needed to do something, to say something that would address any issues of their falling in love.

"This has been nice, but you know I can't stay here forever," she finally said as she looked at him. "I've been thinking that maybe it's time I invite Marlene or Sheri to stay with me at the Dollhouse and get out of your hair."

He held her gaze for an endless moment. "You know that's not a good idea. You wouldn't want to put your sisters in any danger." He paused a long moment. "What did my mother say to you?"

"Nothing." She cast her gaze away again, unable to look him in the eye and fib.

"Roxy."

She forced herself to look at him. "Your mother is worried about our relationship." She felt the warmth that crept into her cheeks. "She thinks you're falling in love with me."

"I am."

Those two words, so stark, so simple, turned her already topsy-turvy world upside down once more. "You can't be. We said neither of us wanted a relationship."

"I didn't think I was ready. I hadn't planned it to happen." He leaned forward, close enough to her that she could smell the scent of him mingling with the faint pine off the mountains. "I thought all my heart could hold was grief over my missing son, but I was wrong. There's space for you there, Roxy."

She got up from the chair and walked over to the deck railing, as if she could remove herself from what he was saying to her. "What about those phone calls you get that you're so secretive about? Are they from some woman who's wondering what happened to you? Somebody waiting for you to say those things to them?"

"Roxy, what am I going to do with you?" he asked with a hint of impatience. "Those calls are from Tanner Cage, the private investigator I've got working on finding Stacy and Tommy."

Her shoulders stiffened. "It doesn't matter anyway. Don't love me, Steve," she said, keeping her back to him. "Your mother is afraid I'll break your heart, and I will if you love me."

She heard his chair scoot back, and she tensed as she sensed him coming to stand just behind her. "If you're about to tell me that you don't care about me, then I won't believe you," he said, his breath warm against the back of her neck.

She closed her eyes and remained facing outward, not wanting to turn and look into his beautiful blue eyes, afraid she would be vulnerable to him. "I do care about you," she admitted. "I care about you more than I've ever cared about a man, but that doesn't change the fact that I never intend to invite a man into my life."

His hands fell on her shoulders, and she allowed him to turn her around to face him. "What are you afraid of, Roxy? Why are you so afraid to love…to be loved?"

She shrugged off his hands and moved several feet away from him but remained facing him. "Love destroyed my mother's life. Men forced her to make bad decisions that destroyed any hope I had of family. She stole and did drugs, she dragged me around like a dog on a chain and sometimes forgot to bring me in from the rain because she was so focused on *loving* some boyfriend."

"And so your mother's downfall was all due to men. She had no part in it," he said softly.

Roxy stared at him, her heart in a turmoil she'd never felt before. She'd never wanted to look at her mother's own culpability in the mistakes she had made. It had always been so much easier to blame her disastrous errors on the men in her life.

"Roxy, I'm not like any of the men in your mother's life, and you definitely aren't your mother," he said. Without waiting for her to reply, he grabbed his coffee cup from the table and went back inside.

Roxy remained on the deck, tears burning her eyes. How she wished Aunt Liz was there to talk to, to tell Roxy that everything was going to be okay.

But at the moment she felt as if nothing was ever going to be okay again, and the worst part was she didn't know if she didn't trust Steve to be the man she needed, or if she didn't trust herself to be the kind of woman she'd always thought she was.

Chapter 16

He'd told her he was in love with her. Steve sat at his desk the next day, trying to forget the awkwardness of the night before.

Sunset had passed by the time Roxy came in from the deck, and she had gone immediately to the guest bedroom and hadn't emerged until morning.

They'd had coffee as if the conversation the night before hadn't taken place, although the tension between them could have been cut with a rusty knife.

He'd been afraid that he'd have to talk her into continuing to stay at his place, but she hadn't said anything about changing up the game when he'd dropped her off at the Dollhouse.

But he knew she wouldn't stay at his place forever, especially now that he'd spoken out loud of how he felt about her. He'd seen the fear that had leaped into her eyes, but he'd also seen a flicker of wistfulness, of yearning.

It was obvious from what little she had told him that she'd seen her mother as a victim and men as the victimizers in Ramona's life. It was as if she'd never considered Ramona's guilt in the choices she had made.

There was no way in this life or in another one that Roxy would ever be a victim of any man. She was Amazon strength and beauty in a pint-size package. She was too savvy to allow any man to push her around for any reason.

And Steve didn't want to push her around or change her. He loved who she was, brash and outspoken, tempestuous and sexy. He loved how she looked at him with those dark chocolate eyes and that take-no-prisoners expression.

He looked up as Frank ambled over to his desk and sat in the chair facing him. "What's up?"

"Absolutely nothing," Steve replied. There was no way he was going to share with Frank his feelings for Roxy, because any further relationship didn't appear possible.

"We've hit dead ends everywhere," Frank said, his frustration mirroring how Steve felt about the current investigations.

"No sign of where Ramona Marcoli might be?" Steve asked.

"The only thing I know for sure is that she isn't dead. No death certificate is listed in any of the fifty states, but that's all I've managed to learn."

"And there's still been no movement on Liz's finances," Steve added.

Frank frowned. "I'm feeling like we're not going to have a happy ending where this is concerned. Late last night I remembered something that doesn't bode well for Liz Marcoli."

"What's that?"

"Two years ago a sixty-year-old woman named Agnes Wilson vanished from her home, and to this day she's never been found."

Steve stared at Frank. "I don't remember anything about this. Where was I?"

"You were crazy. It was during the first weeks that Tommy was taken. Jimmy and I worked the case. I don't know why I didn't think about it until last night, but I came in this morning and pulled the file."

"And?" Steve asked with a sinking feeling in his stomach.

"And the cases are very similar. Agnes was divorced and lived alone. She had no children. Her next-door neighbor, Nancy Williams, came over every morning to share coffee with Agnes. One morning she came over as usual, and Agnes wasn't there. Her car was in the driveway, and so Nancy eventually called out an officer to do a well check. The officer, Wade Peters, went into the house but found no signs of anything criminal. We investigated, but the case went cold. Agnes was just gone, and she's been gone ever since."

The sick feeling in Steve's stomach deepened. "I want to see the file. Maybe somehow there's a connection between the two women."

"They were in the same age bracket. It might be a weak lead, but at least it's something to explore,"

Frank said. He got up from the chair. "I'll get you that file."

An hour later, Steve was immersed in the details of an investigation into a woman who had been missing for a little over two years. Agnes Wilson shared a lot of common characteristics with Liz Marcoli.

Like Liz, Agnes had led a relatively quiet life, enjoying working in her yard and cooking for her church, which provided potluck dinners twice a month for members or anyone else in need of a hot meal.

The investigation had turned up no men in her life, no reason for anyone to want to harm her, and in the past two years her finances had remained intact, indicating that wherever she was, she wasn't spending a dime.

It's hard to get to the ATM if you're dead, Steve thought.

Her house had been paid for, and a younger brother had cut all but the minimum utilities and had kept the taxes on the property paid up. The circumstances of Agnes's disappearance in far too many ways mirrored Liz's.

It was just after noon when Jimmy and Frank insisted he go with them to grab some lunch. They wound up at a Chinese restaurant not far from the station, where they ordered enough food for an entire task force.

While Jimmy and Frank ate as if they hadn't seen food for days, Steve picked at his sweet and sour chicken, his head filled with thoughts of Agnes and Liz.

"We need to check out where these two lives might have connected," he said, giving up on eating and setting his fork down by his plate. "Did they share the same lawn service, go to the same beauty shop? Were they friends with the same people? At some point it's possible that both of them connected with the wrong person, and we need to figure out who that person is."

While the idea of a woman missing for two years was horrendous, Steve was encouraged that perhaps by comparing Agnes's and Liz's lives, they might actually come up with something that had previously been overlooked.

"Are we going to tell any of the Marcoli women about Agnes?" Jimmy asked.

Steve knew that Roxy would react poorly to the news. She wouldn't see it as an opportunity to broaden the investigation; rather, she would see it as a horrifying possibility.

"I think it would be best if we keep it to ourselves until we do a little more digging," he replied.

For the remainder of the meal, Jimmy and Frank kept up a running conversation about Wolf Creek High School's chances to have a decent football team that year, while Steve's head rumbled with thoughts of Roxy.

He'd crossed the line in challenging her about her mother, but he had a feeling that Roxy's belief that her mother was nothing but a helpless victim to horrible men was what kept Roxy from reaching out for any real happiness in her own life when it came to a relationship.

She was so afraid to relinquish control, to simply let go and allow any man to get too close. He understood. He'd been there, but in the past almost two weeks of close contact with Roxy, he'd realized that despite the grief he held in his heart for his missing son, there was still room for a new love to blossom.

He wasn't ready to get down on one knee and propose to her, but he wanted to build on the love he already felt for her, give them time to explore that love and see where it eventually led them.

But he couldn't do that if she wasn't willing. He didn't know how to show her that she could trust him. He didn't know what else he could do to make her understand that she would never make the mistakes that her mother had made, and he certainly would never be the kind of man who would use or abuse her in any way.

"Earth to Steve," Jimmy said, jarring Steve from his thoughts.

"Sorry, got lost in my head," Steve said as he looked at his younger partner.

"I asked if you wanted to get a to-go box. You barely touched your food."

"Nah, I'm good. I'll make up for it at dinnertime."

"Must be nice to have one of the best cooks in the county making your dinner every night," Frank said as they walked out of the restaurant.

"Yeah, I could definitely get used to it," Steve agreed. He could definitely get used to having Roxy around all the time. But he didn't just want her in his guest room. He wanted her in his bed every night. He wanted to wake up with her in his arms every morning.

The sunshine had disappeared as they'd eaten lunch, usurped by a low, heavy-hanging cloud bank that made it feel more like evening than midday.

"Looks like we're in for a big rain," Frank said.

Steve nodded. The darkness of the day mirrored the inside of his heart. All he could think about was the one and only time he'd made love to Roxy and how much he wanted to make love to her again, how much he wanted her to give them a chance to build something together.

But the ball was now in her court, and he had the terrible feeling that she intended to foul out rather than play the game of love.

All day long Roxy had played and replayed the conversation she'd had with Steve on his deck the night before. He was falling in love with her, and she knew in her heart she was in love with him.

But that didn't mean any happily-ever-afters. She'd never planned on love. It had no place in her life. Besides, she was still trying to process what he'd said about her mother.

It had always been so easy for her to blame and hate the men who'd been integral parts of Ramona's life. It had been easy to believe that all the bad choices her mother had made had been the fault of bad men.

But he was right. Ramona's tragic life and choices, her drug abuse and illegal behaviors, hadn't all been because of whatever boyfriend she'd been dating at the time. She'd made choices. She'd ultimately been responsible for the direction her life had taken.

Steve had also been right in that Roxy wasn't her mother. She wasn't anything like her mother. She would never make the kinds of choices her mother had made, no matter how important the man in her life.

She'd spent her entire life trying to justify why her mother hadn't wanted her, and while there had been days she'd hated her mother for abandoning her, most of the time she'd managed to convince herself that her mother had only made that decision because a man had forced her to make it.

Now, stripped bare of that justification, she was left with the bitterness of knowing the truth: her mother's decision had been her own. Ramona had been the captain of her own ship and had willingly relinquished control of it.

What would happen if Roxy relinquished control, if she allowed Steve into her heart, into her soul in a true, meaningful way?

He was a man who loved his son, who, despite the two years' absence, continued to fight for his return. He was a man who had told her she didn't have to change for anyone, that he loved her for the woman she was, not the woman she'd try to be for his benefit.

"Roxy," Josie said, a touch of irritation in her voice. "For the third time, what do you want to do about the afternoon meal? Barbecue chicken or chicken and noodles?"

Roxy shoved herself away from the counter where she'd been leaning, lost in thought. "I don't care. You pick."

Josie raised a dark eyebrow in surprise. "Are you okay?"

"No, I'm not sure I'm okay," she admitted.

Josie looked at her with concern. "Has something happened? Have you heard something about your aunt?"

"No, nothing like that," Roxy assured her. She drew a deep breath. "I think I'm in love with Steve."

Hearing the words spoken out loud jammed them home into her heart.

"Roxy, that's wonderful!" Josie grabbed her and pulled her into a quick hug and then stepped back. "Do you know how he feels about you?"

"He told me last night that he's in love with me."

"Then it really is wonderful," Josie exclaimed.

Roxy stared at her as she felt her heart expand with the love she'd tried so hard to deny that she felt. Somehow the surfer dude detective had managed to get beneath her defenses, make her realize that her thoughts about men, about love, had been skewed by the actions of her mother.

As she embraced what was in her heart, a lightness swept over her and a warmth imbibed her. She was in love with Steve Kincaid, and he loved her back.

"I haven't told him yet," she said to Josie. "I'll tell him tonight when we get to his place." Her cheeks burned as she thought of the night to come. She had a feeling that once she told him what was in her heart, she'd be in his arms and eventually in his bed. And that's exactly where she wanted to be.

At that moment a large group came into the restaurant for lunch. For the remainder of the afternoon Roxy focused on waiting tables, delivering orders and visiting with her patrons.

Outside the weather had turned for the worst; darkness crept in as rain clouds filled the skies. But the nasty weather couldn't take away Roxy's happiness as she thought about Steve and the night to come.

There was only one thing wrong at the moment. She wished that she could share her feelings for Steve with her aunt. The absence of Liz in their lives resonated like a discordant bell in her head.

She knew Steve and his partners were doing everything in their power to find answers, but she didn't need Steve to tell her that the case had gone cold…. In truth, it had never been hot.

There had been no breaks in the case of who had attacked her, either. Her best guess was still Michael Arello. He'd been so angry when she'd fired him, and he hung out at Ling's Studio, which meant he might know other students who were proficient at knife throwing, friends who might be willing to give her the scare of her life.

She couldn't explain how anyone might have gotten into the restaurant to push her into the freezer without breaking in, and she didn't believe that any of her staff members who had keys were responsible.

She supposed it was possible that when the restaurant was open, Michael had come in and hidden until the place closed down, and then he'd waited for her to return.

But suspecting wasn't knowing, and the only thing she knew for certain at the moment was that she was in love with Steve Kincaid and couldn't wait to get to his place and let him know what was in her heart.

She imagined telling him at sunset on the deck, where he'd spoken of his love for her the night before. It would be a beautiful moment…if she could wait until sunset, and if the dark clouds managed to disperse in time for a view of a lovely setting sun.

She was afraid that the minute he walked into the back door of the restaurant to take her home she'd jump into his arms, wrap them around his neck and spill the beans. Now that she'd truly embraced her love for him, she couldn't wait to share it with him.

It was just after five and she was smiling as she had been for most of the afternoon as she and Josie cleaned up the kitchen. Minutes earlier she'd sent Gus and Greg home. The afternoon had been slow, probably because of the dreary weather, and there was no point in them hanging around since they'd already cleaned the dining rooms.

"I'm going to run upstairs before Steve gets here and grab a stack of to-go containers. I see we're running low down here," Roxy said.

"Want me to go?" Josie asked as she put the last of the barbecue chicken in a container for Roxy to take with her to Steve's.

"No, I'll take care of it. While I'm up there I might grab a few more items of clothing to take to Steve's. I'll be right back down."

Josie nodded. "And I'll be right here until Steve arrives."

Roxy bounded up the stairs, energized despite the long day by the events of the night to come. Maybe she'd grab her pretty pink floral blouse and black slacks to change into before dinner. It didn't seem right to profess your love for somebody wearing a chicken-stained T-shirt and jeans.

She raced up to the third floor, grabbed the slacks and blouse in question and quickly added a pair of pink-and-black earrings, then stuffed the items in a small overnight bag.

She carried the bag down to the second level and set it on the floor outside the storage room. The room was dark, with only a single window that emitted the semilight of the darkened day. She flipped the light switch on the wall and muttered a curse when nothing happened.

When was the last time she'd changed the lightbulb in here? She couldn't remember. At least she knew where the foam containers were. Unfortunately they were on a shelf on the back wall, requiring her to maneuver around tables and chairs and a variety of bins and storage boxes.

Although slightly disoriented by the darkness of the room, she headed in the direction of the back wall. The door slammed shut behind her, and with a gasp she realized she wasn't alone.

Instantly she ducked down behind an overturned table. "Josie?" she said softly.

"No, but if you want to yell for her I'll be glad to kill her, too."

Roxy froze at the sound of the feminine voice, a voice she was certain she'd never heard before in her life. She curled up to make herself as small as possible as she heard the sound of footsteps across the floor.

At least she had the near-complete darkness of the room on her side, she thought as she tried to figure out who was in the room with her and what item might be close by that could be used as a weapon.

The footsteps halted, and the only sound was the frantic beat of Roxy's heart. Her instinct was to scream her head off, but there had been a harsh tone to the woman's voice that made Roxy believe she wouldn't think twice about hurting Josie.

She bit her lip, refusing to release the scream that would bring Josie running potentially to her own death.

The next sound she heard was a click, and then a tiny beam of light danced around the room. As Roxy realized the woman had a flashlight, her terror shook through her.

"You can't have him," the woman said softly, her footsteps audible as the beam shot from one area of the room to another in her search for Roxy. "He's mine. He's always been mine. I made a mistake by leaving, but now I've come back for him and you're in my way. I have his son, and we're all going to be a family."

The beam of light landed on Roxy, and she scrambled away at the same time she heard the *thwack* of a knife hitting the table where she'd been hiding.

Stacy. It was Stacy. Roxy tried to wrap her head around what was happening. Neither she nor Steve had ever considered that his ex might return and have a reason to hurt Roxy.

It was Stacy, and she obviously wanted Roxy dead.

As the ray of light struck her again, Roxy raced ahead, crashing into boxes and finally halting behind one of them. Deep sobs welled up inside her, but she slapped a hand over her mouth to hold them in, knowing that this was a deadly game of hide-and-seek.

She suddenly remembered her cell phone in her pocket. She knew that the moment she opened it, the screen would be backlit and would indicate her location. She only hoped she'd have enough time to punch in Steve's number before Stacy saw the light and attacked.

Drawing a deep breath and trying to control the violent tremble of her hands, Roxy pulled out the cell phone, slid it open and punched in Steve's number.

She didn't wait for a response, but instead scrabbled away from the phone.

She pulled herself into a ball behind a storage bin and heard the strong footsteps that strode across the floor. There was a loud stomp and a splintering noise, and the light from the phone instantly blinked out.

Roxy had no idea if the call had gone through or not. She had no idea if there was any help on the way. She refused to scream for Josie, even though she knew that there were only so many places in the room where she could hide.

Eventually this game of hide-and-seek would end, and Roxy knew with every fiber of her being that she was locked in this room with a woman who intended to kill her, who wouldn't stop until she was dead.

Chapter 17

"That's odd," Steve said as he got up from his desk and stared at his phone.

Frank stepped up next to him. "What's odd?"

"I just got a call from Roxy's number, but she didn't talk to me and then the line went dead."

"A dropped call?"

"Maybe…maybe not." Steve looked up at Frank, an edge of anxiety creeping through his veins. He quickly punched in Roxy's number, but it went straight to voice mail.

"I think maybe something's going on." Steve headed for the door, the thrum of anxiety growing stronger.

"Want company?" Frank asked.

"Yeah, I think that's a good idea."

Steve got in his car and Frank got in his own, and

together they pulled away from the station. Had Roxy sent everyone home because business was slow? Was she alone in the place, and had danger once again crept inside the doors?

His heart nearly jumped out of his chest as he roared down the street to the Dollhouse. When he pulled up in back he was relieved to see Josie's car still parked beside Roxy's. So Roxy wasn't there all alone.

Frank pulled in next to him. "Maybe I overreacted," Steve said as the two of them got out of their cars. "Josie is still here, so Roxy must be okay." *Unless Josie was the danger,* a little voice niggled in Steve's head.

Frank didn't look relieved. "But it looks like it's just Josie and Roxy. It looks like all the men have gone for the day."

The anxiety jumped back into Steve's veins. If Josie wasn't the perp, she was a lightweight like Roxy. It would be relatively easy for somebody to overtake the two of them, especially if that somebody had a weapon.

Steve drew his gun, as did Frank as they approached the back door. Steve would certainly rather be safe than sorry. As he opened the door and rounded the corner in the kitchen, Josie squealed in surprise and threw her hands up in the air.

"Don't shoot me!"

Steve expelled a sigh of relief and lowered his gun. "So you're all okay?"

"I'm okay. Roxy went upstairs to get some containers." She frowned. "But it's taking her a long time."

Once again that screaming anxiety leaped into Steve's brain and into his heart. He motioned for Frank to follow him, and they climbed the stairs silently.

Steve turned on the light against the looming darkness that encompassed the second floor and the narrow, dark stairway.

The door to the storage room was closed, and Steve heard the sound of movement behind it. There was a scuffle, a dull thud and a stifled squeal.

Steve threw open the door, and the illumination from the hall light shone in. He froze at the sight of Roxy on the floor on her back and Stacy straddling her, a large dagger held in both hands over her head.

Stacy? Where had she come from…and what was she doing to Roxy?

As if in slow motion, Steve saw the knife in Stacy's hands begin a descent. Roxy screamed. A gunshot deafened him as he tried to make sense of everything.

The scent of cordite filled the air as Stacy's blouse blossomed with red. The knife slipped from her hands, and she fell to the floor next to Roxy. Roxy's deep sob broke Steve's inertia, and he ran to her side as she got up on all fours.

"Are you okay?" He crouched down next to her. "Roxy, did she hurt you?"

Roxy shook her head and struggled to her feet, and Frank drew her close to him. Steve stared over at Stacy, a new horror filling his head.

No…no! his brain screamed.

He ran to where she lay on her back. She was still alive, although he didn't know how. "Stacy…Stacy, where's Tommy?" Steve's heart beat so frantically he felt as if he were on the verge of a heart attack or a mental breakdown.

Stacy smiled up at him. "If I can't have you, then

you can't have him." Her voice was barely audible in the utter stillness of the room.

"Stacy, for God's sake, just tell me where he is," Steve begged, his vision blurring with tears.

She coughed and gurgled as a trickle of blood escaped from the side of her mouth. "You'll never know." They were her last words. She turned her head slightly and died.

Steve stared at her. *No.* It couldn't end like this. It couldn't. He grabbed Stacy by the shoulders and shook her. "Tell me—tell me where he is."

He was wild with grief, aware someplace in the back of his mind that his last hope to find his son was with a dead woman. *No...no...no.* The word thundered over and over again in his brain. This couldn't have happened.

"Steve." Frank placed a firm hand on his shoulder. "She's gone. Leave her be."

Steve stared up at his partner, tears streaming down his face. "I'm sorry," Frank said, his voice breaking slightly. "I'm sorry that I had to shoot her, but she was going to kill Roxy."

Like a robot, Steve turned his head to see Roxy standing in the doorway, embraced by Josie, who had obviously run upstairs during the drama.

"Yeah, you did the right thing," Steve heard himself say as he got to his feet and swiped his face, numbed by what had just occurred.

"I've already called for backup," Frank said. "Go home, Steve. Get out of here. I'll handle the details."

He saw the guilt and grief that deepened the lines on Frank's face and knew Frank felt bad for pulling the trigger that ended all Steve's hopes, his dreams of ever seeing his son again.

Although logically Steve knew Frank had had no other choice, right now he didn't have the words to assuage Frank's guilt. Steve was utterly destroyed.

"She wanted to be with you. She thought I was in the way," Roxy said, her voice trembling from the residual terror she had to have felt. "She's the one who threw the knives at me and locked me in the freezer. She wanted me dead so you could all be a family." Roxy turned her head into Josie's shoulder and began to weep.

Steve walked over to her and pulled her from Josie and into his embrace. But he felt nothing. He patted her on the back as she cried into the front of his shirt. "It's going to be fine," he said by rote. "Everything is going to be fine now."

At that moment the thunder of footsteps sounded on the stairs, and Steve knew the backup had arrived. He released Roxy, still feeling as if he were in a haze, trapped in a terrible bad dream and couldn't wake up.

"I'm going to head home," he said to nobody, to anybody. "I'll be there if you need me."

He met several other officers, including Jimmy, coming up the stairs, but nobody spoke to him and for that he was grateful.

Alone. He just wanted to be alone to process what had happened, to grieve what now would probably never happen. Still in a numbed fog, he got into his car and drove to his house. As he drove he found himself playing and replaying the last seconds of Stacy's life.

In those last moments, why hadn't she just told him

what he needed to know, given him what he wanted so much? She'd taken joy in denying him.

He'd always known she was selfish and crazy; he just hadn't realized the utter depths of her madness. He pulled into his driveway and dropped his head to the steering wheel, despair making him too weak to move.

The only hope that remained was that on her body they'd find something that would indicate where she'd been staying, but it was a hope barely realized as he knew Stacy was probably smarter than that.

Like an ancient man, he finally got out of his car and went into the house, where for the past week laughter and joy had lived with Roxy's presence. Now the silence screamed at him as he climbed the stairs.

There was no doubt where he was going. He needed to be as close to his son as possible. He stumbled down the hallway to the bedroom at the end.

He opened the door and headed straight to the bed, where he collapsed and pulled the stuffed horse tight against his chest—and only then did he weep for the child he feared he would never see again.

The night was endless for Roxy. Somebody screwed in the lightbulb that Stacy had apparently unscrewed in the ceiling of the storage room, and men tramped in and out, taking pictures, collecting evidence and doing their jobs.

She was questioned by first one person and then another. Josie was also interviewed for a long time. Somehow word had gotten to Marlene and Sheri, who both showed up, their faces fraught with worry as they provided emotional support for Roxy.

Stacy's body was finally removed, and Roxy was allowed to go upstairs to her own quarters with her sisters while the police finished up their work.

Despite the horror of what she'd been through, despite how close death had come, all Roxy could think about was Steve. Tonight was to have been the night she confessed her love for him, and instead he'd been dealt a kick to his heart that she feared he would never survive.

She knew the implications of Stacy's death, the agonizing secret she'd taken with her, and she'd seen the hope die in Steve's eyes, his soul shut down in agony.

She sat at her kitchen table while Marlene made coffee and Sheri rummaged in the refrigerator for sandwich makings. "It's almost midnight. You have to eat something," she said as Roxy sat numb and slightly disconnected from everything that was happening around her.

She knew there would never be a happily-ever-after with Steve. She would always represent to him the reason he didn't get his son back, the reason Frank had pulled the trigger to kill the only woman who had answers for him. The whereabouts of Tommy had been sacrificed to save her life. How could he ever forgive her for that?

This night had not only destroyed Steve. The collateral damage had been Roxy's hope for a future with him and the dark shadows of guilt from killing that filled Frank's eyes.

"Here you go," Sheri said as she placed a paper plate with a ham-and-cheese sandwich in front of Roxy. Marlene poured them all coffee, and then the two of them joined Roxy at the table.

"Eat," Sheri commanded.

"You two should be home where you belong, not here taking care of me," Roxy protested.

"And why wouldn't we be here taking care of you?" Marlene asked. "You've been through a traumatic night. Whether you believe it or not, you need us, Roxy."

To Roxy's horror, tears filled her eyes. "I always wanted to be the strong one for the two of you. I wanted to be the one to take care of you."

"And you have," Marlene assured her. She covered one of Roxy's hands with hers. "You've been the best big sister we could ever have. You are so strong, but so are we, Roxy, and it's okay if once in a while you need to lean on us."

"Roxy, you've done your job. You and Aunt Liz taught us how to be strong, independent women," Sheri said.

Her words were followed by the silence of loss, by the knowledge that each of them shared that nobody was even close to figuring out what had happened to Liz.

"I'm spending at least tonight with you," Marlene said and gazed at Roxy with her ice princess look that brooked no argument. "I'll be here to do the baking in the morning."

Roxy sighed. "I don't think I plan to open tomorrow. I already told Josie to take the day off and to contact any other help to tell them the same thing." She picked up half of the sandwich and took a bite.

"Maybe it's a good thing not to open. You could come out to my place and spend the day with me," Sheri said. "There's nothing better than fresh air and taking care of little creatures to set your mind straight."

Roxy smiled at her youngest sister. In many ways Sheri was so uncomplicated. "Maybe I'll do that," she agreed. "In fact, maybe I'll head to your place with you for the rest of the night." She smiled apologetically at Marlene. "Not to offend you, but to be honest, I don't think I want to be here tonight."

"No offense taken," Marlene replied easily. "I just want you to know that we're both here for you, for whatever you need."

A knock fell on the door, and Marlene jumped up to answer it. It was Frank. He stepped inside, his eyes still haunted with grief and guilt. Roxy got up from the table to greet him.

"Frank," she said softly and gave him a quick hug. "Thank you for saving my life."

"I didn't know what else to do. I had a split second to make a decision." His eyes darkened. "I just wish things had turned out differently for Steve."

"Me, too," Roxy said as her heart squeezed tight in her chest.

"I just came up to tell you we're all finished. I'm sure in the next couple of days we'll need you to come in to finish up some reports, but somebody will call you and arrange a time that's convenient for you."

"Whenever is fine with me. I just want to get this all behind me now."

"At least we can close one of the cases we've been working on." He glanced over at Roxy's sisters. "And you all know we're doing what we can to find your aunt."

"We know," Sheri said.

"Do you want us to lock up as we leave?" he asked Roxy.

"I'll take care of it. In fact, I'm packing a small bag and heading to Sheri's for the night," Roxy said. "And the restaurant will be closed at least for tomorrow."

"I understand. The good news is you're safe now, Roxy. Your attacker is dead, and now you can breathe easier."

She forced a smile at him and nodded. "Thanks again, Frank."

After he left it didn't take Roxy long to pack for the night, and then the three sisters headed downstairs. They stepped outside, where the rain clouds had finally moved on, leaving behind a slice of moon and a million stars.

Marlene looked up and then back at Roxy. "Seems like the worst has passed. Now we just have to wait for Aunt Liz to come home."

"And even if that doesn't happen soon, in the meantime we've got each other," Sheri said, her words ending in a group hug.

It was only when she was in Sheri's car on the way to her sister's mountain cabin that Roxy replayed Frank's words in her head. He'd told her that now she could breathe easier.

But how was that possible when her love for Steve still filled her soul, and when she knew that once again his heart was full of grief, leaving no room for her or her love?

For the next three days Steve remained at home, lost in a fog of despair like he'd never known before. He knew he should get back to work. He knew he needed to talk to Frank, to speak to Roxy, but he couldn't get past the black abyss he'd fallen into with Stacy's death.

His mother came by each day, forcing him to eat something, simply sitting in a chair near wherever he was to offer silent support. She knew him well enough to know that there were no words that could pull him from the darkness. He'd have to fight his way out on his own.

It was finally on the morning of the fourth day that he woke up on the sofa, unshaven and in the same clothes he'd been wearing for the past two days, that the fog of grief that had encased him lifted enough for rational thought to occur.

Just because Stacy was dead didn't mean that Tommy was. Nothing had really changed except that Stacy would never be able to tell him where Tommy was, but Tommy was still out there someplace and Steve needed to pull himself together and move forward. There was still that fragile thread of hope inside him, the hope that somehow, someway, he'd find his son.

With a renewed burst of life flooding through his veins, the first thing he did was check the messages on his phone that had piled up while he'd been in his dark cave. There were two from Frank, just checking in, and one from Jimmy letting him know they'd found nothing on Stacy to indicate where she'd been staying. There were also a couple of hang-up calls from a number he didn't recognize, and one from Chief Krause telling him to take as much time as he needed to get back to work.

He headed for the bathroom, where he leaned

against the shower wall and let a hot spray of water hit his back. He was ready to go back to work, ready to get back to life. He still had to find Liz Marcoli, and he still needed to find Tommy. Stacy might be gone, but she'd obviously been staying in the area.

As he stood, his thoughts went to Roxy. Thank God Frank had taken that shot. Although Steve would have liked things to have had a different ending, the one ending he couldn't have lived with was Roxy's death.

Steve had been so stunned to see Stacy that he'd done the unthinkable and froze. If Frank hadn't been with him, Roxy would be dead and Stacy would have probably either been arrested or dead, as well.

He owed Frank a debt of gratitude for saving Roxy's life. He had no ill will toward the partner who had done what he had to do. Frank needed to know that.

Once showered, he dressed in a pair of black slacks and a white shirt, deciding he wanted to look like a real detective on his return. As he strapped on his gun, his thoughts once again went to Tommy. He'd call Tanner and let the private investigator know that Stacy had been in the area. Maybe he could figure out where she'd been staying and if Tommy was someplace close.

He left the house with a new sense of purpose. He needed to find out where Stacy had been and where Tommy might possibly be. He wanted to continue the investigation into the missing Liz Marcoli, and he wanted—needed—to see Roxy.

Walking into the police station felt right, and the first person he saw was Frank, who looked like hell. Steve walked up to his partner and placed a hand on his shoulder.

"Hey, Steve," Frank said, and Steve couldn't help but see the shadows in Frank's eyes, shadows he hadn't seen in Frank's eyes since Frank's wife had committed suicide.

"It's good to see you back."

"I realized over the last couple of days I need my partners in my life," Steve said. "I especially need the kind of partner I can depend on to do the right thing when I'm mentally shut down."

He saw the flicker of relief dash into Frank's eyes. "I'm so sorry how it all went down, Steve."

Steve dropped his hand from Frank's shoulder. "There's nothing to be sorry about. You did the right thing, and that's that. I couldn't have lived with myself if Stacy had managed to kill Roxy, so I thank you for taking that shot. Now tell me what's been going on since I left."

"Nothing much. Jimmy has been checking out the similarities between Agnes Wilson's and Liz's cases, and I've been tying up the ends of what happened at the Dollhouse."

"Have you seen Roxy?" Despite the pain in his heart, a tiny ray of joy shone through as he thought of her. "I should have called her over the last couple of days, but I've been in a pretty dark place and didn't want to talk to anyone until I got my head back on straight."

"She's doing fine. She closed the Dollhouse for a day, but she's back up and running now. In fact, she's due in here anytime now to sign off on some final reports," Frank said.

The last time Steve had seen Roxy, he'd let her down by not shooting the woman who was about to stab her to death. And before that, he'd told her he loved her and she'd turned her back on him, but that didn't halt his heart from reacting to the anticipation of seeing her again, of finding out how she was doing.

Even though she'd basically told him she didn't want a relationship with him, that didn't mean he'd stopped caring about her, didn't mean his love for her had magically disappeared.

He made the rounds, chatting with everyone who was working, and then finally made it to his own desk, where he sat and tried to figure out what was the first thing on his agenda.

He'd just settled in when Roxy came through the door. Clad in her usual pair of tight jeans and wearing a hot pink T-shirt with the Dollhouse in black lettering across her midsection, she looked every inch the Foxy Roxy he'd come to know and love.

Her eyes widened and softened as he stood and approached her, and he didn't realize who reached for who first, but suddenly she was in his arms, the warmth of her, the scent of her, snaking into the places in his heart where only love could fit.

"I'm so glad you're okay," he said as she broke the embrace.

"Are you okay?" A dainty wrinkle creased her brow as she gazed at him with her beautiful brown eyes. "I've been so worried about you."

He wanted to pull her close again, to lose his grief in the warmth of her body, in the sweet scent of her that smelled like home, but instead he nodded. "As okay as I can be," he replied.

Although it had only been four days since he'd

seen her, it felt like a lifetime. "How's business at the restaurant?"

"Good." There was an awkward moment of silence. "Speaking of which, I'd better get this paperwork done and get back to work."

With murmured goodbyes, she headed for Frank's desk and Steve went back to his own. He'd only been there a moment when the uniform on duty in the civilian area poked his head in the door. "Steve, you got a minute? There's a guy here who wants to speak to somebody."

"Send him in," Steve said, wondering what crime was about to be reported now.

The man who entered appeared to be in his early thirties and looked like a stoner. Clad in dirty jeans and a grungy white T-shirt, he was painfully thin and had a bad complexion.

"Can I help you, Mr. ....?"

"My friends call me Chopper," the man said as he sat in the chair in front of Steve's desk. "Look, I let this crazy chick flop at my cabin for the last couple of weeks. She came and went as she pleased, but the last time she left my place she never came back, and I'm not about to take care of a kid that isn't mine."

Steve's heart stopped beating. "Slow down. What was the woman's name who was crashing at your cabin?"

"The boy is a good kid, but I ain't no babysitter, and I knew that chick was trouble the minute I met her. But I felt bad for the kid, and they needed a place to crash," Chopper continued.

"Her name. What was her name?" The question

seeped through the tiny space of Steve's narrowing throat.

"I don't know her last name, but her first name is Stacy. You need to find her and tell her to come get her kid."

Steve continued to stare at the man as the implications of his words pierced through his brain, arrowed into his heart. "The boy…where is he now?" Steve felt light-headed, almost nauseous with the surge of hope that slammed into his heart.

"He's out in the waiting room. I'll go get him." As Chopper jumped up from his chair, Steve rose more slowly, afraid of the hope, afraid of the tumultuous emotions that pressed so tight in his chest he could scarcely draw a breath.

The door opened, and the boy walked in. Everyone in the entire room stopped what they were doing. It was as if the whole world halted at the sight of the little boy with shaggy blond hair and eyes the color of the ocean. His jeans were dirty and torn at the knees, his T-shirt stained, but Steve knew that face. He'd loved that face since the moment it had come into being.

He choked out a sob and fell into a crouched position. "Tommy?"

Tommy's gaze held his, and Steve saw his beautiful eyes widen and wonder steal across his already handsome little features. "Dad?" Tears filled Tommy's eyes. "Daddy?"

Steve opened his arms and Tommy ran to fill them, his skinny arms winding around Steve's neck. Ah, heaven. His child was in his arms, and as Tommy clung tightly to him, Steve wept unabashedly.

He finally got to his feet, Tommy's legs wrapped

around his waist as he pressed himself against Steve's chest. "I've been looking everywhere for you," he finally managed to say.

"And I've been waiting for you to find me," Tommy replied.

Steve gave no thought to anything else but the child in his arms. The world had shrunk to a tiny picture of Tommy. "Let's go home," he said to his son, and without a backward glance, he carried his son out of the police station and into the beautiful spring day.

There would be time enough later to tell Tommy that his mother was dead. There would be time to catch up on where Tommy and Stacy had been for the past two years. But for now, Tommy was back with him, and for Steve that was more than enough.

Chapter 18

It had been a week since Roxy had last seen Steve, a week that she had held the heartwarming vision of him walking out of the police station with his son in his arms.

Roxy had thought about the two of them a lot in the past seven days. Frank and Jimmy had come in for breakfast one morning and had told her that Steve had taken some time off from work to be with Tommy, but they'd assured her they were still on the case of her missing aunt.

The pain of the absence of Liz had not lessened with time, but Roxy had finally understood Steve's advice. She couldn't control when Liz would be found. She and her sisters had done everything they could in order to help the investigation, but ultimately they had to carry on with their lives.

However, the return of Tommy to Steve after two long years had renewed Roxy's hope that eventually Aunt Liz would be found safe and sound and returned to where she belonged.

As far as Roxy's love for Steve, it remained as hot and as strong as it had ever been, and most nights she fell asleep wondering what if? What if she'd told him she loved him that night on the deck when he'd professed his love for her? What if she hadn't allowed her mother's mistakes to make her too afraid to reach out to the man she knew would only add happiness to her life?

She couldn't stop loving him, but she also knew his heart was filled now, just like that bedroom at the end of his hallway that had been empty for so long.

Tommy was home, and it was obvious Steve's life was full once again. Whenever she thought of the two of them together, her own heart filled with joy.

The restaurant kept her busy, and in the evenings she'd begun spending more time with Marlene and Sheri at the Roadside Stop. The bonding time between the sisters was good, although she still worried about Marlene and the dark shadows that never quite lifted from her pretty blue eyes.

Business at the restaurant had been brisk, and at the end of each night Roxy fell into dreamless sleep, no longer afraid for herself as the danger that had come at her from Steve's past was gone. She told herself life was good, but each night before she slept, her heart filled with thoughts of Steve and Tommy and what might have been.

"Ah, hump day," Josie said as Roxy came down the stairs early Wednesday morning. The room already smelled of the sweets that Marlene had dropped by before Roxy had come downstairs.

Roxy perched on a stool as Josie continued to debone chicken and Gregory finished up the breakfast prep. "I'm thinking about hiring a pastry chef."

Josie looked at her in surprise. "Won't that hurt Marlene's feelings?"

Roxy frowned thoughtfully. "I don't think so. She only took over the job when Aunt Liz disappeared, and I think between the baking for me and her work at the shop, she's burning the candle at both ends. I think maybe she'll be relieved. So you know of any pastry chefs in town?"

"I'll put out the word," Josie replied. "And now you'd better get out there and open the doors. It's almost five minutes after seven."

Roxy jumped up from the stool and hurriedly left the kitchen. As she approached the front door, she smiled as she saw Jimmy and Frank, and then her heart expanded even more when she saw that they weren't alone.

Steve and Tommy were with them. At the sight of father and son together, her heart soared with their joy. She quickly turned the Closed sign to Open and then unlocked the door to allow them inside.

"Well, what a fine-looking group this is," she said as they entered and headed toward their usual table. She tried to quiet the beat of her heart at the sight of Steve smiling so widely, appearing so complete and whole.

"Roxy, I'd like to introduce you to my son, Tommy."

"Hi, Tommy, I've heard a lot about you from your dad," she said. There had been changes in the boy during the past week. His hair was neat and short, his jeans new and his shirt a pearl-buttoned Western plaid. "It's so nice to finally meet you."

"It's nice to meet you, too," he said and gave her a shy smile.

Orders were taken and then Roxy disappeared back into the kitchen, her heart experiencing a battle—happiness for Steve and the deep yearning to be a part of his life with his son.

Josie took the order slip from her, and at that moment Steve stepped into the kitchen. "Roxy, could I speak to you for a minute alone?"

She frowned. "Will Tommy be okay without you?"

Steve smiled. "He'll be fine. He knows he's with big important detectives who would never let anything happen to him. When I left the table, he was explaining to them that he wasn't sure whether he still wanted to be a cowboy or if maybe someday he'd like to be a private investigator or a detective."

He grabbed her by the arm and pulled her out of the kitchen and into the small mudroom that served as a combination storage and prep area.

"I'm so happy for you, Steve," Roxy said. "He's adjusting well?"

Steve's smile faltered a bit. "It was rough telling him that his mother was dead, but he didn't ask many questions about it and seems to be adjusting very well. I know he might have more questions when he's older, but for now he seems happy just to be with me."

"Your happiness shows," Roxy said, fighting the need to reach out and touch him, knowing that she had no right.

The smile on his face disappeared, but his eyes

held a sweet softness as he gazed at her. "For the last two years I believed that if only I got Tommy back, my life would be complete. I thought he was all that was missing to make me whole."

Roxy's heart had begun a rapid tattoo, and she didn't know if it was because he'd taken a step closer to her or because of the desire that shone so sharply from his beautiful eyes as he gazed at her.

"I'm not sure what to say," Roxy finally managed to utter. She had no right to believe something magical might be about to happen. He'd already professed his feelings for her, and she'd shut him down.

He smiled, that slow, sexy upward slide of his lips that melted her heart. "Roxy Marcoli speechless? I never thought I'd live to see the day."

"Don't worry, the moment is already over," she replied. "I'm glad we have this private opportunity to talk because I never got a chance to thank you for everything you did for me. I've been doing a lot of thinking in the last week. Josie used to call me a manhater, and I always told her she was wrong. But what you said to me about my mother and her men and that I would never be like her made me realize just how frightened I've been of letting any man close to me." She paused a moment. "I'm not afraid anymore."

He reached up and placed his palm against her cheek. "That's good, because I'm a persistent kind of man, and I needed to tell you that the piece that's still missing from my life is you. I love you, Roxy."

"I love you, too," she said tremulously.

His eyes lit with flames of love and desire. "So what do you think we should do about it?"

"I think a kiss is a good start," she ventured.

"Ah, Roxy, I love the way your mind works." He took her in his arms and kissed her, and in his arms she felt right. In his lips she tasted a future.

"We'll take it slow," she said when the kiss finally broke apart. "For Tommy's sake. I love him already, Steve. I love him because he belongs to you."

"And now he's going to belong to you, too," Steve replied. "Now, why don't you join us all for breakfast, or at least have a cup of coffee with us."

"I can do that," she instantly agreed. For a moment her happiness was tempered by the fact that her aunt was still missing, but she also knew if there was one thing she'd want for Roxy, it would be love.

As Roxy and Steve left the kitchen and stepped into the dining room, where Jimmy, Frank and Tommy awaited them, Tommy's smile was as wide as the mountains that cradled the little town of Wolf Creek.

Steve had seen her at her best and he'd seen her at her worst, but she was honored that he thought she was the woman to make him whole, to coparent his son.

She knew in her heart, in her very soul, that Steve was in this for the long run, and so was she. Eventually there would be a wedding, and she could only hope on that day of happiness and love that her Aunt Liz was there, as well.

In the meantime she had a breakfast to eat, a man to love and a little boy to get to know. Life for Foxy Roxy had never felt so good.

Epilogue

Sleep was terrifying. Liz worried what might happen when she slept, if her captor would sneak into the bunker and kill her.

However, she couldn't go without sleep forever, and as she now lay on the cot, she tried to hold on to her hope for rescue, but each day it became more difficult.

Instead, as she felt the drowsiness of oncoming sleep drift over her, she focused her thoughts on the three little girls she'd raised as her own.

Roxy, Marlene and Sheri had been Liz's reason for living after her husband had died. They'd brought sunshine and giggles and love into her life.

Liz squeezed her eyes against the burn of tears. Her only hope was that she would be able to see them again, that she'd be found and could embrace the women who were such a big part of her heart.

Hope. She had to hang on in the hope that somehow, someway, she'd be rescued before she died in this terrible place.

* * * * *

To see if Liz is found, stay tuned for more of Carla's books in the Men of Wolf Creek *series in 2014.*

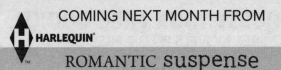

COMING NEXT MONTH FROM

HARLEQUIN®

ROMANTIC suspense

Available January 7, 2014

#1783 LETHAL LAWMAN
Men of Wolf Creek • Carla Cassidy

When heartbroken Marlene Marcoli is targeted by a madman bent on revenge, Detective Frank Delaney vows to protect her while breaking down the walls that shield her heart from love.

#1784 THE RETURN OF CONNOR MANSFIELD
The Mansfield Brothers • Beth Cornelison

Connor Mansfield leaves witness protection to save his daughter's life and reclaim the woman he loves, but to have a future together, they must escape assassins and rebuild lost trust.

#1785 DEADLY ENGAGEMENT
Elle James

Adventure diver Emma is soon in over her head when undercover agent and former SEAL Creed Thomas commandeers her boat, and her heart, in a race to stop a terrorist plot.

#1786 SECRET AGENT SECRETARY
ICE: Black Ops Defenders • Melissa Cutler

Catapulted into the middle of an international manhunt, secretary Avery has no one to rely on but herself...and Ryan, the mysterious spy with a secret connection to the enemy.

YOU CAN FIND MORE INFORMATION ON UPCOMING HARLEQUIN® TITLES, FREE EXCERPTS AND MORE AT WWW.HARLEQUIN.COM.

HRSCNM1213

REQUEST YOUR FREE BOOKS!
2 FREE NOVELS PLUS 2 FREE GIFTS!

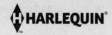

ROMANTIC suspense

Sparked by danger, fueled by passion

YES! Please send me 2 FREE Harlequin® Romantic Suspense novels and my 2 FREE gifts (gifts are worth about $10). After receiving them, if I don't wish to receive any more books, I can return the shipping statement marked "cancel." If I don't cancel, I will receive 4 brand-new novels every month and be billed just $4.74 per book in the U.S. or $5.24 per book in Canada. That's a savings of at least 14% off the cover price! It's quite a bargain! Shipping and handling is just 50¢ per book in the U.S. and 75¢ per book in Canada.* I understand that accepting the 2 free books and gifts places me under no obligation to buy anything. I can always return a shipment and cancel at any time. Even if I never buy another book, the two free books and gifts are mine to keep forever.

240/340 HDN F45N

Name	(PLEASE PRINT)	

Address		Apt. #

City	State/Prov.	Zip/Postal Code

Signature (if under 18, a parent or guardian must sign)

Mail to the **Harlequin® Reader Service:**
IN U.S.A.: P.O. Box 1867, Buffalo, NY 14240-1867
IN CANADA: P.O. Box 609, Fort Erie, Ontario L2A 5X3

Want to try two free books from another line?
Call 1-800-873-8635 or visit www.ReaderService.com.

* Terms and prices subject to change without notice. Prices do not include applicable taxes. Sales tax applicable in N.Y. Canadian residents will be charged applicable taxes. Offer not valid in Quebec. This offer is limited to one order per household. Not valid for current subscribers to Harlequin Romantic Suspense books. All orders subject to credit approval. Credit or debit balances in a customer's account(s) may be offset by any other outstanding balance owed by or to the customer. Please allow 4 to 6 weeks for delivery. Offer available while quantities last.

Your Privacy—The Harlequin® Reader Service is committed to protecting your privacy. Our Privacy Policy is available online at www.ReaderService.com or upon request from the Harlequin Reader Service.

We make a portion of our mailing list available to reputable third parties that offer products we believe may interest you. If you prefer that we not exchange your name with third parties, or if you wish to clarify or modify your communication preferences, please visit us at www.ReaderService.com/consumerchoice or write to us at Harlequin Reader Service Preference Service, P.O. Box 9062, Buffalo, NY 14269. Include your complete name and address.

HRS13R

SPECIAL EXCERPT FROM

H HARLEQUIN

ROMANTIC suspense

Connor Mansfield leaves witness protection to save
his daughter's life and reclaim the woman he loves,
but to have a future together, they must escape assassins
and rebuild lost trust.

Read on for a sneak peek of

THE RETURN OF CONNOR MANSFIELD

by Beth Cornelison, available January 2014 from
Harlequin® Romantic Suspense.

Darby's chin snapped up, her eyes widening. "That sounds
like a threat. What do you mean assure my silence? Connor,
what kind of thugs are you involved with?"

"Not thugs, ma'am," Jones said, pulling out his badge.
"U.S. Marshals. Connor Mansfield is under our protection as
part of WitSec, the Witness Security Program."

"U.S. Marshals?" Darby ignored Jones's badge and scowled
at him. "Since when is it okay for federal agents to kidnap
law-abiding citizens?"

Darby's stomach swirled sourly, and she held her breath,
wondering where she'd found the nerve to so openly challenge
these men. The bulges under their jackets were almost assuredly
guns. How far would these men go to *assure her silence?*

The man named Jones looked surprised. "You haven't been
kidnapped. You're free to go whenever you like."

Darby scoffed. "Childproof locks ring a bell?"

Jones smiled and sent Connor a side glance. "Feisty."

"Just one of her many attributes," he replied.

"Marshal Raleigh," Jones said, still smiling, "would you be so kind as to unlock Ms. Kent's door for her?"

"Roger that." Raleigh pushed a button on the driver's door, and the rear door locks clicked off.

Darby blinked, startled by the turn of events. Was she really free to go, or would they shoot her in the back if she tried to leave? She glanced from the door to Jones, narrowing her eyes as she decided whether Jones was pulling a trick. She tested the door release, and it popped open. Then she paused. *Connor.*

She jerked her gaze back to Connor, the man she'd once loved and conceived a child with, and her heart staggered. This wasn't about a standoff between her and two U.S. Marshals. The important issue was Connor. Who was alive. In Witness Security. And who'd contacted Dr. Reed.

He could well be a tissue match for Savannah's bone marrow transplant. *Connor.*

She exhaled a ragged breath, shifting her gaze from one man to another. And closed the car door. "I… All right. You have my attention."

Don't miss
THE RETURN OF CONNOR MANSFIELD
by Beth Cornelison, available January 2014 from
Harlequin® Romantic Suspense.

Trained to kill, but built for love...

From *New York Times* bestselling author

LINDSAY McKENNA

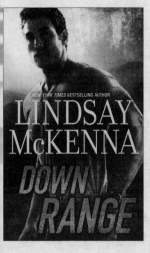

Captain Morgan Boland is at the top of her game, as is navy SEAL Jake Ramsay, her former lover. Then a military computer selects them to partner in a special op. The mission can't be compromised by their personal history—and they have truckloads of it.

But the Afghan assignment might provide the discipline they need to finally get it together—outside the bedroom, that is. A lot has happened over the two years since they last went their separate ways. And there's way more to Morgan than Jake has ever given her credit for....

Available now!
www.LindsayMcKenna.com

Be sure to connect with us at:

Harlequin.com/Newsletters
Facebook.com/HarlequinBooks
Twitter.com/HarlequinBooks

www.Harlequin.com